"I'm confident we could pull it off, Stella. It's not as complex as you might think."

Luke unfolded himself from the love seat and stood up. His height added to his overall impact. He was an impressive-looking man, from his chiseled features to his well-honed body. "I should get going so you can think things through. Thanks for hearing me out."

"Of course," she said, standing up and walking him toward the door. When she pulled it open, Luke paused in the doorway for a moment before turning back toward her. She looked up at him, admiring the strong tilt of his jaw and his chiseled features. What woman in her right mind wouldn't want to pretend date this too-handsome-for-his-own-good Navy SEAL?

He held out his cell phone. "Before I forget, can you put your number in my phone?"

ALSO BY BELLE CALHOUNE

No Ordinary Christmas

Summer on Blackberry Beach

BELLE CALHOUNE

FOREVER

New York Boston

Copyright © 2022 by Sandra Calhoune

Cover design and art by Elizabeth Turner Stokes
Cover images © Shutterstock
Cover copyright © 2021 by Hachette Book Group, Inc.

Forever
Hachette Book Group
1290 Avenue of the Americas, New York, NY 10104
read-forever.com
twitter.com/readforeverpub

First Edition: June 2022

Forever is an imprint of Grand Central Publishing. The Forever name and logo are trademarks of Hachette Book Group, Inc.

The publisher is not responsible for websites (or their content) that are not owned by the publisher.

The Hachette Speakers Bureau provides a wide range of authors for speaking events. To find out more, go to www.hachettespeakersbureau.com or call (866) 376-6591.

ISBN: 9781538736029 (mass market), 9781538736012 (ebook)

Printed in the United States of America

OPM

10 9 8 7 6 5 4 3 2 1

For my sister, Karen. For always being a Stella to my Lucy.

ACKNOWLEDGMENTS

To my husband, Randy, and my two daughters, Amber and Sierra. Thank you for supporting my dreams and always being enthusiastic about my projects. It means the world to me.

To my agent, Jessica Alvarez. I'm so grateful for your wisdom, guidance, and humor. We make a good team.

I am forever indebted to my editor, Madeleine Colavita, for her excitement over this project and for helping me polish up the final version so it shined.

Thank you to Estelle Hallick for working so hard on my behalf and shining a light on my books. And for the entire Grand Central Forever team... You rock!

For my wonderful writer friends who are always in my corner... Piper Huguley, Julie Hilton Steele, Karen Kirst, Jolene Navarro, Lee Tobin McClain, Amanda Peterson Wilson, Dana Lynn, Cate Nolan, Susie Dietze, Tina Radcliffe, and Angela Anderson. Your support means everything to me.

Summer

on
Blackberry
Beach

CHAPTER ONE

Stella Marshall sipped a cup of Earl Grey tea as she sat on her back porch and looked out across Blackberry Beach. The water looked enticing, even though a lifetime of experience had taught her that Maine waters were ice cold, even at the beginning of summer. She wasn't ready to dip her pinky toe in these waters. Maybe by the Fourth of July she'd be raring to go. When she'd purchased this house, the location had been its main selling point. Living by the ocean felt as essential to her as breathing. She didn't know what she would have done with herself if she hadn't been able to walk the length of the beach as a form of self-care during some of the worst days of her life. Being by the sea was a soul-stirring experience and she wouldn't trade it in for anything in this world.

Now that temperatures were heating up, Stella would

open her ocean-facing bedroom windows at night and fall asleep to the sounds of waves lapping against the shore. It would feel heavenly.

She let out a sigh of contentment despite the early hour. June sunrises in Mistletoe, Maine, were spectacular. A band of pink mixed with orange stretched across the horizon as far as the eye could see. Stella felt awestruck by the raw beauty of her surroundings. Despite the fact that the last few years of her personal life had been rough, she really was blessed. Although she knew from listening to her favorite weather forecaster that temperatures were going into the eighties today, right now it was simply glorious and balmy. A slight breeze from the ocean swept across her face, and she closed her eyes and inhaled the sea air. Moments like this one were rare and precious. She'd learned to embrace every second of serenity, knowing it might not last long.

A quick glance at her watch told her she needed to get moving. Today was the last day of school in the Mistletoe district and it was bound to be a bit hectic. Stella could barely stop herself from happy dancing at the thought of the unbridled freedom stretched out before her. Although she would miss the daily interaction with her students, she was ready to fully embrace summer break. It meant she could stay up late watching her favorite classic movie channel and sleep in until midmorning. Perhaps she could do something a little daring and out of character, like kiss a total stranger or go bungee jumping. She could do a road trip with a few friends and check out the Cape Cod National Seashore. Maybe she could even get her younger sister Lucy to come with her if she could get the time off from work and pry herself away from her gorgeous fiancé.

Lucy was head librarian at the Free Library of Mistletoe. Last Christmas, she had reunited with her first love, Dante West, who had grown up with them in Mistletoe before becoming a famous movie star in Hollywood. Over the Christmas holidays, the pair had reconnected and managed to get back together despite their tangled past. Now, Lucy and Dante were planning a spectacular fall wedding. Although she was thrilled for her sister's good fortune, Stella couldn't help but wonder if the tight bond they'd always shared would weaken after Lucy got married. She hated herself for even thinking it, but what if they weren't close once Lucy tied the knot? What if she lost her best friend?

Get a life, Stella Marshall. The sassy little voice buzzed in her head. Ever since her breakup with her fiancé, Rafe Santos, Stella had clung to her sister like a life preserver. Being dumped so close to her wedding day had really done a number on her, both mentally and physically. She wrapped her arms around her waist as the painful memories washed over her. Thankfully, the raw emotions weren't as razor sharp as they had once been. All she felt now was a dull ache and a bad taste in her mouth about romance. With her sister's big day on the horizon, she needed to get over Rafe and the wedding that wasn't once and for all.

Meanwhile, as maid of honor for Lucy, Stella was determined to make their autumnal wedding the event of the season. Lucy deserved every bit of the happiness she'd found with Dante. Her sister was smart and funny and absolutely adorable. And Dante had shown the entire town of Mistletoe that he was head over heels in love with Lucy. Stella had no doubt in her mind that their future was filled with nothing but happiness.

Once she got dressed, Stella didn't waste any time heading out the door. As she drove along the coastal road toward town, the salty sea air floated on the wind through her car window. Soon enough she would be exchanging chalkboards and homework assignments for sea glass hunts and sandals. It was something wonderful to look forward to. Stella easily made the eight-minute drive to school with her hair flowing in the wind and the sun shining down on her. Upon arrival she immediately made her way to the teachers' lounge to grab a cup of coffee and a doughnut.

Paul Whittaker walked over to the coffee station, where Stella was standing waiting for her K-Cup to percolate. Ever since coming on board as principal, Paul had made it clear to Stella that he was romantically interested in her, feelings she didn't reciprocate. For starters, it simply wasn't wise to date your boss. Second, she didn't have the slightest bit of attraction toward him. If nothing else, Stella needed sparks to ignite with any potential love interest. Paul wasn't it.

"Morning, Paul," Stella said, grabbing her mug and stepping aside so he could prepare his own coffee without either of them invading the other's personal space.

"Good morning, Stella." Paul placed his coffee cup in the holder and began pressing the machine's buttons. He looked her up and down in the same objectifying way he always did. "You look very nice for our end-of-school celebration," he said. "We have a wonderful surprise this morning for one of our students." A hint of a smile played at the corners of his lips.

"A surprise? That's great. For which student?" Excitement raced through her at the idea of someone receiving good news. It would be wonderful to end the school year on a high note. Perhaps one of the kids had won an award or been chosen for a special distinction. That would be a great source of pride for the student and the school district. Stella lived for these special moments where talent and hard work were applauded.

Paul pressed a finger against his lips. "All will be revealed at the assembly. Until then it's top secret." His lips were twisted upward in the semblance of a smile that came off as creepy.

Stella fought against the urge to roll her eyes. Paul loved dangling carrots in front of the staff members' noses. He seemed to love knowing things no one else did. She wasn't going to give him the satisfaction of asking any more questions even though he'd piqued her curiosity. Carolina Rivera, her close friend and a fellow teacher, rolled her eyes from a few feet away. She couldn't count the number of times they'd shared inside jokes about their boss. Paul was the gift that kept on giving them something to talk about.

"Would it kill him to spill the beans? Why even mention it in the first place? He just loves torturing us," Carolina said as soon as Paul walked away. She shook her head at the principal's retreating figure. "Maybe Idris Elba is here in Mistletoe visiting."

"Dream on," Stella said, chuckling at the idea of

another movie star visiting their small New England town. Mistletoe had been buzzing with excitement last Christmas when Dante had returned home and ended up romancing her sister. It was hard to imagine lightning striking twice. Her hometown wasn't big enough for two massively famous actors.

Carolina made a face. "Okay, well even if it isn't Idris, I'm dying to know what the big surprise is."

Stella shrugged. "We'll find out soon enough, I suppose." She let out a little squeal. "And it's the last day of school, so it's all good, right? That's reason enough to celebrate."

Carolina's grin lit up her face. "I can't wait for our beach days and the Fourth of July town festivities. We might even be able to squeeze in a road trip if we're lucky."

With wide brown eyes and full cheeks, Carolina was a beautiful woman. She'd proven herself to be a great friend to Stella over the years. Along with Lucy, Carolina had been an amazing support system when the bottom had dropped out of her world. She wasn't sure if she could ever repay Carolina's many kindnesses when she'd been heartbroken and humiliated by her ex-fiancé. She'd shown Stella her big heart by bringing her dinners, going on long walks with her, and passing her boxes of Kleenex. Stella would never forget those moments where Carolina had literally lifted her up off the floor.

"I better head to my classroom," Stella said as she checked the time on her watch. "We have a full day ahead of us."

"I'll need a few more sips of my coffee before I'm

ready to face a room full of second graders," Carolina said as she took a lengthy swig of her aromatic brew. She wiggled her eyebrows dramatically. "I'm still hoping for an Idris sighting though."

"Keep hope alive. See you at the assembly," Stella said with a chuckle as she left the break room and walked down the hall toward her classroom. She also taught second graders, so she understood Carolina's need to caffeinate herself before facing the day. Their students could be a handful. Thankfully, being a teacher was her dream job and she felt lucky each and every day.

As she drew close to her classroom, Stella spotted one of her students standing by the door waving at her.

"Morning, Miss Marshall," Miles Keegan said, grinning up at her as he held the door to their classroom open. Dressed in a Hawaiian shirt, navy shorts, and a pair of white Converse sneakers, Miles was a stylish eight-year-old. With caramel-colored eyes, a close-cropped Afro, and burnished brown skin, Miles was an adorable kid.

"Good morning, Miles. Happy last day of school," Stella said. She smiled back at him, her heart experiencing a pang as she locked gazes with her favorite student. No matter how hard she tried not to favor one student above the rest, Miles held a special place in her heart. He was the sweetest little boy, one who'd been plunged into grief after the death of his mother in a tragic car accident. Despite everything he'd been through, he still managed to be joyful even though he experienced moments of being out of sorts. Stella imagined he was still processing the loss of his mother, and as his teacher it was her role to help guide him on his path.

Stella walked into the classroom and placed her purse inside her desk drawer. When she turned around, Miles was standing in front of her with a bouquet of tulips tied with a bright yellow bow. "This is for you. From my dad and me."

"They're beautiful," Stella said. "What a thoughtful gift." She raised the flowers to her nostrils and inhaled the heavenly aroma. It wasn't every day that she received a lovely bouquet from one of her students.

Miles shifted from one foot to the other. "My dad said most girls love flowers. I wanted to give you a set of Legos, but he wasn't sure if you would like it."

Stella threw her head back and chuckled. "I like Legos, but the flowers are perfect. I'm going to put them in that empty vase on my desk and then take them home with me. Thanks for thinking of me. I appreciate it."

Other students began trickling into the classroom, and Miles moved away from her to join in on the last day of school revelry with his classmates. Laughter rang in the air as the children celebrated the start of summer vacation and no more homework. Normally, Stella would encourage the kids to settle down and sit at their desks before the morning assembly, but since today was a special day, she didn't bother. It was nice to see the students in relaxation mode. They'd worked hard all year. They deserved to have fun and celebrate.

At nine a.m. sharp, Principal Whittaker came over the loudspeaker to announce it was time for the last assembly of the year. Stella led her students in single file as they made their way down the hall toward the gymnasium. Stella had to corral a few who seemed to have ants in their pants and refused to listen to her instructions. She was a firm believer that no student was ever bad, although they did have their moments.

As they filed into the room, Stella led her class to the bleachers where they completely filled out an entire row. Once the assembly began, students were called to the stage to celebrate their achievements. Honor roll students, top athletes, spelling bee and science fair winners. Some students even performed songs and skits they'd learned in choir and drama classes. Stella loved the supportive nature of the students as they cheered and clapped for their classmates.

"And now, to conclude our assembly, we have something very special lined up. Miles Keegan, can you come front and center?"

Stella looked over at Miles, who had a stunned expression on his face. She gave him an encouraging nod as everyone began enthusiastically clapping. Out of the corner of her eye she spotted a tall figure snapping pictures on his cell phone. It was Nick Keegan, Miles's dad. He'd been a friend of hers since middle school. What was Nick doing at the end-of-the-year assembly? Although parents weren't prohibited from attending, it was pretty rare for one to show up. Something was definitely going on. Was Miles the student who had a special surprise in store for him?

Once Miles made his way to the front, Principal Whittaker placed his hand on Miles's shoulder. "Are you looking forward to summer vacation?" he asked, speaking into a microphone. He placed the mic in front of Miles's mouth. With all the attention focused on him,

Miles looked slightly nervous. He placed both hands in his back pockets and rocked on the heels of his Converse sneakers. "Yes, I guess so," he mumbled.

Principal Whittaker chuckled. "You don't sound too sure about that, but I have a surprise for you that might bring a smile to your face. A present just for you. All the way from Afghanistan."

Afghanistan? Before she could ponder what in the world was going on, a man strode into the gymnasium from a side entrance. She sucked in a sharp breath at the sight of him. He was wearing camo cargo pants and a short-sleeved olive-green T-shirt that showed off his sculpted arms. He was tall and muscular with a face chiseled by the archangels. His brown skin was a beautiful russet color, and he had a strong jawline. Suddenly, Stella felt a jolt of recognition. After all, who could forget Luke Keegan? He was all grown up now and incredibly handsome. And seriously, smolderingly sexy.

Being a Navy SEAL had given him a serious glow up. And that was saying something since he'd always been handsome. Nick talked about his brother all the time, so she knew Luke had worked really hard over the years to rise up in the ranks. From the sounds of it, he'd devoted his entire life to being a Navy SEAL. He'd even been injured in the line of duty, which had ended his career.

Miles let out a cry and ran toward his uncle. She couldn't take her eyes off Luke as his powerful arms reached out and wrapped his nephew up in a huge bear hug. Miles clung to his uncle with complete abandon, his little legs wrapped around Luke's waist as if he might never let go. Tears misted in Stella's eyes at the emotional reunion between uncle and nephew. Miles had lost so much over the past few years; it was amazing to see him being gifted with his uncle's presence. On more than one occasion, Miles had gushed about his uncle's bravery and service to his country.

Stella loved these military surprises. She couldn't remember one ever taking place at Mistletoe Elementary, but it was fitting that this special moment between Miles and his uncle had occurred on the last day before summer break. It was a feel-good event for the entire community. But especially Miles. A bunch of photographers stepped onstage and began snapping pictures of Miles and Luke. Stella had the feeling this surprise reunion would be featured on the local news and in dozens of newspapers around the region.

Luke Keegan was definitely the eye candy Mistletoe needed. Not that there weren't good-looking men here in town, but most of them were either already coupled up or strictly in the friend zone. Stella wasn't looking for a summer romance, but if she had been, Luke would have been at the top of her list.

"He's one hot soldier," Carolina said in a hushed voice as she leaned over and poked Stella in the shoulder. Carolina began fanning herself with her hand in an exaggerated way.

"Even hotter than when we were in high school," Stella murmured. "And that's saying something."

"You went to high school with him?" Carolina asked in a raised voice, her eyes widening.

Stella put her finger to her lips and made a shushing sound. The last thing either of them needed was for their students to overhear their conversation and take it home with them. "I sure did," she confirmed in a low whisper, turning her head to make eye contact. Stella didn't want to get into it with Carolina, but Luke had been voted as the senior most likely to get a girl in the back seat of his car. He'd been hot stuff. Girls had practically lined up to get with him. Stella had crushed on him from afar since they hadn't hung out in the same circles.

"And Dante West as well? What's in the water in Mistletoe? This place is full of gorgeous men." Carolina wrinkled her nose. "Not sure why I'm still single though. I've got to step up my game." She patted her hips. "I need to lose a few pounds."

"Don't you dare," Stella objected. "You have curves in all the right places. You'll find someone special before you know it. And you don't have to lose a single ounce to make that happen." It was easy to see Carolina coupled up with a wonderful partner. She was smart and vivacious with a killer sense of humor. And she was way more confident than Stella herself was. She let out a little sigh. If only she could be a little bit bolder, a little bit braver. If only her romantic past with Rafe hadn't sucked all the life out of her. Why was it so much easier to imagine Carolina finding herself coupled up with someone than herself? Rafe had really done a number on her. He'd stomped all over her heart and left her incredibly jaded.

"Be careful. You're drooling," Carolina whispered in Stella's ear.

"I am not," she said, trying to keep her composure. "It's not like I've never seen a hot guy before."

"He's not just any guy. The whole Navy SEAL thing

is pretty awesome. And he is just as smoldering as Idris. Maybe even more so."

"Well, I'm not looking to date anytime soon, so he's all yours," Stella said. Her heart twinged when she said it. Seeing her friend with her former crush would be slightly difficult to bear.

Stella didn't need to turn around to see her friend rolling her eyes at her. Carolina, along with half of Mistletoe, had tried on many occasions to set her up on dates. Even though it had been almost two years since Rafe had informed her that she wasn't his soulmate, the very thought of someone hurting her again was still terrifying.

The sight of Luke Keegan standing in the middle of the gymnasium was a nice visual to get her mind off her own problems. A girl could at least dream, couldn't she? He'd developed into a fine-looking man, and there was something very appealing about a guy who put his life on the line for others.

Seeing him again after all these years was a shock to the system. He was all grown up now and smoking hot. Was it her imagination or had it suddenly gotten warm in the gymnasium? She was feeling a bit flushed. It brought her back to the days when she'd had a gigantic crush on him. Stella had been one year below Luke in school, and although they'd known each other since they were little, there had never been a friendship or any type of rapport between them. Not that Stella wouldn't have moved heaven and earth to make it happen, but Luke had gazed straight through her. It was a little bit painful to remember how she'd been so enthralled by a boy who hadn't even noticed her. She couldn't really blame him though. He'd always been highly sought after by all the girls in town, and she'd been on the shy side with her nose always stuck in a book. There had been zero chance of them getting together back then.

And even though she'd outgrown her awkward teen-aged years, Stella still felt like the younger version of herself on the inside. Luke was still way out of her league. Smoking hot Navy SEALs could generally get any woman they pleased. And if she knew the ladies in town like she thought she did, not a single one would say no to Luke Keegan.

She wondered how long he was staying in Mistletoe. And just how long would it take for all the women in town to make a beeline in his direction?

CHAPTER TWO

Luke Keegan stood in the middle of the basketball court in the gymnasium of his former elementary school and looked out at the audience composed of students and faculty members. His gaze swept over the packed room, searching for his younger brother. His chest tightened as he spotted Nick waving in his direction as the crowd headed out of the assembly. Nick couldn't hide the raw emotion from showing on his expressive face. He had always worn his heart on his sleeve, while Luke tended to be more stoic, keeping it all on the inside. It had served him well as a Navy SEAL, but he wasn't certain it had benefited him in his personal life. While Nick had been destined to settle down with the love of his life, Luke was the poster boy for failed relationships.

You're not meant for the long haul. To this day, those words rang in Luke's ears, courtesy of his ex-girlfriend,

Allison Teague. It hadn't hurt at the time, but in the past few years the insult had been festering inside of him. He couldn't help but wonder if she had been right. Was he meant to be alone for the rest of his days?

Luke shoved those emotions down and reminded himself to savor this moment with his nephew. He was miles away from covert missions and stealth operations, instead standing next to Miles, who he'd missed like crazy, in his old stomping grounds. When he'd been a student here, the building had seemed gigantic. He couldn't help but feel stunned at the reality. It was actually pretty small. Perspective was a funny thing.

Ever since he'd arrived in Mistletoe last night, Luke had been in full nostalgia mode. After being in the Middle East for the better part of six years, his hometown felt like paradise. He hadn't even realized how much he'd needed to be back in Maine and experience some normalcy after living the military life for so long. Although he loved having proudly served his country, Luke knew his time was up. He needed to move on with something else. It was both nerve-racking and exciting to create a new life for himself.

Once a Navy SEAL, always a Navy SEAL. It would forever be a part of his identity if not his reality. Medal of Honor. He wished this distinction could trump the bomb blast that had ended his career and killed two of his SEAL team members.

"I want you to meet my teacher, Miss Marshall." His nephew's voice drew him out of his thoughts. Miles tugged at Luke's hand and began to pull him forcefully toward the bleachers. For a little kid, Miles sure had some super strength going on. *He must be eating his Wheaties*, Luke thought with a chuckle.

"Sure thing, buddy. Slow down. What's the rush?" Luke asked. His nephew's excitement was contagious. Seeing such joy in a pint-sized version of his brother lifted him up to the stratosphere. It was thrilling to know they'd be in the same zip code for the foreseeable future. He had so much to catch up on in both Miles's and Nick's lives.

The woman standing before him was nothing short of spectacular. Luke dragged in a ragged breath. It had been a long time since he'd been in the presence of a woman who looked like his nephew's teacher. Miss Marshall had big, brown eyes framed by thick black lashes. Her skin was mocha colored. A heart-shaped face with full ruby lips and gorgeous cheekbones put her in the category of absolutely gorgeous. He had to remind himself to pick his jaw up off the ground.

Back when he'd been a student in this very building, Luke hadn't had a single teacher who looked like Miss Marshall. It had probably been a blessing in disguise. He wouldn't have been able to focus on reading, writing, and arithmetic if the teacher at the front of the classroom had been as stunning as this woman.

"Miss Marshall. This is my uncle, Luke." Miles craned his neck looking up at him, wonder etched on his face. "He came all the way from Afghanistan to see me." Luke's heart cracked open a little at the pride emanating from Miles's voice. Every time Luke talked to Nick, his brother told him how much his nephew looked up to him. He couldn't even put into words how Miles's hero worship made him feel. Planning this surprise reunion had been Luke's way of creating a special experience for him.

Miss Marshall's grin caused Luke's chest to painfully tighten. He wasn't used to being so affected by a woman's smile or her close proximity. There was something slightly familiar about his nephew's teacher, but he couldn't put his finger on it.

"Hi there, Luke. Nice to see you again." She stuck out her hand. "I'm Stella. Stella Marshall. We grew up together in Mistletoe."

Stella Marshall? The name came out of nowhere, surprising him in the process. He had a vague recollection of a gangly girl with long legs and an overbite. Surely this couldn't be the same person. Miles's teacher was a knockout. Stella had been in his brother Nick's circle of friends, and she'd been quiet and studious— the type of girl who'd never walked on the wild side. It was strange how he remembered those details and yet he hadn't recognized her at first.

Luke slid his hand into hers. "Stella! Of course. You were the grade below me, right?" They hadn't been friends, but in a small town like Mistletoe, everybody knew everybody on some level.

She nodded. "Yes. You might remember my sister Lucy as well."

He grinned back at her. "Of course I do. I recall reading a headline not too long ago about Dante West getting engaged to a certain hometown librarian named Lucy Marshall. Dante and I used to play football together. Do you still hang out with Nick?"

"We do. A group of us do dinner and a movie when he can get a sitter," Stella acknowledged. "Nick is a good friend."

"She was friends with my mom too," Miles said in a quiet voice. Luke looked down and placed his arm around his nephew's shoulder. There had been a little hitch in Miles's voice when he said the word *mom*. Although Luke knew grief didn't have a timetable, he found himself wishing for his nephew to be completely healed. Losing a parent was the single most devastating thing that a child could endure. Most times, it stayed with a person throughout their lives. One of his objectives was to be a support system for both Miles and his brother while he was in town. Help them with their grief in any way he could.

"I always tell Miles that his mother was the best dancer in town, maybe in all of Maine," Stella said. "She put the rest of us to shame with her moves. I seem to remember her being a big Rihanna fan." Her eyes seemed to warm up to a lighter shade of brown when she smiled.

A huge grin began to break out over Miles's face at the mention of his beloved mother. Clearly, Stella had developed quite a rapport with his nephew. Their relationship was a special one. Luke could tell by the way his nephew responded to her that they had a tight bond. And Stella was gazing down at Miles as if he'd hung the moon.

Luke felt a clapping sensation on his back, and his brother's voice washed over him. "Hey, guys," Nick said. Miles was the spitting image of his dad, sharing the same features and warm brown complexion, as well as similar mannerisms. All of the Keegan males tended to resemble each other, including their father.

"Daddy!" Miles said in an excited voice. His face lit up with happiness at the sight of his dad.

"Hey there," Nick said, raising his hand up to Miles in a high-five gesture. "Great job up there. You were as cool as a cucumber." Miles high-fived him back with gusto, slapping Nick's hand extra hard. Nick muttered an "ouch" that made his son giggle.

"Did you know Uncle Luke was going to show up today?" Miles asked.

"I may have known a little something," Nick said in a teasing voice. "But I was sworn to secrecy." He made a twisting motion against his lips as if he were turning a key. "Life isn't any fun without surprises."

"It was a great surprise." Miles threw himself against Luke's chest. "I can't wait to show you my classroom." He looked over at Stella. "Is it okay if Uncle Luke comes back with us?"

Stella nodded enthusiastically. "Of course it is. We love having guests." She turned toward Luke and locked gazes with him. "We're actually having a little end-of-the-year celebration with punch and cupcakes. You're welcome to come. You too, Nick."

"You made me an offer I can't refuse," Nick said, glancing at his watch. "I don't have to be back at the office for a bit."

"I'll never say no to cupcakes," Luke said. "Or spending time with my chill nephew."

"Excuse me. I'm going to head back to the classroom. My students are under the watch of another teacher at the moment, but they look like they're itching to get the party started," Stella said. She looked at Miles. "Why don't you follow behind us with your dad and uncle? I'll see you shortly." Luke's gaze trailed after Stella as she organized her class in single file, then led them out of the gymnasium and into the hallway. The woman looked just as good walking away from him as she had face-to-face. Stella Marshall was seriously messing with his decision to stay away from the ladies in Mistletoe. Dating was a distraction he couldn't afford.

Luke thought his heart might explode the moment Miles reached for his hand to hold as they left the gymnasium. Luke could have sworn he saw tears misting in Nick's eyes before his brother turned his head in another direction. He knew what this moment meant to him. Losing his beautiful wife, Kara, had devastated Nick and turned his world upside down. They'd been high school sweethearts who had never wavered in their love for each other. They'd built a beautiful family with Miles at the center, and it had all been taken away in a matter of seconds due to a drunk driver. Luke still couldn't wrap his head around it.

He hadn't been much help to Nick back then due to the demands of his job. Luke had flown home for the funeral, but he hadn't been able to stay in Mistletoe for long. But now he had nothing but time on his hands to spend with his two favorite people in the world. He meant to make the most of it. Being back in Mistletoe allowed Luke to finally relax, even if he wasn't used to this way of life. Rebuilding his life in Maine was way less harrowing than conducting special op missions and placing himself and his SEAL team in harm's way.

For the moment he could bask in spending time with Nick and Miles. Maybe being with his family would help him heal emotionally from what had happened over in Afghanistan. Maybe if he tried really hard, he could forget that his actions had gotten two members of his SEAL team killed.

CHAPTER THREE

Sleeping in was definitely underrated, Stella realized. It was downright decadent. Walking around her house in her undies and a Spelman College T-shirt felt completely liberating. She'd just devoured scrambled eggs, hickory-flavored bacon, and blueberry waffles smothered in maple syrup for a nice brunch. She'd washed it all down with a Long Island iced tea to celebrate her first day of summer vacation. After placing her dishes in the dishwasher, Stella made her way to the living room and plopped down on her comfy gray couch. She'd been starving, but now she felt absolutely stuffed. Her eyes had been way bigger than her stomach.

She began rubbing her belly just as her dog, Coco Chanel, began scratching at the back door. Stella shut her eyes and tried to ignore it. She'd just taken her out a half hour ago. It figured she was making a fuss and whining.

Her miniature poodle was high-maintenance and a true diva. Although Stella loved her to pieces, she felt completely wrapped around Coco Chanel's little paw.

With a groan she got up and walked to the kitchen, where her poodle was sitting at the door and looking up at her with her big brown eyes. It didn't take a rocket scientist to figure out the message Coco Chanel was sending to Stella. Whatever Coco Chanel wanted, Coco Chanel got.

"Okay, I heard you. I get it," she grumbled. "You better not be yanking my chain. Didn't you get the memo? I'm on vacation."

Stella opened the back door, which led to a small patch of yard fenced in by a white gate. Once you left the property, the beach was steps away. Stella could smell the briny aroma of the sea from her back patio, and it always served as a reminder of her good fortune. Living on the beach was the gift that kept giving. Coco Chanel scampered outside and sprinted toward the small bush in the side yard. Stella sat down in a patio chair and inhaled deeply as a slight breeze swept over her. She would relax for a few minutes while Coco Chanel did her business. Sun, sea, sand. In the distance she could see sailboats and a few wind surfers. The weather was heating up and people were taking advantage of it. Pretty soon the water would be warm enough for swimming, which was one of Stella's favorite pastimes. She couldn't wait to run headlong into the ocean in her new salmon-colored bathing suit.

Stella sat up with a jerk as she saw a white blob of curly hair sashaying away from the yard.

She jumped up from her chair and howled. "Nooooooo!" Somehow her poodle had found a way out of her fenced-in yard and was now on the loose.

Coco Chanel loved to take off at lightning speed and run across the long stretch of beach until she was exhausted. There wasn't a single hope of Stella catching up with her unless Coco Chanel stopped running. Because her dog was so small, Stella always had to worry about her making her way into the road. Stella wrenched open the gate and began jogging down the beach in sand that felt like quicksand. Her feet couldn't seem to get any traction, and it felt like she was running in place. Within seconds, Stella realized trying to run was futile.

At first Stella thought it might be a mirage brought on by the heat and her panic. A shirtless man was running on the beach, heading her way. Abs of steel. Sweat glistening on his perfect torso. He was coming toward her with Coco Chanel in his arms. She let out a sob of relief that quickly turned to disgust. Her snobby, fickle poodle was licking this man's golden-brown arm as if they were the best of buddies.

Hold up. This wasn't just any man sprinting in her direction. It was Luke! And he was looking finer than ever.

"Hey, Stella. Is she yours?" Luke asked when he came within a few feet of her.

Holy Hotness. He wasn't even panting hard. Meanwhile, Stella was completely out of breath and feeling as if her chest might explode from her pathetic attempt at running. She didn't want to stare, but she thought he might have an eight pack.

"Yes, she's mine," Stella said after a brief pause, reaching out to pluck Coco Chanel from his arms. Her fingers grazed Luke's torso and she sucked in a steadying breath. His skin was silky soft but his stomach was hard as a rock. It had been a long time since she'd been in such proximity to a man, let alone one who looked this fine.

"Naughty dog," she scolded. Coco Chanel gazed at her with a calm look that served as a slap in the face for all the mayhem she'd caused. "Don't look at me with those big brown eyes of yours. You scared me to death."

"She's a runner, huh?" Luke asked. "She was moving pretty fast."

"That's putting it mildly," she said, forcing herself to look away from his extremely kissable lips. What was wrong with her? Combined with the heat, Luke's presence was making her a little loopy.

"Umm. Did you forget something?" Luke's gaze lowered to her legs. He took a moment to drink her in before dragging his eyes back up to meet hers. He was clearly trying to hide a grin that tugged at the corners of his mouth. And what a nice mouth it was, Stella thought for the gazillionth time.

All of a sudden it dawned on her that she hadn't put any pants on before she'd fled her yard in pursuit of Coco Chanel. The oversized T-shirt covered all of her unmentionables, but she still felt like an idiot. She must have looked ridiculous running down the beach with her arms flapping like a pelican and showcasing an ample amount of leg and thigh. All because of her spoiled and undisciplined pooch. She tugged at her T-shirt, trying to pull it down farther so she wouldn't run the risk of flashing too much skin. The fabric wouldn't cooperate and didn't budge an inch.

"I was in a rush trying to catch Coco Chanel," she explained. "When she takes off like this I always worry that she'll run into the road."

He raised an eyebrow. "Did you say Coco Chanel?"

"That's her name," Stella said. "She's a French poodle so I thought it was fitting. It was either that or Marie Antoinette. And we all know how that ended." Stella sighed and bent her head down to place a kiss on the poodle's temple. No matter how badly Coco Chanel acted, Stella ended up forgiving her. She would go to the moon and back for her pampered pooch.

Luke made a face. "That's...different. I don't think I've ever known a dog with two names."

"Poodles are one of a kind," Stella said as she shifted Coco Chanel onto her hip and winced. Sprinting had caused an uncomfortable stitch in her side. She was trying to play it off and not let Luke see how out of shape she was. A ridiculously fit Navy SEAL wouldn't be able to relate to her situation. He could probably bounce quarters off his abs while she could barely make it through a Zumba class.

He drew his brows together. "Are you all right? You seem a little...winded."

"I am," she admitted. "I'm not used to doing the one-hundred-yard dash on wet sand."

"Running on sand is tough, but it makes for a great workout."

If he weren't so cute, Stella might want to push him in

the ocean. But with his rock-solid chest and abs of steel, Stella doubted she could swing it.

"Yeah, it's a great workout if one survives it," Stella quipped. The words jumped out of her mouth before she could rein them back in. It wasn't as if she was trying to impress Luke or anything, but she didn't want him to see how nonathletic she was.

Luke let out a deep-throated chuckle that sounded rich and inviting. It went straight to her belly, causing all sorts of tingles and prickles of awareness. *Uh oh.* Although it had been a while since a man had given her the warm and fuzzies, Luke was giving her all the feels. *Dang it!* They were too similar to how she'd felt about Rafe during their relationship. And that had ended disastrously. She wanted to avoid these emotions at all costs. They made her feel too vulnerable, yet here she was crushing on Luke all over again. And now she was staring at him, mesmerized by the strong tilt of his jaw and his glorious brown skin dotted with little droplets of moisture.

"Do you want a cold water or something?" she asked him, willing herself not to stare. In the cold light of day, he was even more smolderingly handsome than she'd realized. "My house is right over there. The white one with the blue shingles." She pointed to her house in the distance. It always gave her a sense of pride to tell someone she was a homeowner. She'd put a lot of blood, sweat, and tears into renovating her beach cottage, and the end result had been a smashing success.

"Nice place. I ran by it earlier." Luke looked at her quizzically. "Didn't Mr. Jackson live there back when we were in school?"

"Yes," Stella said with a nod. "He sold it to me three years ago. He had a few health setbacks and went to live with his daughter in Boston. It was a bit of a fixer-upper, but I made it my own and added some new features." Stella couldn't help but smile. Buying a home on her own had been one of her proudest moments. It had been her haven when the bottom fell out of her world.

"I'll take that water," Luke said, wiping his brow with the back of his hand. "It's getting hot out here."

Yes, indeed. It was getting downright scorching out here. Feeling slightly flustered by his close proximity, Stella began walking back down the beach toward her house with Luke right beside her. "So how is Mistletoe treating you so far?" she asked, curious about how Luke was acclimating to life in his quaint New England hometown. Although it suited her perfectly, she knew small-town living wasn't for everyone.

"Not bad at all. The town has changed a lot since I was last living here, but it's fun to scope it out."

Stella wrinkled her nose. "I guess it has transformed a bit over the years, although I've always lived in Mistletoe so it's hard for me to spot the changes. The only time I've lived elsewhere was during college."

Luke jerked his chin in the direction of her T-shirt. "Spelman, huh? Atlanta is a beautiful city. I spent some time there a few years ago with one of my SEAL team members." Luke couldn't contain his enthusiasm. "It was fun hanging out with my buddy and his big, gregarious family. They showed me all the major sites and the best restaurants in town. It was a great example of Southern hospitality."

Stella nodded. "There's a warmth that you don't find in too many places. I loved going to college there. It gave me a chance to spend some time in a city and expose myself to museums and restaurants and concerts at big venues. I enjoyed it, but I prefer the intimacy of a small town." She stopped as they reached her house and pushed open the back gate. "Mistletoe has a lot to offer. You'll see."

Luke grinned at her. "This town is lucky to have such a passionate resident. Are you sure you don't work as part of the tourism bureau here in town? If not, they need to hire you." Luke's tone was slightly flirtatious. She couldn't remember the last time she'd been receptive to a man's flirtations. But before she knew it, Stella was engaging in banter with him.

She giggled. "You're not a tourist, Luke. Mistletoe is your hometown. So I'm just refreshing your mind about the wonderful place you've come back to. That's all."

"Well, it's a far cry from Afghanistan," he said, his features slightly pinched. His tone had suddenly shifted, going from upbeat to somber in the blink of an eye.

Something about the way he'd spoken set off a warning bell. She didn't really know him well enough to ask any questions, but she sensed he was reflecting on something specific. Stella knew from Nick that Luke had gone through some tough times while serving overseas. At the moment it was lurking in the depth of his eyes and pulsing in the air around them. She couldn't remember the details, but she knew he'd earned a medal for his heroism. The local news had eaten the story up, eager to profile Mistletoe's town hero.

"Let me go get that water," Stella said, wanting to ease the tension.

Stella brought Coco Chanel back inside, then grabbed a cold water from the fridge. When she returned, Luke was standing with his hands on his hips, facing the ocean. Her eyes lingered for a moment on his back and shoulders. He radiated strength. She didn't know all that much about Navy SEALs, but she'd heard a lot about their discipline and bravery.

At the sound of her footsteps, Luke turned away from the glorious view of the water.

"Here you go," Stella said as she handed Luke the bottle, her fingers grazing his as he took it. She felt a frisson of electricity as their skin came into contact, but she quickly shrugged it off. That's what happened when a person went two years without being touched or kissed or embraced.

"Thank you," he said, twisting off the top and raising it to his lips. As Luke guzzled down the bottle of water, his Adam's apple convulsed. Stella didn't think she'd ever seen a man drink with so much gusto. Or finesse. He resembled one of those buff male models on a healthy living commercial.

"Thanks for the hydration," Luke said. "I need to finish this run before I lose my momentum."

"You're welcome," Stella said, reaching out to take the empty bottle off his hands.

"In a town as small as Mistletoe, I'm sure I'll see you around," Luke said. "Stay cool."

He was probably right. In a small town like Mistletoe, they were bound to run into each other. Not to mention the fact that someone like Luke would stand out in any setting. He was the type of man whose presence would always command attention.

Stella turned around and snuck a last look at Luke as he ran off down the beach. Although she had no business gawking at him, Stella couldn't resist. She wasn't sure, but he appeared to be limping slightly on his right leg. And he was wearing some type of wrap on it that she hadn't noticed before. Perhaps he'd pulled a muscle or strained something. It served as further proof that running was a dangerous activity.

As far as she was concerned, he was the sexiest man who'd ever set foot in Mistletoe, Maine. And, if she wasn't so dead set against getting involved in any romantic entanglements, she might just consider something completely out of her comfort zone—a smoldering summer fling with the handsome Navy SEAL.

Humph! She was certain that Luke was causing a lot of temperatures to rise all across town. He was a one-man heat wave.

As she turned to head back inside, she spotted her neighbor, Patsy Sampson, standing on her back porch with her eyes glued on Stella. She sighed. Patsy was the nosiest gossip in town, and it was just Stella's luck that she lived right next door. Widowed for the past decade, Patsy was fond of saying she was on the lookout for love and if it ever came knocking, she would open up her door in a flash. Strangely enough, her nose seemed to be planted in everybody's business but her own.

Stella raised her hand and waved. "Hey there, Patsy. It's a beautiful day, isn't it?"

"Glorious," the older woman called out. Patsy's eyes trailed after Luke as he sprinted away. "And I'm not talking about the weather," she said with a chuckle. "I'm so glad you're putting yourself back out there, Stella. He's quite the catch."

Stella's heart sank. "Oh no, Patsy. It's not what you think. He's just a friend," Stella said, eager to correct Patsy's misassumption. Shoot. Her imagination had probably run amok seeing a shirtless Luke hanging out with Stella on the patio. From where Patsy had been standing it had probably looked very intimate between them. *Good grief.*

Patsy shook her head. "Whatever you say, Stella. All I know is I'd sure like a friend who looks like that in a tiny pair of shorts."

Stella's jaw dropped as Patsy turned on her heel and went back inside her house. There wasn't a single doubt in Stella's mind that her neighbor would spend the rest of the day calling all of her girlfriends and gossiping about seeing her and Luke together. There was no telling how salacious the details might be. Patsy had a vivid imagination and a talent for embellishment. She really knew how to spin a juicy tale. Stella wasn't sure if she should walk over and set Patsy straight face-to-face. But, if she did, it might look as if she was trying too hard to snuff out any potential rumors. Playing it cool might be her best option. Hopefully luck would be on her side, and nothing would come of it.

She groaned. All she could do was wait and see

how things unfolded. Stella hoped that there were other stories brewing in Mistletoe that might distract the residents from any unfounded gossip about her and Luke. She'd already been at the center of town chatter when Rafe had called off their wedding and reunited with his childhood sweetheart. It had been humiliating to be the object of the town's pity when Rafe had gotten married so quickly. Then Tabitha had gotten pregnant and the rumor mill had revved up again. Throughout that painful period, she'd held her head up high and pretended it didn't crush her. As a teacher in the district, Stella hadn't wanted to be the talk of the town for such an awful reason.

All she wanted was to be able to move past the entire Rafe fiasco and not be an object of pity. There was a lot to be said about living peacefully with no dark clouds hanging over her head.

Last winter Lucy and Dante had been the subject of numerous rumors involving their whirlwind romance. Considering he was a famous actor, it was understandable. He'd blown into town to film a movie and had quickly become the focus of everyone's romantic fantasies. Getting engaged to a hometown girl had endeared him to everyone in Mistletoe. The fact that they were getting married in their hometown was the icing on the cake. Everyone loved a happy ending.

Stella bit her lip. Maybe Patsy wouldn't say anything about seeing her and Luke together. Perhaps for once she would keep her mouth shut. Who was she kidding? Patsy's flapping lips were tantamount to a runaway train barreling off the tracks. And having a gorgeous

Navy SEAL land in Mistletoe added a juicy element to the story.

Stella had the feeling her and Luke's names would soon be on the tongues of town gossips, and there wasn't a single thing she could do to stop it.

CHAPTER FOUR

Mistletoe had really come a long way in the past few years, Luke thought as he made his way back to Nick's house. A coffeehouse called the Coffee Bean had sprung up in the Main Street area, as well as a small independently run bookstore called the Bookworm. Over by the marina he'd spotted a dozen or so artist shanties doing a brisk business with loads of customers, some of whom he presumed were out-of-town tourists. He made a mental note to make a coffee run later on today so he could check the new place out. It was one of the major things he'd missed out in Afghanistan—his favorite java.

By the time Luke made it back to the house, his right leg felt as if it were on fire. He knew he'd been pushing himself, but he wanted so badly to be better. The doctor had warned him to avoid straining his leg or run the risk of backsliding. It was frustrating to be in this situation six months after he'd been wounded. He just wanted his body to go back to normal and for the residual pain to subside. Being classified by the Navy as permanently disabled still made him angry. He was merely bent, not broken.

Shame roared through him. He had no right to complain. Not when two members of his team hadn't made it back home. Not when two families were grieving the loss of their loved ones. Normal had flown out the window the day his SEAL team had come under attack. Everything had fallen apart in an instant. He shuddered as painful memories crashed over him like a tsunami. Heat. Fire. Chaos. Searing pain. As always, his mind prevented him from going too deep.

Crossing paths with Stella had been a sweet surprise. She wasn't just easy on the eyes. Stella was funny and sweet natured and smart. She was the type of woman his mother called "the whole package." If he was even remotely interested in dating anyone in Mistletoe, pursuing the stunning teacher would be a no-brainer. But he couldn't go there. He wasn't in any shape emotionally to invest in another person. Rebuilding his life and mapping out his future would take every ounce of strength he possessed. He'd already taken a first step by positioning himself as a support system for Nick and Miles. Meeting with the families of his two team members who'd died in the explosion would be trickier. Now might not be the right time, but he was determined to see it through.

The sight of Nick playing catch in the side yard with Miles greeted him as he walked past the front gate. From the outside, Nick's house resembled a story-book New England home with its white façade and black shutters. A hanging flowerpot filled with bright red flowers hung from the ceiling of the wraparound porch. He couldn't remember the name of the flowers, but they'd always graced his own home growing up, courtesy of their mother. Zora Keegan was now cruising the Mediterranean on a thirty-day cruise with their dad, Curtis. Although his parents had offered to cut the cruise short in order to come back to Mistletoe for his return, Luke had quickly rejected the idea. After retiring from their thirty-five-year careers in medicine, they both deserved some rest and relaxation. It also gave him a chance to get his game face on before his mother gave him the once-over and began worrying about him. It was the last thing he wanted—to have his parents lose a moment of sleep over him.

"How was your run?" Miles asked, dropping the ball and running toward him at breakneck speed. Luke opened his arms for a hug, catching Miles as he vaulted into his arms.

"Whoa!" Luke said, laughing at the impact his small nephew made as he crashed into his body. "For a little dude, you're pretty strong."

"Thanks," Miles said, beaming at the compliment. It felt nice to see his nephew smiling despite the various issues he'd been dealing with since his mother's death. Seeing Nick bring up his son in the aftermath of tragedy made him Luke's own personal hero. He always thought of his son's needs before anything else, and he'd done a bang-up job of raising him.

"Easy there. Don't break your uncle," Nick said, bending down to collect the baseball. "Why don't we head inside for a water break?"

"Race you," Miles said, issuing the challenge to Luke. Before he could agree, Miles took off running toward the house. Luke shook his head and followed behind his nephew. Once they were inside the house, Nick pulled out three bottled waters from the fridge and placed them on the counter. Miles dipped his hand into a cookie jar and pulled out a chocolate chip cookie.

"Can I go watch TV in the playroom?" Miles asked, a hopeful expression on his face. Before Nick could even answer, Miles was halfway down the hall. Luke and Nick both chuckled as they watched him disappear.

"Thanks again for letting me stay." Luke hadn't had time to find a place in Mistletoe before heading back home from Afghanistan. Truthfully, he wasn't even sure if he would remain permanently in his hometown. For most of his adult life, he'd been stationed in various hotspots around the world or undergoing rigorous training to be a member of an elite SEAL team. Planting roots in this quaint Maine town might prove to be challenging. He wasn't sure if he would fit into this laidback place as an adult. He was still trying to figure out what he was going to do with himself for the rest of his life. He'd been an exemplary Navy SEAL. There weren't many other things he was good at.

"No problem. We love having you stay with us," Nick said. "It's like old times. It's been awfully quiet around here without Kara." The longing in his brother's voice gutted him. Luke had never loved any woman enough to feel the pain Nick was going through, although he still empathized with him. Sometimes when he thought about Nick and Kara's love story he wondered if he was even emotionally capable of experiencing a love like that. The realization that he might not be made him feel empty inside.

Luke looked around the spacious, all-white kitchen. It had been Kara's pride and joy, the place where she'd cooked meals from the heart to nurture her family. Luke remembered when they'd first bought this home and created the nursery for the child they'd dreamed of having. Kara, with her warm smiles and vivacious personality, had been the heart and soul of their home, as well as a beloved member of the Mistletoe community. There had just been something about his sister-in-law that had made loving her the easiest thing he'd ever done. He'd always wanted a sister, and Kara had been the perfect addition to the Keegan family.

"I know how hard it's been to try and move forward without her. She was your rock. Your true north." His throat tightened with emotion. The wounds were still fresh for all of them. If it was this hard for him to talk about Kara, he could only imagine how badly Nick struggled to deal with it all. She'd been the perfect partner for his brother with her sweet, giving personality. Kara had nurtured everyone in her world, especially Miles and Nick. And him. How many care packages had she sent him through the years. *Packaged with love.* That's how she'd always signed the letters inside.

Pain passed over Nick's face. "I try to be strong for Miles, but some days are tougher than others. It still seems so unimaginable that she's gone. Everyone says it gets better, but I still feel stuck in the weeds."

Listening to Nick's heartfelt words made Luke feel as if his heart might crack wide open. His brother had been so strong ever since his life had been torn apart. He'd needed to hold it together for Miles so his son's life would still be filled with sunshine and rainbows and Batman figurines.

"So, on a lighter note," Nick said, "it seems that your presence here in town is causing quite a stir." A huge grin broke out on his brother's face. His deep brown eyes twinkled with mirth. Luke knew this look like the back of his hand. His brother was trying to play it cool, but something was up.

"Really? Why?" he asked, playing along. Something told him he might not want to know the answer, but he wasn't going to leave Nick hanging when he was clearly enjoying himself.

Nick went into full-on smirk mode. "It seems that you've been given the title of Most Eligible Bachelor in Mistletoe."

Luke spit out his water. It sprayed in Nick's direction. "Me? You've got to be kidding."

Nick wiped water off his shirt. "Thanks for the shower, but I had one earlier."

"Sorry about that, but you can't just spring something like that on me without expecting a reaction." Luke reached for a paper towel and began wiping up the water. "I've only been in town for a few days and I've barely seen anyone. How is my name even out there?"

Nick shrugged. "Word of mouth, I guess. You strutted out onto that gymnasium floor and wowed all those teachers. And they must have spread the word about you around town." Nick placed his hand over his mouth in a gesture that did nothing to hide his grin.

"I didn't strut," Luke said through gritted teeth. "I've never strutted in my life."

Nick smirked. "Well, you clearly made an impression. My cell phone has been ringing off the hook ever since yesterday. Everyone wants me to fix them up with you." He shook his head. "I feel so used." His brother's twinkling eyes belied his comment. Nick appeared to find the situation comical.

Luke felt his eyes going wide. "You're getting requests?" Maybe Nick was playing a prank on him. Before Kara's passing, Nick had been the biggest joker out there. These days he was a bit more somber, so it was nice seeing him smile even if it was at Luke's expense.

Nick nodded. "It's no joke. More than a dozen at the moment, but who's counting? They all want to go out with you. Coffee meetups. Dinner invitations. Picnic on the beach. Movie nights at Casablanca's. It's all on the table."

Luke shook his head in disbelief and reached for one of the apples sitting in a large bowl on the kitchen table. He took a huge bite out of it. A dozen women wanting to get with him? He wasn't being humble, but it baffled him. His whole life he'd been given his fair share of female attention, but nothing like this. Nick began rattling off names, some that he was familiar with from his school days. One was even a girl he'd dated back in high school. Regina Dawkins. She'd done everything in her power to get him to marry her before he went off to the US Naval Academy in Annapolis. He had no desire to revisit their relationship. Just the thought of it made him shudder.

"What about you? Why aren't you being chased by the single women in Mistletoe?" Luke asked his brother. "Everybody loves you." With Nick's sweet personality, he'd always been beloved. Someone like him shouldn't go through life alone. Kara was too special to ever be replaced, but he wanted his brother to find love again. This home needed a woman's touch, especially for Miles.

Nick quirked his mouth. "I'm the heartbroken widower. No one wants to push me into anything romantic before I'm ready. And trust me, I'm not. But I'd like to find love again someday. Just not now."

Luke's guilt rose up leaving him breathless. Up until now he'd been overseas focusing on his military career. He'd been MIA during some of his family's lowest moments. With the exception of the funeral, he hadn't been around to hold his brother and nephew up as they mourned their huge loss. If it was possible, he intended to make up for it now that he was home. But he drew the line at going out on dates with the single women in town as a way to make Nick happy. Luke knew his brother would love nothing better than to see Luke settle down with someone in their hometown.

Nope. It wasn't happening. Not in a million years. Being in Mistletoe was about settling into a new life. Now he could finally meet with the families of his SEAL team buddies who'd died in the explosion. Luke owed them a face-to-face. Being back in Mistletoe was about saying goodbye to the demands of being in the military and getting his body back in the condition it had been in before the IED explosion. He was no longer fit for duty as a SEAL, but he wasn't useless.

"Honestly, I'm not really interested," he admitted, bracing for his brother's response.

Nick's lips twisted. "Are you serious? You're turning down the chance to date some of Mistletoe's finest ladies?" Nick was staring at him with disbelief. "I remember the days when you would have jumped at an opportunity like this. What's up with that?"

"I don't really...date." Luke forced the admission out of his mouth. Saying it out loud made it all too real. And he knew it must sound strange to Nick.

Nick snorted. "What does that even mean? You're single. And pretty good-looking according to the ladies. Even back in high school you had them wrapped around your finger. Frankly, I don't see the appeal," he teased, his handsome face lit up with a grin. "But there's no accounting for taste." He waited a beat then asked, "When was the last time you were coupled up with someone?"

Luke nodded. "Not in a while." Not since Allison. They'd met during one of his deployments when he had headed to Hawaii for some rest and relaxation. Maintaining a relationship while employed as a Navy SEAL had been near impossible due to the demands of his profession. He'd never told Luke the details about the way their relationship had ended. He hadn't wanted his little brother to think badly of him for breaking her heart. That situation had revealed so much to him about himself. He wasn't a good partner, and he didn't think he ever would be.

"It's not like I could actively pursue a relationship while deployed," Luke explained. "Things get way too intense for me to be able to dedicate myself to another person. Or keep up a long-distance relationship."

"I get that," Nick said, taking a swig of water. "It's not exactly conducive to a steady partnership."

"I'm not proud to admit it, but in the past few years it's been more hookups than anything of substance," Luke confessed. His brother had always been easy to talk to. When they were growing up, they'd shared secrets in the quiet hours after lights were out in their bedroom. Both had kept those sacred words in confidence, never telling them to another soul. It wouldn't be any different now.

Nick nodded. "I get it. But, word to the wise, it's definitely not smart to be hooking up with a bunch of women in a small town like Mistletoe. I'm sure you remember how fast gossip spreads around town. I'd hate to see you caught up in the rumor mill." Nick sent him a warning look.

"No thank you. I'll pass on all that." Luke shuddered. "From what you told me, Dante and Lucy were in the thick of it last Christmas. It sounded like the whole town was in their business."

"Yeah," Nick said with a chuckle. "But look how that ended. He put a ring on it."

Luke let out a low whistle. "Good for them, but I have

no intention of getting hitched any time soon. I don't even see myself being in a relationship."

"Keep an open mind, Luke. Now might be the time to connect with someone in a meaningful way. And if you end up planting permanent roots here, you might just find yourself wanting to settle down."

He moaned. "I'm not good at making connections. You know some of what happened in my last relationship. Things got really complicated." Heat suffused his face. In a perfect world he would be friends with his exes, but it never worked out that way for him. His profession hadn't allowed him to be present in relationships, and when things went south there were always bad feelings.

Nick held up his hands. "I'm not pressuring you. I just wanted to give you a heads-up about your name coming up as Mistletoe's most in-demand bachelor."

Luke winced and placed his hand over his chest. "You make it sound so stressful. No pressure."

Nick locked eyes with Luke from across the table. "If I haven't said it a hundred times already, I'm really happy to have you back."

"Glad to be here, bro," Luke answered. "Thanks for welcoming me with open arms." And he meant it. He hadn't had a home in quite some time. Mistletoe was a soft place to fall. And he needed one now more than ever. He'd made the mistake of believing that the Navy SEALs were his family, until it had all fallen apart and he'd been forced to realize that he was damaged goods. The last thing he needed was to be booed up with someone who dreamed about white picket fences and a house full of kids. He wasn't the settling-down type. A host of failed romances had driven home the point.

How could he ever be worthy of a normal future when his actions had cost two of his SEAL team members their lives?

CHAPTER FIVE

"Lucy, you look radiant," Stella gushed, admiring her sister, who stood before her in a stunning ivory gown with a tulle skirt and dazzling rhinestones gracing the bodice. Set against her sister's tawny-colored skin, the dress was spectacular. And achingly romantic. Stella sighed as Lucy preened in front of the full-length mirror.

"Do you love it?" Lucy asked, her eyes filled with such joy it made Stella want to weep. Lucy deserved the world, and it was so wonderful to see her getting it. She flashed back to when they were kids playing wedding and dressing up in their mother's lacy nightgowns. Back then they'd each had their own fantasies about what it would mean to be a bride. Only now for Lucy, it would soon be a reality.

Stella reached out and touched the gown's fabric. "It's perfect. You knocked it out of the park."

Stella tried not to think of her own wedding dress, which had never made it down the aisle, but the vintage silk gown flashed before her eyes. It still hung in her closet as a memory of what might have been. Although she'd tried on several occasions to donate the dress to Goodwill, she hadn't been able to go through with it.

Their mother, Leslie, dabbed at her eyes with a tissue. "I can't even come up with a word to describe how you look. Dante is going to be blown away when he sees you gliding down the aisle."

"It's even prettier than I remember from last time," Lucy said, twirling around for her audience. Stella, along with her mother and little sister, Tess, had gathered at Rosie's Bridal Shop in order to weigh in at Lucy's last fitting before the wedding. Between the four of them there wasn't a dry eye in the gown shop.

"You look like a princess," Tess added, gazing up at her sister with an expression resembling worship. At ten years old, Tess was enthralled by the idea of her big sister getting married to a movie star. Not to mention the fact that she was thrilled to be in the wedding party as a junior bridesmaid. Stella's heart ached a little bit at the realization that Tess was growing up so fast. She'd always been an adult masquerading in a child's body, but as of late she was maturing by leaps and bounds. Next month they would be celebrating her eleventh birthday. It didn't seem possible that she was so grown.

Lucy leaned down and pressed a kiss on Tess's cheek. "Thanks, Tess. A princess bride. That's one of my favorite books."

"You Marshall girls sure make my wedding dresses shine," Rosie said, her voice shimmering with pride. She gasped and turned her gaze to Stella, a sheepish expression on her face. "Me and my big mouth. I'm sorry, honey. I didn't mean to bring up a sensitive subject."

"No worries," Stella said as heat suffused her cheeks. She'd been waiting for an awkward moment like this one ever since their arrival. Two years ago Stella had stood in this very bridal shop and modeled her own wedding gown for her mother, sisters, and Carolina. Rosie had fawned all over Stella, telling her she was the most stunning bride-to-be she'd ever seen. But for her fiancé calling off the wedding, Stella would be married right now. She might even have a little one on the way. Most days Stella could stuff the memories down into a little black hole, but standing in Rosie's shop brought it all back again in vivid detail. Lucy sent Stella a sympathetic look. Stella winked at her sister, letting her know she was fine. She didn't want Lucy to spend a single moment worrying about her feelings when the focus should be on her upcoming wedding. This was her special day.

"Let me help you out of the dress," Rosie said to Lucy. Rosie's voice sounded way more subdued than usual. Stella had the feeling she was still kicking herself for her slip of the tongue. "We don't want a single sequin to come undone when you change back into your clothes."

After Lucy and Rosie went into the dressing room, Tess filled the air with chatter about summer vacation and her plans to become a famous Olympian swimmer. Stella felt grateful for the way her little sister was able to effortlessly ease the tension. A late-in-life baby for her parents, Tess was truly the heartbeat of the Marshall family.

Lucy returned a few minutes later without Rosie. "I need to head back to the library," she said, casting a glance at her watch. "I hate to dash off, but I have some new programs to set up for guest lecturers. I'm really thankful for all the support." Lucy reached out and squeezed Stella's hand. "I know it hasn't been easy for you seeing me in the wedding gown and helping me with my planning, but I truly appreciate it, Stella. You're the best."

"I always want the world for you, Lucy. And that's never going to change." Tears misted in her eyes as she hugged her sister. Helping Lucy was second nature to Stella. The two of them had always been joined at the hip. She couldn't ask for a better or more loyal best friend. With only a year separating them, they had walked through life side by side and shared an unbreakable bond. Seeing her walk off into the sunset with Dante gave Stella a glimmer of hope that it was possible to find love, even though the thought of trusting someone again terrified her. Every time she imagined getting close to a man, Rafe's betrayal came back into sharp focus.

"You two are getting mushy," Tess complained. She rolled her eyes and folded her arms across her chest.

"If this isn't the time to get mushy, then I don't know what is," Leslie said, tugging at her daughter's pigtail. "Happiness is something to rejoice about."

"I've got my swim practice, Mama," Tess said, pulling at her mother's hand. "We need to get going before I'm late."

Leslie reached for her cane and stood up. Although

her movements were slightly jerky, Stella appreciated the fact that her mother's multiple sclerosis had improved in the past few months. At the moment, she was able to drive and work part-time hours. They were all aware that the situation could regress, so it was all the more poignant to see her doing so well.

"Let's do Mexican takeout this week at my house," Lucy suggested. "We can watch that new show *Love Connection*." Lucy's house was located right across the street from their childhood home, where her parents and Tess still lived. It was a cozy situation for all involved, although Stella still loved living by Blackberry Beach with the ocean a stone's throw from her house and the sea air filling her nostrils. She hadn't known it at the time she'd purchased the cottage, but being by the sea had served as a refuge from the storms of life.

"Sounds good," Stella said, reaching out to hug her sister. "I'll see you guys later. Rosie asked me to stick around so we can finalize the bridesmaid dress order." After another chorus of goodbyes, Stella found herself standing alone in the salon surrounded by dozens of bridal gowns.

So. Many. Wedding dresses. In all shapes, sizes, designs, and shades. Sweetheart necklines. Mermaid style. A-line. Strapless. Sheath. It felt like her worst nightmare brought to life. Was this some sort of sign? A visual reminder that she was miles away from being settled in her life?

Being at the bridal shop had truly been taking one for the team. *Team Lucy and Dante.* But, if she was being completely honest, she couldn't wait to get as far away from this shop as humanly possible. What in the world was taking Rosie so long? Maybe she should just leave and come back another time.

Finally, Stella thought, as footsteps echoed in the hall. A few seconds later when Rosie reentered the salon she wasn't alone.

"Sorry to keep you waiting, Stella. You remember my nephew, Tucker?" Rosie was looking back and forth between Stella and Tucker with a rapturous smile stamped on her face.

Stella nodded and fixed a smile on her face. In a million years Stella could never forget Tucker Riordan. "Of course I do. Nice to see you again, Tucker." Ugh. It really wasn't, but Stella was nothing if not polite. Her mama had raised her right.

Tall and blond, Tucker was a decent-looking guy, but his personality needed an overhaul. He was pushy and needy, as well as being a bit of a narcissist. Tucker's sudden arrival was obviously a setup by Rosie. Clearly, at some point she had given Tucker a call and invited him down to her place of business to see Stella. *Surprise!*

Without any warning, Tucker leaned in and hugged her. The smell of strong cologne rose to her nostrils. Stella froze up at the overly intimate gesture and stepped away. Six months ago she'd gone on a coffee date with Tucker after Rosie had relentlessly hounded her to meet him. It had been a complete disaster as far as Stella was concerned. Tucker had mapped out their entire future together, even going so far as to call her his new girlfriend. After an hour of torture, Stella had slunk out of the café claiming a migraine. She'd been ducking Tucker's calls ever since.

"You're a hard person to track down, Stella Marshall." Tucker grinned and wagged his finger at her. "I've been wanting to see you again since our last date. Where have you been hiding?"

All of a sudden, Stella felt tongue-tied. It wasn't as if she could tell him the cold, hard truth—she'd rather have a root canal than go out with him again. She'd been avoiding Tucker like nobody's business ever since their disastrous coffee date. Mistletoe was a quintessential small town that made such efforts nearly impossible. Yet, somehow, Stella had managed to pull it off like a pro. "I've just been so busy with work and my sister's upcoming wedding. I'm the maid of honor so I'm up to my elbows in planning."

Tucker winked at her. "You know what they say about bridesmaids? You'll be the next one walking down the aisle. So don't worry about it."

Hmm. Kind of an inconsiderate comment considering she'd been dumped right before *her* wedding. She couldn't miss Rosie jabbing her nephew in the side.

"I'm not worried," Stella said, trying not to show her annoyance at Tucker. Why did people always say things like that to the sister of the bride, as if she was staying up at night fretting over her single status? She would bet her last dollar that no one ever made comments like this to the best man. Or any man for that matter!

"Good," Tucker said with a grin, seemingly oblivious to her irritation. "Now how about we pick up where we left off? I'd love to take you out to dinner. Maybe I'll add in a movie if you play your cards right." He winked at her in an exaggerated fashion.

Rosie rolled her eyes and shook her head. Even she seemed to know that Tucker was a fool.

"So let's make a date," he said. His expression reflected his eagerness. He was practically panting. He reminded her of Bucky, the St. Bernard her family had owned during her childhood.

"I-I can't, Tucker. I'm actually seeing someone," she fibbed. Other than sheer desperation, Stella didn't know why that humongous lie had come out of her mouth. In a small town it was unlikely that people wouldn't know if she was dating somebody. Now that she'd stepped into it, Stella didn't know how to get herself out of the sticky situation she'd created. Why hadn't she just told him the truth? *Tucker, I'm just not that into you.*

Tucker's face fell. A frown replaced his over-the-top smile. "What do you mean? How is that possible?"

Stella sputtered. "Excuse me. What is that supposed to mean? You want to go out with me, so why wouldn't someone else want to date me?"

"I'm sure he didn't mean it like that, Stella," Rosie interjected, sounding apologetic. She jabbed her nephew again in the side. Stella felt a sense of satisfaction when this time he grunted.

Tucker shrugged. "Word around town is that you've been single ever since Rafe dumped you at the altar. That's why I'm surprised."

Rosie moaned and put her head in her hands. Stella opened her mouth to check him, but other than being a rude jerk, he hadn't told any lies.

"So who is he?" Tucker asked. He'd quickly transformed from happy-go-lucky to angry. Red splotches colored his cheeks, and his hands were tightly clenched at his sides.

"Tucker, this is a relatively new relationship, so for now we're keeping it under wraps," Stella said, hoping she wasn't going up in flames for telling such a whopper.

"So you're not even going to give me that courtesy?" Tucker asked. By this time, he was pacing back and forth in front of Stella and looking more upset by the minute.

"I really can't," Stella murmured. At least this was the truth! She couldn't name someone who didn't exist. Ha!

In response, Tucker stormed out of the room, his footsteps loud and clunky.

"I'm sorry. He's always been a bit of a hothead," Rosie apologized. "Let me talk to him for a minute. Then I'll come right back."

Stella slapped her palm against her forehead. She really needed to get going. This trip to the bridal salon was becoming an all-day affair. And even though she was relieved that Tucker would no longer be pursuing her, she still felt nervous that her lie would unravel.

She could hear more footsteps, the opening and closing of a door, then a mixture of voices. One sounded low and masculine. She sincerely hoped Tucker hadn't returned to grill her about her mystery man. She wasn't sure how long she could hold up against any further interrogation. She might fold like a deck of cards.

"We're actually looking for a baby's christening gown." The deep gravelly voice drifted into the room where she was waiting. It was one Stella knew as well as her own, and her entire body tensed up at the sound of it.

"Can you believe Lily is almost four months old?" a female voice rang out. She knew it must be Rafe's wife, Tabitha. To Stella it sounded like nails on a chalkboard.

Stella felt as if her heart might jump out of her chest. She pressed her eyes closed and pinched herself. *No way! This cannot be happening.* Not on the heels of being blindsided by Tucker. Not when she was standing in the same bridal salon where she'd been fitted for her own breathtakingly gorgeous gown. Not when the man standing in the next room with his wife and baby had turned her entire world upside down a few days before their wedding. Sheer panic seized her, and she began taking shallow breaths to calm herself down.

"Oh, she's lovely. What a perfect name." Rosie's voice sounded a bit muffled as if she didn't want Stella to overhear her.

Stella battled against feelings of anger toward Rosie. She knew it didn't make any sense, but it hurt to think her friend was praising Rafe and his family. Everything he now had in his life had come about due to his decision to call off their wedding. He had broken Stella's heart in the process and made her a laughingstock in Mistletoe. The only thing he deserved was a swift kick in the rear.

She didn't want Rafe or his wife to see her. And she really didn't want to come face-to-face with them or their baby. Especially the baby! Laying eyes on her ex-fiancé would bring up too many emotions she wouldn't be able to stuff down. And she wasn't going to give Rafe the satisfaction of seeing her crumble right before his eyes. Grabbing her purse from the sofa, Stella scoured the room for a way to exit the salon without entering the hallway. There was literally no way out.

Stella eyeballed the window. No, she couldn't. What if someone saw her? Even when she wasn't on the clock, she tried her best to comport herself as a professional. Just then the sound of Rafe's laughter drifted into the salon room. Desperate times called for desperate measures. With a huge sigh, Stella leaned forward and began tugging at the window frame. After a few attempts, it lifted so that she could easily push up the screen. She bent forward and catapulted herself onto the ground, landing on a mound of pink peonies. She crouched down low in case of any passersby, then jumped to her feet and partially closed the window behind her just as Rosie came into view. Stella quickly moved to the side of the building where traffic was traveling past at a trickle. She smoothed down her hair and wiped dirt off her slacks as her brain tried to catch up with her actions. If she circled back to the lot, Rosie, Rafe, and his wife might spot her. If that happened, the ground might just open up and swallow her with mortification.

The honking sound of a slow approaching vehicle unnerved her. Had someone seen her climbing through the window? Goodness! Could this day get any more humiliating? The navy-blue truck slowed down and came to a stop beside her. The passenger-side window rolled down and Luke's gorgeous face was peering out at her. "Hey. Are you okay? You look like you're about to jump out of your skin," he called out. As usual, Luke radiated the kind of raw sex appeal that made her knees go weak.

She barely had time for that thought to register before dread washed over her.

"I need to make a quick getaway," Stella said, advancing toward the vehicle. Before she could even think about what she was doing, she wrenched open the passenger-side door and jumped inside. "Get me out of here, Luke," she said in a trembling voice. "Now!"

* * *

Luke had no idea what was going on with Stella, but he pressed his foot on the gas and took off down the road and away from Rosie's Bridal Shop as fast as he possibly could. He couldn't remember the last time he'd been involved in rescuing a woman fleeing a bridal shop, but as a Navy SEAL he was ready for anything. *Former Navy SEAL*, he corrected himself. It was going to take him some time to come to terms with his early retirement. Every time he thought about it, Luke felt as if he'd been run over by a Mack truck.

A quick glance in Stella's direction showed she was breathing heavily. He tried his best not to let his gaze linger. He didn't want to ogle her during a crisis. Everything about her behavior indicated that something bad had gone down. *Look at the road before you get into a wreck*, he cautioned himself. He let out a deep, steadying breath as he focused. This woman did something to his equilibrium. It had been a long time since he'd felt anything quite like this. She was a sucker punch to his gut.

Seconds ticked by without Stella saying a single word. He needed to fill the silence by saying something.

Anything. There was nothing worse than this type of quiet when you weren't alone.

"I don't mind being your getaway driver, but where am I headed?" he asked. Being in such close confines with Stella was all kinds of wonderful. A sweet floral scent hovered in the air. He had to admit he liked it. It had been a long time since Luke had been this up close and personal with perfume and he'd missed it.

"Anywhere is fine. I don't care." As Stella shrugged, dark strands of hair swirled around her shoulders. She really was beautiful with her warm brown skin and striking features. At the moment she looked vulnerable, and he wondered what exactly he'd rescued her from. A hundred different theories were bouncing around in his head. Had he been her getaway driver after she'd robbed Rosie's salon? The thought made him want to laugh out loud.

"Nice ride by the way," she mumbled.

"I just bought it," Luke answered. "It's been invaluable taking me to all of my old haunts. I've been thinking about driving Miles to Old Orchard Beach and staying for a few days." His nephew didn't have anything major on his schedule for a few weeks, so Luke thought he might enjoy a short getaway. It would also give Nick a little bit of a break.

"He'd love that, especially the amusement park."

"I'm not sure which one of us would love it more." After all these years he was still a big kid at heart. He loved roller coasters and Ferris wheels.

"How about I drive to Main Street or the lake? Or I could drive to Blackberry Beach or the marina," he suggested. She wasn't giving him much direction, which made him all the more curious about why she'd fled the store like she'd just robbed a bank. He'd endured his fair share of panic attacks in the past few months. Was that what was going on with Stella?

"I don't know. My car is still parked in the lot by Rosie's salon." She groaned. "Can you just drive me around for a little bit so I don't run into him…them? If it's not too much trouble."

Him? Them? Yep. There was definitely a story brewing here. And he really wanted to know the reason she'd escaped via a window as if her pants were on fire. But he wanted to ask her in a way that didn't make her feel as if she were under a microscope.

"It's not any trouble at all." He tightened his grip on the steering wheel. "So are you okay? Do you want to talk about what happened back there?" He still couldn't believe he'd seen her somersault out of an open window. Had someone been chasing her? With every second that went by he became increasingly concerned. He needed to know if someone had harmed her in any way.

"Let's just say my past came rearing up to bite me," she answered in a low voice. "So thanks for the rescue. You were in the right place at the right time. I'm grateful."

Another quick glance in her direction revealed slumped shoulders and a downcast expression. Seeing her so dejected caused a squeezing sensation in his chest.

"It can't be that bad. Can it?" Luke didn't mean to pry, but he figured Stella might benefit from a sounding board. His fellow SEALs had always told him he was a good listener. Out of the corner of his eye he could see her fiddling with her fingers.

Stella let out a deep breath. "It's my ex. He came into the shop with his wife. He was in the hallway, so he didn't see me, but when I heard his voice I just panicked. So instead of coming face-to-face with him like a normal person would, I fled the premises."

Luke sputtered. "Through a window?"

"Yep. It was the only way to avoid seeing Rafe," Stella acknowledged. "I'd rather pitch myself out a window than look into his beady little eyes."

Luke turned to look at her. "So you're running from an ex? Wouldn't it be better just to deal with the situation head-on?" Luke immediately felt the heat of Stella's glare in his direction.

"He's not just any ex. We were engaged." She spit out the words like they were poison.

A surprised sound slipped past his lips. "Oh. Wow. Engaged." Curiosity pricked at him, but it wasn't the time or the place to ask. If Stella wanted to tell him, he'd be all ears.

"It's only fair to tell you since you're probably wondering why I'm avoiding him like the devil himself. I was planning to spend the rest of my life with Rafe when he decided two days before the wedding that I wasn't the one. And to make matters worse, he hightailed it back to his hometown and tracked down his high school sweetheart and married *her* a few weeks later."

Luke winced. Ouch. Her ex had delivered several crushing blows in rapid succession. It sounded like Stella had dodged a bullet with this Rafe character, but he knew better than to say it out loud. Stella's nerves were seriously on edge, and he didn't want to push it by saying something wrong. He steered the truck onto the stretch of road parallel to Blackberry Beach, pulling into one of the main parking lots. Luke brought the vehicle to a stop and put it in park.

He turned toward Stella. It was near impossible for him to imagine anyone treating Stella so poorly. "I'm so sorry he put you through all of that," he said. He wished he could say more, do more to make the sad expression on her face go away.

Stella let out a brittle laugh. Her eyes looked moist. "Yeah, well it was a really sorry situation. Do you want to know what the icing on the cake is? It's not just the two of them anymore. They have a baby girl, Luke. And Rafe had the freaking audacity to steal my baby name."

CHAPTER SIX

Once the words flew out of her mouth, Stella wanted to rein them back in. Why had she just blurted out something so personal to Luke? So far, the only person she'd discussed the baby-name situation with was Lucy, who'd wanted to hunt Rafe down and bloody his nose on her behalf. Stella hadn't objected on principle, but due to Lucy's position as head librarian and her engagement to a certain famous actor, it might have landed Lucy on the cover of the *National Enquirer*. That type of negative publicity would have been disastrous. Thankfully, Stella had talked her out of it. Ever since they were little, it had been Stella's job to rein Lucy in. She still wondered if she should have let Lucy do her thing just that one time.

As it was, Luke probably thought she was having a nervous breakdown, which was a distinct possibility under the circumstances. Her face felt warmer than usual and her heart was beating really fast. She was talking a mile a minute and there was nothing cool, calm, or collected about her at the moment. That was unusual for her. Normally she held things together quite well. Her fight-or-flight response to hearing the sound of Rafe's voice had taken her by surprise. Although she knew she wasn't over the Rafe situation, she hadn't expected to react so strongly to his nearness.

She turned her head and met Luke's gaze. The smell of pine and the outdoors hovered around him. Being in such close confines in his truck brought his attributes into sharp focus. He had a strong jawline, nice bone structure, and broad shoulders that a girl could comfortably lay her head on. It was hard not to stare. She felt certain that women must ogle him all the time.

Stella suppressed the urge to reach out and graze her fingers against his warm brown skin. He looked extremely rugged, no doubt due to his military training. She'd heard how rigorous the requirements were, not to mention the actual conditions they faced while being deployed. Luke was the real deal. No question about it. He'd earned his swagger.

"He did what?" Luke's eyes were bulging, and there was an angry-looking vein on his forehead. She shivered. This was not a man to be messed with. He didn't strike her as the type of person who would back down to anyone or anything.

"Yep. To add to his other crimes, he's a thief. I made a list of names for our future children, and he used the one at the top of my girl list. Who does that?" Just thinking about it made her face burn with outrage. "It's just such a low-down thing to do in addition to everything else he put me through. Of all the names out there in the universe, did he really have to poach mine?"

Luke clenched his jaw. "You won't get any argument from me on that front. Not to rub salt in the wound, but it seems hard to believe it wasn't deliberate."

She let out an indelicate snort. "I'd bet my last dollar it was." Stella had no idea why Rafe seemed to want to twist the knife in her back. Hadn't he done enough by calling off their wedding and marrying another woman? Buying the old Victorian they'd talked about and stealing her baby name were acts of aggression.

Luke made a loud sucking sound with his teeth. It felt good to know Luke felt her pain. Or at least understood.

"And then my friend Rosie who owns the bridal shop blindsided me with her nephew, Tucker, who just happened to find his way over to the shop while I was there. I've been dodging his calls and texts for months now, so it was awkward to say the least," she explained. She felt a bit breathless after talking a mile a minute.

"Wouldn't it just be easier to tell him you're not interested?" Luke was looking at her with his head cocked to the side as if he couldn't figure her out. For a millisecond she got lost in his soulful brown eyes. At this close proximity she could see little caramel-colored flecks in his orbs. Stella slowly dragged her gaze away and focused on the sight of the ocean in the distance. Usually it brought her a sense of calm, but at the moment it wasn't doing anything to bring Stella peace.

She let out a pent-up sigh. "Of course it would be. But

that would be the mature thing to do, right? Surely you don't expect that from a woman who threw herself out of a shop window. That's why I hate people trying to play matchmaker on my behalf. I have trouble saying no. It's the same thing with my parents. They're always trying to set me up on blind dates." Stella made a face.

"Okay, so it's not as bad as you might think," Luke said, his voice calm and sexy. "Just tell the nephew you don't think the two of you are a good fit. Let him down easy, but firmly. Put some bass in your voice if you have to. And as for your ex, I think avoiding him at all costs is the smart thing to do." He quirked his mouth. "He sounds pretty awful."

Stella didn't know how to explain it, but hearing Luke speak so poorly about Rafe made her feel defensive. For better or worse, she'd loved him like nobody's business. Sometimes she wondered if she still did. Every now and again, late at night in the hours between darkness and dawn, thoughts of Rafe kept her awake. She wondered when he'd stopped loving her and why. Had there been some pivotal moment that she'd missed? Something she'd done to turn him off?

"He wasn't always such a complete jerk," she said quietly, wrapping her arms around her midsection. It felt like Luke's condemnation of Rafe was a reflection of her and the poor choices she'd made in her romantic life. If he was the world's biggest tool, why had she planned to marry him? What was wrong with her? Why was she feeling some kind of way about Luke's description of her ex? Rafe had jerked her around and treated her horribly. He'd left her broken and embarrassed and empty. The entire town of Mistletoe had borne witness to her humiliation. If she lived to be 102, Stella didn't think she would ever forget how awful it had felt to be unceremoniously dumped.

"When we were together, he was far from perfect . . . but not a monster." Her voice was a lot softer now. "Trust me, I have moments where he seems worse than Hannibal Lecter, but he wasn't always that way." Otherwise, Stella never would have fallen in love with the handsome charmer.

"I'm sorry if I overstepped. I don't even know the guy. But the way he treated you . . . I hope you know you didn't deserve that." The intensity radiating from Luke's eyes made Stella feel comforted and valued. It was amazing how a few words from someone she didn't even know all that well could lift her up.

"I do," she said, blinking away tears. And she did. It was just so hard to move past the promise of the life she'd mapped out. *Wedding, honeymoon in Fiji, buying the sweet Victorian home, babies.* She'd planned on being happy and paired up with a man who was committed to her. And yet, in the end, she'd been left with nothing. Although Stella had chosen not to showcase her heartache to the entire town, she'd been completely shattered by Rafe's actions. Strangely, folks just expected her to get over it and move on to someone else. She wasn't built that way.

"Do you know what it's like being the older sister of someone who's getting married to Mistletoe's favorite son? Everyone and their mother wants to pair me up with someone. They seem to think I can just find my soulmate by snapping my fingers." She let out an indelicate snort. "As if I want all of that. Those dreams went up in smoke a while ago. If another person asks me when I'm getting hitched, I'm going to lose it. And things might get really ugly if anyone tries to set me up with their nephew or brother or the random guy who sells CDs out of the back of his car."

Luke wasn't saying anything. He was gazing pretty intensely out the window toward the endless miles of ocean. Stella imagined there were a lot of thoughts running around in his brain, such as wondering how he'd gotten stuck with her inside his vehicle in the first place.

"I'm sorry for ranting. I promise you I'm not usually like this," she said. She felt deeply ashamed. Luke hadn't signed up for all of this. All he'd offered her was a ride, not a therapy session. It was just so frustrating to have to suck up her feelings all the time and pretend as if all was right in her world when in reality it seemed like she might be falling apart.

He turned back toward her. "There's nothing to be sorry for. You've really been through it. Believe it or not, we have more in common than you might think."

"Really?" she asked. What could she and this rugged military hero have in common? It was unlikely that his personal life was as messy as her own unless he had some major skeletons in his closet. And if he did, she would really like to hear all about them so she didn't feel like such a mess.

"Yeah," Luke said. He cleared his throat. "It seems I may have captured the attention of a few dozen ladies here in town. They've been blowing up Nick's phone and asking to go out with me." He raised his fingers and began massaging his temple as if he had the world's biggest headache. "It's getting a bit awkward."

There was absolutely nothing shocking to Stella about Luke being a hot commodity in Mistletoe. She'd predicted it the very first day he'd shown up at her school. Navy SEAL plus tall, dark, and handsome was a nobrainer in these parts. Stella was slightly surprised they weren't showing up unannounced at Nick's house to try and woo Luke with cakes, casseroles, and skimpy outfits. Or anything else that might tempt him.

She made a tutting sound. "I hope you realize that these women aren't playing around. You've only been in town for a few days so they're probably trying to pace themselves. Just wait until they get their bearings." Stella chuckled. "I can't say I'm surprised though. Everyone in Mistletoe is eager to be booed up with someone."

"Everyone except you?" Luke asked with his eyebrows knitted together.

"You got that right. I'm not interested in being someone's other half," Stella admitted. "Been there done that. I'm not going down that road again. I mean if it happens that would be good, but I'm not going out of my way looking for it."

Luke sighed. "I should give you a pep talk and convince you to give romance another try, but considering I'm content being single myself, it would be disingenuous."

They sat for a few minutes in companionable silence. Stella liked the fact that Luke didn't make her feel like a lunatic. He really listened to her and responded with sincerity and kindness. *Thank you, Mrs. Keegan, for raising Luke right.*

"I think I'm ready to head back to the parking lot. I doubt Rafe is still at the shop." Stella bit her lip. She sure hoped he wasn't. As it was she would have to dart to her car in case Rosie happened to be looking out her window. The thought of explaining her Houdini disappearing act was cringeworthy.

"Are you sure? I don't mind hanging out for a bit longer. You're making a great case for staying single," he said, the corners of his mouth twitching with merriment. And what a nice mouth he had, Stella thought once again. His lips were full and perfectly shaped. Extremely kissable.

"I'm sure," she said with a nod, slightly distracted by her unruly thoughts. "Thanks for the getaway car. It felt a little bit like we were Bonnie and Clyde taking off like that."

Luke grinned at her, flashing a Colgate smile. "Anytime, Stella. I've always been partial to that movie. Do you mind if I turn on the radio?"

"Go for it," Stella said. Music always lifted her mood. Spending time with Luke and being surrounded by his calming presence had made her feel so much better. "There's a great new R & B station. 107.9."

Luke fiddled with the dial and programmed the station in. The upbeat rhythms of Kem filled the truck, and Stella found herself humming along with the song. For the duration of the ride back to Rosie's they listened to the soothing tunes with no conversation taking place. Strangely enough, it felt comfortable and natural. She didn't know why being around Luke felt so natural, since they hadn't known each other very well back in school. Not to mention the years standing between the present and the last time they'd seen each other. But there was no denying their easy rapport. She wondered if he felt it too.

"Well, we're back where this little adventure began," Luke said as he pulled into the lot behind Rosie's salon. He looked around a little bit and said, "Looks like the coast is clear."

Relief flowed through her. "Thank goodness. I'm parked right over there." Stella pointed to her dark compact vehicle. Luke pulled his truck alongside her car and put his vehicle in park.

Stella unlatched her seat belt and grabbed her purse. "I appreciate what you did for me today, Luke. I owe you one."

"I'm definitely going to call you on it. When you least expect it, you're going to have to repay this debt." Luke's eyes twinkled and he let out a devilish laugh. Her heart lurched a little bit. This one could charm all the ladies in Mistletoe without even trying.

"Whatever you say, Godfather," she said, referencing her favorite Francis Ford Coppola movie. With a final wave, Stella got out of the truck and shut the door behind her. Luke's laughter trailed after her, warming her insides and serving as a reminder that she'd made it through this storm. She was way stronger than she believed herself to be. As she started up her car and made her way back home, Luke permeated her thoughts.

After all these years, Luke Keegan was still one of

the most swoon-worthy men she had ever known. And he wasn't just eye candy either. He brought so many things to the table—loyalty, honor, humor, and strength. If Stella wasn't so gun shy about men and relationships, she might just be tempted to give it a whirl with the scrumptious Navy SEAL.

CHAPTER SEVEN

You heard what?" Stella asked Lucy in a raised voice that she hoped hadn't carried into the living room, where her mother and Tess were playing cards. She lowered her tone. "Please tell me you're not serious." She didn't know why she was surprised. Stella had suspected this would happen after Patsy's comments about her and Luke.

Lucy looked back at her with wide eyes. "Yep. Today at the library I overheard Laura Jean and Violet talking about you hooking up with Luke. Something tells me they wanted me to hear them because they were not being discreet at all with their gossip." Lucy made a tsking sound. "I imagine they were looking for confirmation from me, so at first I just pretended not to hear them."

Laura Jean Samuels was a former classmate of theirs while Violet Stewart was an older woman who considered herself a matriarch in Mistletoe. As far as Stella was concerned, neither one had any sense. Laura Jean liked flirting wildly with other women's husbands, while as town historian, Violet was rumored to carry around a notebook detailing all of Mistletoe's scandals. She was second only to Patsy in the gossip game.

"That's absolutely ridiculous," Stella sputtered. "Why on earth would they say something like that?"

"They said Patsy told them," Lucy said with a shrug. "No big surprise there."

Stella pressed her hand to her forehead and groaned. "Patsy! I should have known it was her. She loves finding a bone and running with it."

Lucy sent her a knowing look. Patsy was legendary in Mistletoe for being a chatterbox, and that term was being kind. With all the luck, Stella just happened to live next door to her. Violet was no better. She was a notorious gossip with zero remorse about spreading lies all over Mistletoe.

"I eventually walked over and told them it wasn't true," Lucy added, "but I don't think they believed me." Lucy leaned in toward her. "It's not true, is it?" she asked in a low whisper.

"Lucy!" Stella gasped and swatted her sister with her hand. "You know it isn't. I totally forgot that Patsy saw Luke at my place the other day. We were out on the patio. Even though I tried to shoot down her comments about us being involved, she wouldn't listen to me." Stella threw her hands up in the air. "You know how she can be. Completely intractable."

Lucy rolled her eyes. "I sure do. That woman spreads

gossip like it's a paying job. And she convinces herself it's the truth."

"Well, I have a few choice words for her when I see her again." Stella stabbed a fork into the salad, then poured dressing in the bowl and tossed it. "Did you get a sense of what exactly she's saying?"

Lucy bit her lip then turned toward the stove so that Stella could no longer see her expression. Stella knew her sister well enough to know she was low-key trying to avoid the question, which meant it was bad. "Lucy. It's okay. I can take it. What is Patsy saying?"

"That she caught the two of you half-dressed on your patio," Lucy said, turning back around to face Stella. "She made it sound like the two of you were getting frisky right out in the open."

Stella sucked in a shocked breath. "What a liar!" she seethed. "I was simply getting Luke some bottled water."

Lucy bent over and took a sheet of taco shells out of the oven, then placed them on the stove. "Leave it to Patsy to turn a simple act of kindness into a torrid affair."

"It was all perfectly innocent," Stella explained. "Coco Chanel got loose so I chased her down the beach where I ran into Luke who was out on a run. He managed to catch Coco Chanel, so as an act of gratitude I offered him a cold water. Patsy saw us together and decided to go hog wild with the details."

"Ugh. She really has been relentless ever since Frank died. Maybe being a widow is leaving her with too much time on her hands," Lucy said with a shrug. "She needs a hobby. Or a man of her own."

"There are no excuses for spreading lies and gossip. Luke just arrived here in town and now he's caught up in the Mistletoe rumor mill." She groaned. "It's embarrassing."

"Stella!" Lucy put her hands on her hips. "Luke is a smoke show. There's absolutely nothing humiliating about having rumors flying around town that you're involved with a smoldering Navy SEAL. In fact, it's pretty thrilling." Lucy wiggled her eyebrows.

Stella frowned. "I don't recall you saying all this when your name was being tossed around town last Christmas."

"Well maybe I was taking myself a little too seriously," Lucy said sheepishly. "After all, Dante and I did have a happy ending."

"Well, these rumors aren't true, so there's that. I barely know the man." She didn't want to tell Lucy about how Luke had rescued her from the awkward situation at Rosie's salon. If Stella told her about her near run-in with Rafe at the shop, Lucy would be filled with guilt about taking off right after the fitting. Stella didn't want to say or do anything to take away from her sister's prewedding bliss.

"But it's progress from being talked about due to the... situation with your ex. At least this gossip isn't like having a knife driven through your heart. It isn't talking about you when you've been knocked to your knees. Am I right?" Lucy locked gazes with Stella. They both knew how deeply Stella had suffered after being dumped by her fiancé.

Lucy made a good point. This wasn't her first time at

the gossip rodeo. After Rafe called off their wedding, the whispers, fake stories, and stares had been brutal. She'd been the object of pity in her hometown and she'd hated every second of it. *Poor Stella. Can you believe that he married someone else? I wonder what really happened to make him call off the wedding.* Stella hadn't been able to avoid the wagging tongues, and bit by bit, the unrelenting gossip had worn her down. She'd even momentarily toyed with the idea of moving away from Mistletoe. In the end, she'd stayed, and the gossip eventually died down.

"What's taking you guys so long with the tacos? I'm a growing girl and I need to nourish my body." Tess stood in the kitchen entryway with her hands folded across her chest. She was tapping her foot on the hardwood floor.

"Take it easy, Tess," Lucy warned. "Dinner is almost ready." She made a shooing motion with her hands.

"Why don't you go back in the living room and keep Mom company?" Stella suggested. Tess was the last person who should overhear their private conversation. Despite her tender years, Tess had a natural inclination to gossip. The Marshall family had learned the hard way not to tell her anything they didn't want to be repeated.

Tess walked into the kitchen and sat down at the butcher block–style table. She propped her elbows up and leaned her body forward. "So what are you guys talking about? You look really intense."

"Grown folks' business," Stella said, trying not to smile. Tess was too mature for her own good, and Stella knew that her family, including herself, let her get away with bloody murder. She was the very definition of ten years old going on thirty.

"Oh, is this about you and the military dude?" Tess asked with an angelic expression. Her eyes darted back and forth between Stella and Lucy. "Mama and I were just discussing it. She's really pleased you're dating again."

Stella's jaw dropped. She was too stunned to even reply to her sister. How in the world had Tess heard rumors about her and Luke? And her mother knew about it as well? "W-what did you hear?"

"Where did you hear that?" Lucy asked at the same time.

Tess laughed and rubbed her hands together. "It was at summer camp in archery class. I heard two of the counselors talking about the new guy in town and how it's a shame he's already taken. Then I heard your name being mentioned. And then there was some discussion about Luke being hotter than a summer's day. Georgia said she'd seen him running and he has buns of steel. Cinnamon buns." Tess giggled.

"Okay. That's enough," Stella said, holding up her hands to ward off any further commentary from her little sister. She couldn't believe camp counselors had nothing better to do than talk about her nonexistent relationship with Luke. However, it wasn't surprising that Luke had left an impression on the camp counselors. It seemed to be happening all over town.

Stella saw a huge grin breaking out on Lucy's face right before she busied herself in the cupboard with her face hidden. Stella wished she could find the situation as amusing as Lucy did. It would be nice if she could lighten up and laugh it off. But she wasn't built that way.

She was too worried about what people thought about her. Perhaps her goal this summer should be to let loose a little and walk on the wild side. Images of Luke grinning at her in a flirtatious manner flashed into her mind, startling her. She felt a little bit flustered that she was fantasizing about Luke. Getting involved with him would be thrilling and very un-Stella-like.

"Tess, go tell Mom that dinner is ready," Stella said after gathering her thoughts. As soon as Tess left the kitchen, Stella turned toward Lucy. "I guess there's no point in telling Tess and Mom the rumors aren't true, is there?"

"Not really," Lucy said, making a face as she spooned the food from its pot on the stove to a serving dish. "A silver lining is that if Mom thinks you're dating Luke she won't try to set you up on any awkward blind dates."

"Now that is a definite bonus to this bogus rumor," Stella said with a grin. Just having that pressure off her back for a short bit of time would be wonderful. It was honestly the only upside of Patsy's loose lips.

Stella busied herself with setting the table and helping Lucy lay the food out. Why was it bothering her so much that the rumor mill was dishing about her and Luke? Like Lucy had tried to tell her, it wasn't the worst thing in the world to be linked up to a gorgeous guy like Luke. Once upon a time she would have been over the moon to have her name said in the same breath as his. But that had been back in the day of high school crushes. Now, after being at the mercy of town gossip over the wedding that wasn't, Stella felt a bit salty about Mistletoe's rumor mill. It always seemed to be at her expense and could turn cruel in an instant. She didn't want to be on the receiving end of it ever again.

"Take deep breaths, Stella," Lucy advised. "This too shall pass. Next week Patsy will be spreading dirt about someone else." She placed her arm around Stella's waist and pulled her close to her side. "And if I happen to hear any other library patrons gossiping about you, it's going to be on." She held up her fists and made a swinging motion. Stella burst out laughing at the idea of her younger sister getting into a fight. Lucy was a gentle soul with a heart as wide and deep as the ocean.

"What would I do without you?" Stella asked, blinking back tears. No matter what was going on in their lives, Lucy was always there holding her up. A sister and a best friend all wrapped up in one.

"You'll never have to find out," Lucy whispered. "Not ever." Stella didn't know what she'd ever done in this world to deserve having Lucy as a sister, but she was grateful for her love and loyalty.

"Ditto," Stella said. They held up their pinkies and joined them together as they'd done a million times before, ever since they were kids.

Within minutes they were all seated at the dining room table and holding hands as Leslie led them in the grace and offered up thanks for the meal set out before them.

As soon as their mother finished, Tess piped up. "May I add something?"

Stella nodded a bit reluctantly. "Go ahead, Tess." Her baby sister was notorious for adding special prayer requests for outlandish things such as Appalachian owls, solar eclipses, or the freckle-faced object of her ten-year-old affection.

Tess began speaking. "And thanks for bringing a new man into Stella's life, someone who is ten times hotter than Rafe and who has abs you can bounce a quarter off of. May their romance be filled with roses and moonlight. And lots of kissing. Amen." Tess, looking very pleased with herself, began digging into her food with gusto.

Stella tried her hardest not to laugh at her sister's outrageous prayer. She felt her lips twitching and she bit down on her lip to stop it from bubbling up inside her. One look at Lucy's mirth-filled expression and Stella broke. It started as a giggle, then morphed into a full-out cackle. Lucy joined in, along with their mother. Laughter rang out in the dining room, serving as a reminder to Stella that even when it felt like she was standing on shaky ground, family was everything.

* * *

Luke laid his newspaper down and locked eyes with Nick. "What's up with you? You've been staring at me for the last ten minutes." Luke had tried to ignore it, but it was getting on his nerves. They were hanging out in the living room after Luke prepared his famous chicken parmigiana with a side of seafood chowder and home-made biscuits. He wasn't exactly sure, but he thought Miles might have gone back for seconds. It had brought Luke back in time to his teen years when his grandfather taught him everything he'd known about cooking. The night had been going smoothly until he'd noticed Nick's pointed stare.

"I was waiting for you to tell me something, but it seems you're not going to do it." Nick's tone hinted at annoyance. Nick sat back in his chair and propped his feet up on the coffee table. His stern expression reminded Luke of their father.

"What are you talking about?" Luke asked. He wasn't sure if Nick was playing a prank on him or being serious.

Nick jutted his chin at Luke. "You and Stella. The town grapevine is in overdrive about your relationship. Guess I'm the last to know."

Relationship? Him and Stella? They were just friends and nothing more, even though he viewed her as the most beautiful woman in Mistletoe. No doubt in the entire state of Maine. But he barely knew her other than rescuing her fancy poodle and providing her with a getaway car during the awkward situation with her ex. That did not put them in the romance category.

A buzzing sound filled the air. Nick picked up his cell phone and studied the screen, his brows knitting together as he read. He held up his phone. "See. I'm getting tons of texts and calls. The same women who wanted to date you are now waving the white flag and surrendering. Listen to this."

Nick hit play on one of his voicemail messages. "*Hey, Nick. It's Gillian. I heard the news about Luke and Stella. I don't want to step on any toes, so disregard my previous messages about Luke. Thanks.*"

Luke groaned. "What news is she talking about? This

is insanity." He flexed his fingers. "Gossip should be outlawed in Mistletoe."

Nick shook his head. "You won't get any argument from me on that one."

Luke folded the *Mistletoe Gazette* and placed it down on the side table. "Surely the residents have better things to talk about than who I'm spending time with. Why do they even care?"

"Evidently they don't have anything more pressing to discuss," Nick said, a smile playing around his lips. "And they're invested in you because you're a home-town boy. And a hero. Your Medal of Honor designation made headlines all over the state, but particularly here in town. You're the perfect mix of brooding hero and heartthrob."

Luke stiffened. He hated the H word. Losing two of his men in a mission gone wrong hadn't made him feel heroic. Getting a medal for valor didn't erase his feelings of guilt and shame. On the surface Luke knew how he came across—brave, rugged...and heroic. Nick was one of the few people who knew that there was a lot more to him than met the eye.

"Oh, wait. There's more messages." Nick hit play again on his voicemail. *"Hey, Nick. It's Laura Jean. I wish you'd told me that Stella had already scooped Luke up. Thanks for wasting my time."* Luke shuddered at the anger that emanated from Laura Jean's voice. Clearly he'd dodged a bullet.

"Whoa. Sounds like Laura Jean needs to chill out. I haven't seen her since high school. She's acting like we were engaged or something."

Nick held up his phone. "I've got at least six more messages. Don't get me wrong. I'm happy for you and Stella. She's amazing, but a lot of women in town are disappointed."

Luke needed to set Nick straight and let him know there was absolutely nothing going on. "Sorry about that, but Stella and I are—"

"A perfect fit," Nick said, leaning forward and clapping Luke on the shoulder. "I approve. Stella is simply incredible. Miles adores her. He's given her the title of Best Teacher Ever."

"Yeah, she seems to be," Luke said feebly. How was he going to get off this runaway train? Now Nick was all excited. He knew that his brother worried about him and his future. Nick wanted him to stay in Mistletoe, settle down and find a career that didn't involve explosive devices and a high risk of not making it back home. Luke couldn't blame Nick for not wanting to endure any other losses after losing Kara.

"I wish you'd told me sooner," Nick continued. "And here you had me thinking you weren't interested in dating." Nick coughed. "Or am I jumping the gun? Maybe the two of you are just spending time together and seeing where things go. Nothing wrong with that."

Luke didn't know why he wasn't setting Nick straight. The happy expression etched on his brother's face was one he hadn't seen in quite some time. Nick usually looked worried, even when they Skyped during his deployment. He had so much to worry about in his personal life in addition to being employed in a very high-stakes profession. Search and rescue had one of the highest burn-out rates of any job, not to mention the high stress level and trauma. Nick shouldn't have to be concerned about his older brother.

"I wasn't sure what to say," he hedged. Much like right now. He had no clue how to break it gently to Nick that he wasn't dating Stella. But maybe he didn't have to. Maybe he could allow Nick to believe he was coupled up with the most beautiful sweetheart in Mistletoe for a little bit, as long as the woman in question didn't have any objections. It would be nice to have Nick stop worrying about Luke's single status.

He and Stella had grown up together, but they'd never really been friends. He recalled a shy and introverted young girl who'd never really put herself out there. He was ashamed to admit that he'd really never given her the time of day. Luke had been way too busy being popular and hanging around with his football player friends. His life had consisted of family, football, and friends and not necessarily in that order.

"Bro, don't worry about it. I'm actually relieved. It felt awkward being in the middle. Looks like I won't be fielding any more phone calls from your admirers. Judging by all of my messages, they're either pretty ticked off or waving the white flag." Nick flashed a wide grin. "Either way you can focus on finding a new career path and acclimating to life stateside."

Nick was right. The women of Mistletoe would no longer be hounding Nick about fixing them up with Luke if they thought he was taken. The pressure. He didn't have to worry about women stopping him at the coffee shop or on his morning run. He wouldn't have to avoid certain establishments in town like the Bookworm or the artist shanties by the marina. The female attention he'd been receiving had been pretty intense. Not to mention awkward! A small part of him had been flattered, but it overwhelmed him at the same time. Because of the Navy SEAL moniker, women tended to have certain stereotypes and expectations about him. It was rare that a woman took the time to peel back his layers.

If everyone in town believed the story about him and Stella, the heat would be off, and he could focus his energy on trying to connect with the family members of the two SEALs on his team who'd perished, as well as figure out what he was going to do with the rest of his life.

But it wouldn't take long for people to figure out that he wasn't romantically involved with Stella if they were never seen together. He and Stella had one big thing in common. They were both single and not looking for a relationship. At the same time, folks in Mistletoe were trying to pair them both up with people. What if they could use the town gossip to their advantage? What if this turned out to be a huge gift for both of them?

Luke needed to get her on board with his plan. Stella had mentioned being hounded due to her single status. Didn't she tell him that she just wanted to be left alone by the town matchmakers? That she wasn't ready to date? From what she'd said, even her parents were trying to fix her up.

Luke realized he didn't have her cell phone number. So much for them being a power couple in Mistletoe. Just the thought of it made him smile. If he was going to be mistakenly paired up with someone, he couldn't really complain about the fact that it was Stella. He liked her brand of sweet and sassy.

Now he just had to track her down and convince her that the two of them could be Mistletoe's hottest fake couple of the summer.

CHAPTER EIGHT

Stella parked her car and made her way across her pebbled driveway toward the front door of her cottage-style beach house. A soft glow from inside the front window greeted her, providing the warm atmosphere she'd tried to create in her home. The smell of the sea air washed over her, and she could hear the waves crashing against the shore in the distance. On certain summer nights Stella slept with her windows open and let the sea sounds lull her to slumber. It offered her a type of serenity nothing else ever could.

In the daylight her beautiful geraniums and rhododendrons were visible, gracing the area by the walkway. Although she didn't have a green thumb, Stella had worked hard to cultivate these particular flowers. She paused for a moment to enjoy the spectacular supermoon lighting up the night sky. It was a champagne color and seemed to glow brighter and bigger than any moon she'd ever seen in her life.

All day Stella had been processing what she'd learned last night about the false rumor about her and Luke. She'd felt some stares and whispers during her yoga class, but no one had come right out and said anything.

She'd been wondering if she should reach out to Luke and apologize. *No, that would be ridiculous.* It wasn't her fault that Mistletoe was filled with nosy residents who enjoyed stirring the pot. She hadn't asked to be the subject of the town's grapevine. And she certainly hadn't done a single thing to put him in the line of fire other than giving him bottled water. Perhaps it was best to ignore the talk and try to ride it out until things died down.

"Stella." The deep voice coming out of the shadows caused Stella to let out a high-pitched scream and practically jump out of her skin. A tall figure stepped forward, illuminated by her front porch light. Luke.

She pressed her palm against her chest. "Oh, man. You scared the life out of me."

He winced. "I'm sorry. I didn't mean to frighten you. I thought you would have seen my car parked there."

She shook her head. Her heart was still racing. "I was distracted by the moon. It's fairly magnificent tonight."

He looked up at the sky and sighed. "You're right. It's amazing."

"What brings you over here, Luke?" Stella experienced a flash of pure panic. Had he heard the rumors and come to her house to confront her? Did he think she had something to do with it? If that was the case, all she could do was tell him she was a victim just like he was.

Luke met her gaze. Looking into his eyes didn't reveal anything about his reasons for stopping by her house, but it reinforced the fact that the man was gorgeous. *Focus, Stella.* It wasn't the time or the place to ogle Luke, although he didn't make it easy. His body alone was a thirst trap.

"I came by to talk to you," Luke said. "It's important."

Oh no! He wanted to talk. And it was important. There really wasn't much that he could possibly want to discuss other than the obvious. *Yep.* It stood to reason that he wanted to talk about the raging rumors he'd been dragged into. *Dear God.* Did he think she was responsible?

"I'm sorry, Luke. I know what you're going to say, and I need you to know I had nothing to do with it." The words tumbled out of her mouth, and she couldn't seem to stop herself from babbling. "I'm so grateful for your helping me out the other day, so the fact that you might think I'm somehow at fault for this is not only awkward but it's a tad bit hurtful." Stella paused to take a breath.

Luke furrowed his brow as he looked at her. "Stella. I have no idea what you're talking about. I'm not mad or annoyed with you. Can we go inside for some privacy?"

Lucy quickly opened the front door, then ushered him into her cozy living room. "Make yourself comfortable." Luke sat down on her eggshell-colored love seat, making the room seem small with his larger-than-life presence. Suddenly her throat felt dry as he shrugged out of his thick sweatshirt. The muscles in his arms were on full display and his brown skin glistened. This man was fine!

She dragged her gaze away, reminding herself not to stare. Or drool.

"Would you like a cold drink? A snack?" Stella asked. She would love to be in the kitchen for a few minutes taking calming breaths and putting a cool cloth on her face.

"No, I'm fine. Thanks." Stella sat down in the seat across from him. She felt a bit uneasy as he locked gazes with her. "Let me get straight to the point. It seems that the good folks of Mistletoe think we're involved...or hooking up or having a passionate affair." He shrugged. "Something like that."

"I know, Luke," she said, unable to look him directly in the eye. She resisted the impulse to cover her face with her hands or sink into the floor. "I'm really sorry."

"Really? I'm not." A huge grin threatened to take over his entire face. His smile showcased white, even teeth and an impish attitude.

"Wait. What? You're not upset?" Stella asked, relief flooding her entire body. She felt like doing a jig on her hardwood floors. She'd been bracing herself to be on the receiving end of a few choice words from Luke. As usual she'd jumped to conclusions. She really needed to have more faith in people.

"Upset? Of course not." He frowned at her. "Why? Are you?"

"Honestly, yes. I hate town gossip, especially when my name is part of it." She didn't want to tell him that she was sensitive to rumors due to the wild stories that had circulated after Rafe called off their wedding. It wasn't something she liked to think about. After all this time the whispers still hurt.

"I agree that gossip can be annoying and at times damaging, but in this instance it might serve both our purposes. If we let it." Luke folded his sculpted arms across his chest and looked at her with a satisfied expression on his face.

Stella frowned. "I'm not following. What are you talking about?"

"Think about it, Stella. It would make a lot of sense for both of us to have people believe we're an item. Guys like Rosie's nephew wouldn't pester you. And your parents would stop trying to fix you up. Your ex-fiancé will see you've moved on. I can't speak for you, but I'll be able to breathe better without having so many people trying to orchestrate my life."

Stella was completely blown away. Luke wanted to turn the rumors on their head and engage in a show-mance. Even though he'd made some stellar points, it was still fairly shocking. The idea of pretending to date Luke Keegan had its appeal, but there were also a host of drawbacks. For starters, she had the world's worst poker face, so it would be a challenge to play her part without messing things up. Secondly, what if everyone found out they were only pretending to be a couple? That would be embarrassing and hard to justify. As a teacher, Stella always stressed the value of honesty to her students. Would this make her a total hypocrite?

"I definitely feel what you're saying. I'd like to be able to process my romantic future on my own terms without anyone pressuring me to couple up with someone new." Stella knew people might find it strange that she was still stuck in limbo, but she thought it spoke to her commitment to the future that had been snatched away from her. Was there really a timetable for moving on?

There was no getting around the fact that it would be nice to not feel as if she was constantly being suggested as a candidate for *The Bachelorette* or *Love Island*. Truthfully, she wasn't so sure if she felt the same way anymore about love, but she imagined that someday her heart would heal. She just needed to be patient and give it time. And being pushed into the dating world wasn't going to make her fall in love again. It just made her feel smothered and confused.

Stella immediately pictured Tucker's face. He was still calling her and leaving messages. Clearly she hadn't been very convincing that day at the salon about having a boyfriend. If she went along with Luke's idea it would take care of the big fib she'd told about dating someone. Luke would be the perfect fake boyfriend. Just for a moment she allowed herself to imagine the looks on certain people's faces if she walked around holding hands with Luke Keegan. The very thought of it made her want to puff out her chest.

But committing to such a bold plan wouldn't be easy. They'd have to spend lots of quality time together. And while Luke was absolute eye candy, she had no idea if their personalities would mesh. Tucker was a handsome man, but she'd learned fairly quickly that she didn't want to hang out with him. And what if Luke met someone else in Mistletoe he truly wanted to date while they were fake dating? Stella knew he desperately wanted to get off the radar of a multitude of ladies in Mistletoe, but would this really accomplish it? And would it be worth all the effort? She just wasn't sure he'd fully planned this thing out.

"It wouldn't have to be for a long time. Maybe just for the summer," Luke suggested. "That way we wouldn't have to play our roles long-term."

Stella knit her brows together as she thought it over. Was she crazy to even consider this? If she was being completely honest with herself, it sounded like a mutually beneficial arrangement. But it involved tricking the entire town, including her parents. She wasn't sure that she could pull it off without cracking.

"I can't lie to Lucy," she admitted. "She'd figure things out in a heartbeat anyway."

"I wouldn't expect you to. One of my main reasons for wanting to do this is Nick. He worries about me, and I can't watch him buckle under that weight. He has enough on his plate as it is. Miles should be his focus. Not me."

Miles. Her favorite student. A genuine sweetheart. He was a plucky and warm kid. He and his father deserved peace after all they'd been through. Nick didn't need to consume himself with worry over Luke. Doing so wouldn't allow him to move forward in his own life.

Stella played with her fingers. "I'm going to have to sleep on it, Luke. I don't want to make a rash decision." It wasn't her way to jump headfirst into things without pondering the pros and cons. That wouldn't work for her.

"That's fine, Stella. Personally speaking, I don't want to be Mistletoe's catch of the season. I want to be under the radar so I can...figure things out."

Figure things out? She had no idea what he meant by his comment, but his voice sounded serious. Nick had discussed Luke's heroic service in the military, along with the tragic details regarding the loss of two of his SEAL team members. From what she remembered, Luke had been wounded in the incident. Perhaps that explained the wrap on his leg and the reason he was no longer in the military. It must feel strange to be awarded a Medal of Honor when his friends had lost their lives.

"So how would this even work?" Stella asked. "I'm not saying I'm down with your idea, but if it will save me from intrusive matchmaking schemes and men like Tucker, I'm intrigued."

Luke began waving his hands around. "We would show up together at a few town events, meet up for lunch or dinner maybe twice a week, and do our best to convince the good folks of Mistletoe that we're booed up. It'll be a piece of cake."

"Then at the end of the summer our romance will fizzle out? Is that what you're thinking?"

He nodded. "Yes, that would be the plan."

She nibbled on her fingernail, an old habit she couldn't seem to break when nerves got the best of her. "I don't know, Luke. It sounds complicated. And isn't it a bit unrealistic to think we could pull this off in a town filled with so many nosy residents? It wouldn't take them very long to sniff us out."

"I'm confident we could pull it off, Stella. It's not as complex as you might think." Luke unfolded himself from the love seat and stood up. His height added to his overall impact. He was an impressive-looking man, from his chiseled features to his well-honed body. "I should get going so you can think things through. Thanks for hearing me out."

"Of course," she said, standing up and walking him toward the door. When she pulled it open, Luke paused in the doorway for a moment before turning back toward her. She looked up at him, admiring the strong tilt of his jaw and his chiseled features. What woman in her right mind wouldn't want to pretend date this too-handsome-for-his-own-good Navy SEAL?

He held out his cell phone. "Before I forget, can you put your number in my phone?"

Stella took the phone from Luke and quickly added her information. When she handed the phone back, their fingers touched, making Stella very conscious of his nearness. If the mere touching of their hands made her shiver, she couldn't imagine what a kiss might stir up inside her. A little sigh escaped her lips. It had been such a long time since she'd been kissed. And she would bet her last dollar that Luke Keegan knew how to kiss a girl senseless. Her eyes drifted to his lips for what felt like the hundredth time. She was living proof of what it did to a person to go too long without being kissed.

His oh-so-perfect lips curved upward into a smile. "I'll be in touch soon, Stella. Have a good night."

Luke's voice brought her back to her senses. "Night, Luke," she responded, feeling a bit relieved that he would soon be out of her vicinity. He was pure temptation with his perfect lips, amazing facial features, and russet-colored skin. And she didn't even want her mind to dwell on his perfectly honed physique. Like the commercial said, milk did a body good.

He walked off into the night, quickly disappearing into the darkness once he stepped away from her porch. As soon as Stella closed the door and walked past the living room, she spotted Luke's sweatshirt. He'd accidentally left it behind. She picked it up and ran back to the front door, just in time to see the rear lights of Luke's truck as he drove away. Stella fingered the fabric as the scent of pine once again rose to her nostrils. Longing swept over her and she didn't quite know what to make of it. Being in Luke's presence had the same effect on her as riding the tilt-a-whirl at the carnival.

It had been ages since she'd felt butterflies like this. Not since Rafe. And she couldn't stop the niggle of fear that she and Luke would end in exactly the same way: with her heart smashed into a million little pieces.

CHAPTER NINE

Luke woke up the next morning to a picture-perfect late-June day. The sun was shining. Not a cloud was visible in the sky, which was so blue it reminded him of a robin's egg. A slight breeze swept across his face. Waking up in Mistletoe was a far cry from being in Afghanistan. This time of year it was a hot eighty-six degrees over there, with Maine being a bit balmier in the high seventies. He couldn't wait to take his first swim of the season soon at Blackberry Beach. Maybe he could ask Stella to join him, although she might not want to give her nosy neighbor any more fodder for gossip.

Last night Nick had asked him to watch Miles today while he was working a search and rescue. "You sure you're okay with babysitting tomorrow?" Nick had asked. "They want me to head out to Acadia Park in the morning.

My sitter can come on Wednesday and take over until I'm back."

Luke hadn't hesitated to reassure Nick. "I would love to hang out with the little man. I'm jobless and have no place to go at the moment, so you can call off the sitter. At some point I've got to figure something out long-term." He sighed. "I never thought I'd be out of commission at my age. I planned to retire with gray hair and a gut." In truth, Luke had always pictured himself being one of the longest-serving Navy SEALs. But life had a way of kicking you in the butt when you least expected it.

"Sounds like you have a lot of savings, which is great," Nick said. Luke had told him about his healthy savings account as well as his retirement money. Losing his SEAL career wasn't about money for Luke. He needed something to get up in the morning for—a vocation he could be proud of. Despite the inherent dangers of his career, Luke had always been proud of his service. Now, he had a gigantic void in his life, and he needed to focus on how to fill it up.

"I'm thinking about flipping some houses," he'd told Nick. He'd come up with the idea after reading an article from the *New York Times* about successful house flippers in the New England area. He knew he was probably grasping at straws with the house flipping idea, but he needed to do something to help jump-start his new life. There were so few career options open to him as a retired SEAL.

"That's a big undertaking." Nick's expression had been shuttered, but Luke knew his brother well enough to read between the lines. He sounded skeptical. Luke couldn't blame him. What did he really know about flipping houses other than watching the occasional episode of *Flip or Flop* or *Fixer Upper*? It was all fun and games until he invested in a property he couldn't sell. Or the repairs were too costly to turn a profit. Truthfully, the only thing he'd ever been passionate about was serving his country, and he could no longer fulfill the duties of his former job. He needed to find something to bring in an income stream and to keep him occupied. Life in Mistletoe might get stale if all he did was visit the Coffee Bean, hang out with his nephew, and play sudoku games.

"Honestly, I could totally see you being part of the search and rescue team," Nick said, his gaze full of intensity. "Does that appeal to you at all? It's totally in your wheelhouse as far as I'm concerned."

Nick's comment piqued Luke's interest. Search and rescue was a profession he could see himself acclimating to very well. He'd performed numerous search and rescue operations while deployed, and he was certified in CPR. "That would be amazing if I met the qualifications." Being part of a search and rescue team would be exciting and impactful—just what he was looking for. But he wasn't going to even let himself get excited about the possibility of working with Nick. It sounded too good to be true.

Nick grinned. "I don't think that will be a problem given your SEAL training in search and rescue. I'll put in a good word with my boss and give her your contact information. You can take it from there if you're really interested."

"That's awesome, bro. Thanks for always having my back," Luke said, bumping fists with Nick.

"Just like you always have mine," Nick responded.

So now here he was, hanging out with the coolest nephew on planet Earth. Rather than do the cooking honors himself, Luke had suggested to Miles that they grab a meal in town. Miles's reaction had been epic. Luke wasn't sure he'd ever seen his nephew ditch his pajamas and get dressed so fast.

Walking down Main Street with Miles at his side was as idyllic as it got. The quaint shops and the cobblestone sidewalks were distinctively New England. He'd promised to take his nephew to the toy store, which was a mind-blowing experience with a million and one things to choose from. In the end, Miles picked a vibrant yellow-and-orange kite. Now that he'd fulfilled that promise to Miles, they were off to get breakfast at the Starlight Diner. Luke's stomach grumbled in anticipation of the elaborate breakfast he planned to order. Blueberry pancakes with sausage, home fries, and eggs. With a serving of grits on the side.

"I love the kite, Uncle Luke," Miles said, beaming up at him. His nephew looked so much like Nick that it caused a squeezing sensation in his chest. It brought him straight back to childhood when his younger brother hung on his every word. *Those were the days.* Life was much simpler back then.

"It's pretty cool, Miles. You've got good taste," Luke said, giving him a thumbs-up sign. "Later on we can head to Blackberry Beach to try it out." Maybe he'd catch a glimpse of Stella with Coco Chanel while they were there. The thought of her scurrying after her feisty poodle on the beach made him smile. If he wasn't at such a difficult crossroads in his life, Luke would love to get to know her better. Just knowing how badly her ex had wounded her made him extra leery of starting anything with her he couldn't finish. And if his romantic history had taught him anything at all it was that he wasn't in it for the long haul. His ex had been right.

He hadn't slept well last night. A nightmare had woken him up at two a.m., making it impossible for him to go back to sleep. As usual, it had been about the ambush and the two men he'd lost.

Kenneth Smith and Aaron Baldini. They hadn't just been his SEAL team members. They had been members of a tight-knit band of brothers. Family. Bound by their duties to serve and protect. Tethered by shared experiences and devotion to their country. The dream was always the same. Luke figured out that his team was in trouble—unlike in real life—and he attempted to abort the mission. It always ended in blood and fire and screams of anguish, and he awoke crying out in pain. It didn't take a genius to figure out what it meant—he was wrapped up in guilt.

Some days he wasn't sure he would ever see the light again, but being with Miles felt like pure sunshine. There was something about being in his presence that made Luke feel hopeful. After all he'd been through, the kid was still a champ.

"Here we are, kiddo," Luke said as they arrived at the diner. The brick-and-white façade welcomed Luke like an old friend. How many times had he hung out at the diner after football practice with his group of friends? Nick and Kara had always been joined at the hip, along with Dante and Lucy, who'd gone from best friends to coupled up. He'd gone from girl to girl, never establishing anything solid with any of them. Not much had changed in that regard. He was still a lone wolf.

The Starlight Diner hadn't changed much either. It still had the same old-fashioned vibe. Truth be told, the sign by the roof looked as if it hadn't been updated at all. *If it ain't broke don't fix it.* That had been his grandfather's credo. It made Luke chuckle to recall his wise, ornery, and occasionally salty Grand Pop. Wilbur Keegan had been a pragmatic man. After serving his country as one of the Tuskegee Airmen, he'd headed to Maine to forge a future for himself with his new bride. For close to forty years Wilbur had worked as a carpenter, and despite the fact that they were the first African Americans to settle down in Mistletoe, the couple was embraced with open arms by the community.

As soon as Luke and Miles stepped inside the diner, one of the waitresses told them to take a seat wherever they liked. They sat down across from each other and studied the menu. Within seconds, Luke felt someone hovering over him. When he looked up, Saffron Jones was grinning at him. He wanted to let out an exasperated groan. Saffron was one of the women who'd been bugging Nick to set them up on a date. Luke hadn't seen Saffron since their senior prom. She'd been his date and they'd been crowned prom king and queen. Judging by some of her messages, she was keen to pick up where they'd left off.

"Luke! Where have you been hiding? Back in the day

you were the one chasing me." Saffron's perfect white teeth and polished appearance hadn't changed a bit. She was still a looker. But there was something about her intense gaze that he found slightly alarming. It felt like she had him in her crosshairs.

"Hey, Saffron. I've been hanging out with my nephew and Nick since I've been back. Just enjoying what Mistletoe has to offer," he said, trying to keep things casual. "Do you know Miles?" he asked, desperate to change the subject.

Saffron bent over and tweaked Miles's cheek, causing him to grimace. "Of course I do. It's nice to see you, Miles. If you're not just the spitting image of your daddy," she gushed.

"Hi," Miles muttered, barely making eye contact with Saffron. Luke knew he was annoyed at the face pinching, and he couldn't really blame him. As a kid, he'd hated being randomly touched by adults.

"Well, I just wanted to pop over and say hello. And to give you this." She reached into her shirt and pulled out a small piece of paper folded into a tiny portion. She placed it down on the table and slid it toward him. She winked at him and said, "Call me, Luke. We can catch up on old times." He didn't even have a chance to respond before she began sashaying back to her table. He didn't think he was imagining the extra sway of her hips.

"I think she likes you," Miles said. "She was making all those funny faces and batting her eyelashes at you."

"Among other things," Luke mumbled. Maybe he was looking at this all wrong. Perhaps he should just give in and take someone like Saffron out. But then what? She'd get all possessive and angsty like she'd done back in the day. He didn't have time for that type of entanglement. Luke grimaced as he remembered how crazy things had gotten when she found out he was enlisting. She'd had a full-fledged meltdown that was permanently etched in his memory bank.

"Do you have any change, Uncle Luke?" Miles asked. "I wanna pick a song while we wait." With his short-cropped 'fro and gap-toothed grin, he really was a doppelganger for Nick when he was eight.

Luke reached into his jeans pockets and fished around. He let out a sound of triumph as he pulled out a bunch of coins and placed them on the table. "Here you go. This should get you a few songs."

Miles's face lit up as he scooted over and turned the dial on the jukebox. "Whoa. These songs are old. I don't know any of 'em."

"Hey, these are classics. You need to know these tunes because they're never going out of style." Luke let out an excited sound. "'Purple Rain.' Who doesn't love that song?" Luke grabbed a quarter from the table and placed it in the slot, then plugged in the numbers for the song. As soon as the music began to play Luke closed his eyes and strummed an imaginary guitar. "*Purple Rain. Purple Rain,*" he belted.

Miles groaned and covered his face with his hands. "Uncle Luke! Stop. You're killing me. People are staring." He began to giggle uncontrollably. Luke chuckled along with him until their laughter became giddy.

"I see your summer vacation is off to a great start."

The familiar-sounding voice served as a jolt to Luke's system. When he swung his gaze up, Stella was standing by their table smiling down at Miles. Dressed in a sky-blue sleeveless dress, she looked sensational. It was sort of funny how he'd spent most of the morning thinking about her and now she'd showed up at the diner.

"Miss Marshall." Miles jumped up from his seat and threw himself against Stella's chest. She seemed completely overwhelmed by the gesture. Luke watched as a huge grin broke out on her face. Her head was thrown back in laugher, revealing a beautiful and graceful neck. She had a regal look about her—sleek and classy. Maybe it would be a stretch for people to think they were a couple, he thought. He was all rough edges and not a hint of elegance.

"Easy there, Miles," Luke cautioned. "If you're not careful you might knock her off her feet."

Miles let go of Stella and sheepishly gazed up at her. "I'm sorry. I was just so excited to see you."

Luke understood where his nephew was coming from. It was pretty obvious Miles thought Stella was sheer perfection. Luke couldn't say he blamed him. Some tool named Rafe had turned her world upside down, and it made him way angrier than it should. He didn't know Stella all that well, even though they had grown up in the same small town, but he found himself feeling protective of her. And for the life of him, he couldn't imagine what kind of a fool would leave a woman like her at the altar.

This Rafe character must have lost his mind. Not to

mention the fact Rafe was a coward and a liar, two weaknesses Luke hated the most.

"It's okay, Miles," Stella said, still chuckling. She placed her hand on Miles's shoulder. "Most of my students barely want to say hello once school ends, so this warm welcome is really special."

"Can you eat with us?" Miles asked. He was tugging at Stella's hand and slightly pulling her toward the table. Luke made a mental note to talk to his nephew later on about overstepping. He appreciated his enthusiasm, but he still needed to be mindful of boundaries as well as manners.

Miles sat back down in the booth and looked over at Stella with sad puppy dog eyes. *He's really working it.* Luke wondered if this was how he got his way with Nick. Although he was in no position to judge, Luke sensed that Nick allowed his son way too much leeway. Now that he was living under their roof, Luke had seen his nephew getting his way more times than not. It was a delicate subject to broach with Nick, and Luke wasn't even sure he had the right to do so.

"Oh, I really don't want to intrude," Stella hedged. "I just had a random hankering for waffles. It's one of those things I never have time to make on a school day, so Miles isn't the only one celebrating."

Luke motioned for her to sit down. "Then you're in the right place. I'm partial to the blueberry pancakes myself. Join us, Stella. You'll save my nephew from having to hear me belt out another Prince song."

Stella hesitated for a moment, then sat down in the booth next to Miles. "Well, there are far worse things than being exposed to one of the most brilliant musical geniuses the world has ever seen."

"You're a Prince fan too?" Luke asked, unable to mask his surprise. In his opinion, far too few people appreciated The Purple One.

Stella nodded. "When I was in college, a few friends and I took a road trip to New York City because we had second-row seats to his concert. To this day it's one of the most exciting things I've ever done." Stella's eyes were bright with excitement and her mocha-colored skin appeared flushed. He couldn't take his eyes off her if he tried.

Luke whistled. "That's amazing. I saw him in concert three times. All of which were unforgettable." He'd been in his early twenties, when his life was a bit more carefree. Sometimes when he thought back to those days, he wished he'd appreciated them more. Attending concerts was one of the things he was looking forward to now that he was no longer bound to the military.

"You really are a superfan," Stella said with a nod of appreciation.

"Are we going to order?" Miles asked. "My stomach is making grumbly noises." Luke and Stella laughed at his humorous delivery and the exaggerated way he rubbed his stomach. Luke had almost forgotten Miles was sitting there. He'd been wrapped up in his conversation with his nephew's intriguing teacher. He still was having a hard time reconciling her cool demeanor with the quirky side of her he'd witnessed as her getaway driver. Two sides of a coin. He liked a woman who was a bit unpredictable.

Stella leaned in toward Miles and said, "Mine too."

Just watching her interaction with Miles told Luke a lot about her teaching style. She radiated kindness. He couldn't help but think if she'd walked down the aisle, she might have a baby by now. Clearly she wanted kids since she'd brought up the stolen baby name. What kind of man hijacked his ex's baby name? Luke might have a few choice words for Rafe if they ever happened to cross paths.

Just then their waitress arrived and took their order. Between the three of them they were going to keep the cooks in the kitchen busy. Waffles, blueberry pancakes, eggs, sausage, grits, bacon. They'd ordered it all. As they waited for their food to arrive, Stella did hilarious impressions of a few town residents. None of the impressions were mean spirited, but they were spot on. Luke's heart warmed at the sight of Miles being so lighthearted and joyful. He truly had a connection with Stella and it filled the air between them.

When the food came, Luke dug in with gusto. There really wasn't much in life that could rob him of his appetite.

"Uncle Luke? Can I go over to Liam's table for a minute?" Miles asked. "I just want to ask him if he's going to be around this summer so we can plan some sleepovers."

Luke nodded and said, "Sure, buddy. But only for a little while, okay? I think his family is eating."

"Okay," Miles agreed. "Excuse me, Miss Marshall. Can I please get by?"

"Of course you can." Stella stood up, allowing Miles to pass by. Within seconds he was dashing toward his friend's table and exchanging high fives with him. Luke shook his head. It was nice seeing Miles in such an exuberant mood. "It just dawned on me. I think he has a crush on you."

Stella nodded her head as if she wasn't the least bit surprised by his comment. "It's not uncommon for young students to have those feelings towards their teachers," she conceded. "It's harmless. By the time fall arrives those feelings are long gone." She reached for the carafe of syrup and poured a liberal amount on her waffles. He watched as she popped a forkful in her mouth, then let out a little moan of appreciation.

Suddenly, Luke realized that several diners were looking over at him and Stella. At first he hadn't thought anything of it, but with more and more folks gaping and whispering, Luke knew something was up. Dean Granger, the diner's owner, grinned at him from behind the counter as if he'd won the lottery. Dean's gaze flitted back and forth between Luke and Stella, clueing him in to the fact that he was eyeballing them because they were enjoying a meal together.

Stella put her fork down and frowned at him. "Is something wrong? You keep looking behind me."

He really didn't have any choice now about telling her. It would be obvious once they left the diner and everyone's attention was focused on them. She had a right to know that people were gawking.

Luke leaned forward across the table. "At the risk of ruining breakfast, it seems our table has captured the attention of many patrons of this fine establishment."

"Seriously? Why?" she asked, turning to look behind

her. As soon as she turned back around, Stella let out a huff of air. "Mayor Finch gave me a thumbs-up sign. And Saffron Jones gave me the stink eye." Stella's eyes went wide. "Is this about the rumor Patsy started?"

"It seems to be. I can't think of another reason why their eyes would be bugging out of their heads." Although the gossip linking him with Stella hadn't bothered him one bit, the stares and the whispers were annoying. He didn't want Stella to be the subject of flapping tongues. And Saffron was downright scary.

She lowered her voice to a whisper. "I think the mayor just gave us her approval. I feel like I've entered an alternate universe."

Luke snorted. "Or the Twilight Zone. Who would ever think a sleepy little town in Maine would be a hotspot for gossip?"

"It's always been this way," Stella said, taking a swig of her orange juice. "Don't get me wrong. Most people in Mistletoe would give you their last dollar, but the town hobby is gossip. Don't you remember when we were kids there was a wild rumor about Miss Botts the nursery school teacher and Kyle Williams." Stella made a tutting sound. "Poor Miss Botts was a wreck."

Kyle was the owner of the Lobster Shack, one of the most popular restaurants in town. "I don't remember that at all," he said with a shake of his head. "I was too busy playing football and chasing girls."

"Yeah," Stella said with a smirk. "From what I remember, you caught an awful lot of them."

Luke chuckled. "You're right about that." He narrowed

his gaze as he looked at her. "Not you though. You stayed under the radar."

"You can say it, Luke. I was a nerd. Braces, glasses, and Afro puffs." She covered her face with her hand. "And I was woefully underdeveloped. This may be TMI but I wore a training bra well into high school."

Luke had to bite his tongue so he didn't tell her how she'd sure made up for it. She was stunning in every way imaginable. He had the feeling she didn't even know how appealing she was. He figured the breakup with her ex had done a number on her self-esteem.

"Well, you certainly glowed up," Luke said, his eyes roaming over her with deep appreciation.

"Thanks for saying so," she said with a smirk. "When we were in high school, I would have swooned if you'd ever said that to me. I had a gigantic crush on you."

"You did?" Luke asked, flabbergasted by Stella's admission. Once again, he found himself wishing they'd been friends. He'd been stupid not to give her a passing look. But he'd been a popular jock back then with dreams of NFL glory emblazoned in his mind. How could he have failed to notice Stella's warmth, kindness, and sense of humor? Hanging out with her would have added greatly to his life back then. Thankfully he'd evolved into a man who appreciated those qualities.

"I truly did, Luke. I even memorized your schedule so I could pass you in the halls." Stella grimaced. "That sounds obsessive, but I promise you I was well meaning. Just a teenaged girl crushing on the hottest boy in school." Luke heard a little sigh slip past her lips.

He raised an eyebrow. "You thought I was hot back

then? Tell me more," he said in a teasing voice. Luke knew he'd been in demand back in the day. No doubt all the attention had given him a big head. At the moment it gave him a warm and fuzzy feeling to know that someone as special as Stella had been crushing on him too.

"I think I've said more than enough." Stella pushed her plate away from her and wiped her mouth with a napkin. "That really hit the spot, but if I eat another bite, you'll have to roll me out of here."

"We should probably just get the check," Luke said, his eyes widening as he watched Dean come striding over to their table. "Incoming," he muttered, trying his best to give Stella a heads-up. Dean was a nice guy, but he tended to be a bit loud and boisterous. And judging by the way he'd been eyeballing the two of them from behind the counter, Luke had a hunch Dean was on a fishing expedition.

"Luke Keegan!" Dean said in an exuberant voice as he clapped Luke on the shoulder. "It's been a long time. It's great to see you in one piece. I read all about your Medal of Honor award. And Nick has kept us all posted on your achievements. That's one proud brother you've got there."

"I feel the same way about him," Luke said. As far as he was concerned, Nick was the true hero with his search and rescue career and raising Miles as a single father. But it was nice to hear his service was a source of pride for Nick. As the older brother it was his job to lead the way.

"Breakfast is on me," Dean said, rapping his knuckles on the table.

"You don't have to do that," Luke protested. "We had a feast and it was excellent."

"It's my way of saying thank you for your service," Dean said. "This town is mighty proud of you. It isn't every day a hometown boy is honored with a Medal of Honor." He looked over at Stella. "The two of you look good together. Not that it's any of my business, but it's nice seeing the younger generation pairing up. It's a beautiful thing." Dean winked at them before making his way back behind the counter.

"Something tells me Dean heard the rumors about us," Stella quipped once he walked away.

Luke wanted to laugh at the look on Stella's face, but he didn't think she would appreciate it at the moment. "Yeah, it seems so. You know how fast the rumor mill works in this town." Luke darted a glance around them. He beckoned to Miles to come back to the table.

"We should have corrected him," Stella said in a low voice. "Now there's one more person who is going to spread the news that we're together." She wrinkled her nose. "Trust me, I've been at this rodeo before. It's just going to blow up."

"So why didn't you tell him?" Luke asked. "I was kind of waiting for you to set him straight." Luke felt his lips twitching, but he managed to keep a straight face as her eyes widened. Stella was adorable and it would be easy to yank her chain.

Stella bit her lip. "Because I'm still trying to figure out whether or not to participate in this ruse."

"Come on, Stella. Ruse sounds so...negative. We

need to think of this as something positive." He raised an eyebrow at her. "For both of us."

"I suppose you're right, but it's so out of my comfort zone. But, at the same time, it's actually perfect." Stella appeared contemplative, and he had the feeling she was weighing the pros and cons. Was it possible she might change her mind?

"I should get Miles home," Luke said. "He's bouncing off the walls over there." He cast another glance at his nephew. He was having a fork duel with Liam, and the boys were jousting a bit too enthusiastically. Luke smiled as his own childhood memories came into sharp focus. It was great to see Miles enjoying himself in such a carefree manner.

When he and Stella stood up to leave the diner, several pairs of eyes trailed their every move. Stella was probably not too happy about it, but a quick glance at her face showed a placid expression. Whatever she was feeling, Stella was keeping it under wraps. He wagered that it was the teacher in her—cool, calm, and collected under pressure. Unless of course she was fleeing a bridal salon.

Suddenly, Luke felt the pressure of Stella's hand in his own. He looked over at her, shocked at the gesture. Stella knew that there were prying eyes throughout the restaurant. The bold move could only mean one thing, but he needed to hear it from her lips.

"Does this mean…?" he began, searching her eyes for an answer.

Stella leaned in toward him. "I'm down with the plan, Luke," Stella said in a low voice, cutting him off. "I agree with you. This setup could really work for both of us. And if it means I'll have a peaceful summer, I'm all in. I need that." She reached up on her tippy toes and pressed a kiss against his cheek, causing a warm sensation to spread across his face. Her hand rested on his shoulder as she did so, making it feel all the more intimate.

Luke thought he might have to pick his jaw up off the floor. A kiss had been the last thing he'd expected from Stella. He was also blown away by her agreeing to his idea that they become a fake couple. Luke had honestly thought Stella would continue to be reluctant. Miles looked at their entwined hands and grinned from ear to ear as he observed Stella's gesture. The wheels were definitely turning in his young head. As they left the diner as a threesome, Luke could feel the heat of numerous stares focused on them like laser beams. He couldn't be certain, but out of the corner of his eye he thought Saffron might have been making a rude gesture with her finger.

Once Stella, Luke, and Miles left the Starlight Diner, they walked down Main Street, passing by the town's unique shops and the Free Library of Mistletoe, where Lucy worked. After a bit of window-shopping, they cut through the town green. Luke had always loved this part of Mistletoe's downtown area. The huge expanse of lawn was a rich emerald-green color, and a profusion of cherry trees were in full bloom. June in Maine was spectacular. Luke had been all over the world and there wasn't anything quite like his picturesque hometown. Even though he hadn't wanted to be disability retired at the age of thirty-two, Mistletoe was a nice place to lay his head while he figured things out. With each and every day it was growing on him until he was starting to feel like he was part of the town's fabric.

"I'm going to run over to the gazebo. Time me, Uncle Luke. My record is fifty-six seconds." Miles put one leg out and bent his opposite leg as he readied himself for the countdown.

"Okay. Ready. Set. Go," Luke called out, and they watched Miles fly like the wind across the town green.

"He's really fast. You might have a future track star on your hands," Stella said with a knowing smile. "Look at his form. You can't teach that at his age."

Stella was right. He was really focused on pumping his arms and legs. Luke planned to mention it to Nick so he could ask Miles if he wanted to get involved in a track program this summer. When Miles reached the gazebo, he let out a triumphant cry. Luke looked down at his watch. He had a feeling Miles was about to celebrate.

"Fifty-three seconds," Luke called out to him. Miles let out a loud hoot and began dancing the way football players did in the end zone after scoring a touchdown. His exuberance was contagious. Stella and Luke whooped and hollered right along with him.

Luke cast a glance at Stella. Her expression was one of pure joy. If he had his Nikon camera, he could capture her for all time. Her beauty and grace. The tinkling sound of her laughter. The way she lit up from the inside. Her warm brown skin made even more dazzling by sunlight.

Easy there, Cool Hand. His team members had given him the Paul Newman–inspired nickname because of his calm demeanor under pressure.

There was no question Stella was an exceptional woman, but he wasn't going to let things get messy between them by pursuing her. There was an attraction buzzing between them, and he had the feeling she felt it too. He couldn't pretend that he wasn't tempted by Stella, but he would have to push that to the background in order to make this thing work.

CHAPTER TEN

As they walked down Main Street, Stella kept her hand encased in Luke's. She had to admit it felt good, even though it was just for show. Holding hands was such a simple act, yet Stella had always loved this way of connecting with another person.

"Way to keep me on my toes back there, Marshall," Luke said, grinning as he turned toward her. "You blew me away with that handholding gesture in the diner. I totally wasn't expecting it."

"It was a spur-of-the-moment decision," Stella admitted. She bit her lip. One thing was really worrying her. "I don't want to hurt Miles in the process. In case you didn't notice, he was mesmerized by us holding hands. He might be disappointed when our summer showmance ends." Miles had a tender soul and Stella didn't want to do anything to confuse him.

"Don't worry about Miles. I plan to tell him we're good friends so he doesn't think we're settling down together or anything." Luke quirked his mouth. "Who knows? He might be relieved that I'm not poaching his girl." The twinkle in Luke's eyes made him even more attractive. She didn't remember him being this playful back in high school, although their interactions had been few and far between. Stella had admired him from a distance for years, casting him as the star in all her romantic fantasies. She'd even dreamed of Luke asking her to prom, which had been as unlikely as being struck by lightning.

What am I doing? Was this a smart move on her part? She couldn't deny the fact that she was attracted to Luke. And she'd had an intense crush on him at one time. Yes, the crush had lasted throughout high school, but who was counting?

Would she really be able to play this role without crossing any lines? What if those feelings came roaring back to life? The very idea of falling for someone again made her palms sweat with nervousness. The whole point of this arrangement was to give Stella time to heal without being forced into another relationship. It would be a huge step in taking control of her personal life and moving forward. She didn't need to get tangled up with a too-handsome-for-his-own-good Navy SEAL along the way.

"Your timing is excellent by the way. My aunt Hattie showed up on Nick's doorstep this morning with match-making on her mind." Luke visibly shuddered as he mentioned Hattie. His great-aunt had always terrified

Stella, so she felt his pain. At five two and one hundred pounds soaking wet, Hattie Jackson was a force to be reckoned with. Miss Hattie had led the youth choir and she'd acted like a drill sergeant. To this day Stella got nervous in her presence.

"No offense, but Miss Hattie is like a human version of a pit bull."

Luke chuckled. "But her bark is just as bad as her bite. From what Nick said, Miles is scared to death of her so she's not a great babysitting option." Stella joined in on the laughter. There was something ridiculously funny about Miss Hattie Jackson trying to set up her gorgeous nephew on dates.

"So what made you change your mind?" Luke's eyes were focused on her like laser beams. It wasn't exactly unpleasant to be the center of his attention. It had been ages since a man had looked at her with such intensity. She missed it badly.

"You made a lot of sense with your fake-dating pitch. It will benefit both of our objectives. As long as we keep things platonic." Ugh. Her voice sounded so prim and proper. Why had she just said that? Luke was a bona fide stud muffin who had women literally chasing him around Mistletoe. She'd made it sound like she was drawing a line in the sand in case he wanted to get with her. That hadn't been her intention at all. What was it about this man that made her lose her bearings? She had a serious case of foot-in-mouth disease.

Luke threw back his head and let out a hearty laugh. "A-are you serious? Stella, the last thing I want is a relationship. That's the whole reason I came up with this plan. Sorry to disappoint you, but I'm not secretly trying to get close to you, although I do think you're pretty cute." He wiggled his eyebrows at her.

Heat flushed Stella's cheeks and it had nothing to do with the June weather. Embarrassment washed over her. She'd just blurted out her thoughts and made herself look foolish. "I-I didn't mean it like that. It's just that I wanted to make sure—"

"That you wouldn't have to contend with another admirer?" Luke asked, smirking. "Don't worry, Stella. I'm in this for the same reasons as you. And it's not to get a girlfriend."

"Okay. Good to know," she said, trying to shake off her humiliation. "I'm going to head over to the library to see Lucy. She's probably getting ready to open up." Stella wanted to flee this awkward scene as fast as possible. Luke seemed to be savoring it, judging by his grin, no doubt enjoying her discomfort.

"Well, tell Lucy I said hello," he responded. "And remind her to keep our situation on the down low."

Stella wondered what Lucy would say about their arrangement. She spoke to her sister several times a day and they were best friends. She couldn't make it one day without blurting it out.

"Bye, Miles," she shouted, waving her hand wildly in his direction across the green. Before she knew it, he was sprinting back toward her and wrapping his arms around her waist. Suddenly, it felt as if her heart were cracking wide open. She tried so hard not to have favorite students or to get too attached to any one of them. But having Miles Keegan resting his precious little head against her midsection, letting her know she mattered to him, made her feel as if all was right with her world.

Miles let go of her and said, "Bye, Miss Marshall. If you want to come over to my house, you have an open invitation." He flashed her a wild grin. "Uncle Luke will be there."

Luke raised a hand to his mouth to cover up his grin.

"Thanks for the invite," Stella said with a wave. As she walked away Stella couldn't help but wonder if she was in over her head. Hanging out at the Keegans' house and playing the role of Luke's love interest? Going out on actual dates with Luke so they were seen together?

The short walk over to the Free Library of Mistletoe gave Stella time to clear her mind a little bit. Her entire life she'd always been a rule keeper. Back in school she'd verged on being a goody-goody, never taking a walk on the wild side. As a teacher, she insisted on rules in order to keep her classroom operating smoothly. She didn't lie, cheat, or steal. This arrangement with Luke felt like lying to the entire town. It was a bit unnerving.

Growing up in Mistletoe, Stella had been a quiet book nerd. She hadn't gotten into trouble, not even once. Even though she'd fantasized about riding on the back of Luke's motorcycle wearing a black leather jacket and thigh high suede boots, it had never happened. For the most part, she'd led an exemplary life.

Perhaps that was the problem. She had been so busy walking a straight and narrow path that she'd allowed people like Rafe to trample right over her. She always worried about doing the right thing, but what had that gotten her so far? Nothing but heartache.

The Free Library of Mistletoe was an ornate Colonial-style building—the quintessential small-town New England library. However, Stella had always thought of the library as one of the most charming spots in town mainly because it was Lucy's heart and soul. Even when they were kids, she and Lucy had been enthralled by the magic behind the library's walls. Her and Lucy's professions had both been inspired by this fantastic place.

She walked to the back entrance of the library, opening up the door and walking to the main floor's circulation desk. She spotted Lucy arranging books on a shelf for patrons who'd placed them on hold to pick up. Stella was proud of all of her sister's accomplishments as head librarian. Despite the fact that money had been limited, Lucy had always worked miracles to stretch her operating funds and maintain the integrity of the library's programs and catalog. Last year, Dante's film company had used the building to shoot scenes for his film in exchange for a hefty donation. It had made a world of difference for the library's operations.

At the sound of her footsteps, Lucy whirled around. "Sorry, we're not open yet."

"Not even for me?" Stella asked, quickly closing the distance between them and extending her arms for a hug.

"Hey, Stella! What are you doing here?" Lucy asked, sounding surprised. "Shouldn't you be sleeping in now that school's out? Or walking Blackberry Beach?"

"I had a craving for waffles so I had breakfast at the Starlight... with Luke Keegan." Even as she said the words aloud, it seemed a bit surreal. Most women in town would give their right arm to sit down for a meal with Luke. Let's face it. Back in high school she would have given anything to spend alone time with him.

"Stop it! No you didn't." Lucy's voice rose with excitement and she grabbed Stella's arm. "Are you playing with me?"

"I'm not teasing you," Stella confirmed. "I did. And we are officially Mistletoe's It couple of the summer." Just saying the words out loud caused goose bumps to raise up on her arms.

"Okay. Not funny. Now I know you're joking," Lucy said, scowling at Stella.

Stella had to work hard to keep a straight face. Her sister didn't like being pranked, and she seemed to genuinely think Stella was pulling her leg. "I'm actually not kidding. Luke made me a proposition." She shrugged. "One I couldn't refuse."

Lucy gulped. "What kind of proposition?"

Stella chuckled. "Nothing like what you're imagining. Because of the town gossip about us being an item—"

"Item is putting it nicely," Stella said with a grimace. "The main word I've heard is hooking up."

Stella gritted her teeth. She was determined to lighten up about the rumors. *I will not let it get the best of me.* "Luke came up with a plan to spare both of us the agony of town matchmakers and overzealous admirers. He's been deluged with women wanting to go out with him. Really over-the-top stuff. And he knows that I've been trying to move past Rafe and the wedding that wasn't, as well as being pursued by Tucker and Paul...among others thanks to our parents."

Lucy frowned. "How does he know all of this? When did you tell him all that?"

Stella shifted from one foot to the other. "Well, I believe it was the day of your bridal gown fitting."

"Okay," Lucy said, dragging out the word. She stared at Stella, waiting for further clarification.

Busted. Stella sat down in Lucy's chair. "The only reason I didn't tell you is because I know how you are. You would have immediately felt responsible for my near run-in with Rafe at Rosie's."

"What? How could you not tell me that? What happened?" Lucy glanced at her watch. "And tell me quickly because the library opens in fifteen minutes and my employees and the patrons will be arriving at any moment."

"Okay. So after you, Tess, and Mom left the shop, Rosie blindsided me by telling Tucker to come over..."

Lucy groaned and made a face. "He really needs to take a hint. And get a life."

"Girl, you're preaching to the choir. So I may have told him I was seeing someone so he would stop pestering me. After Tucker stormed out, Rosie followed him. Next thing I know I hear a voice in the corridor. Rafe's voice. He was with his wife and baby looking for a baptismal gown."

"Oh, Stella. That must have been so awkward when you came face-to-face," Lucy said in a soothing voice, patting Stella on the shoulder.

"We didn't. I exited the salon by way of the window, which led me to being rescued by Luke, who was driving by in his truck. Right place, right time. We ended up driving around a bit to kill some time," Stella explained. "I kind of owed him an explanation since he'd seen me escaping through the window. So I told him all about Rafe and our canceled wedding and how I couldn't bear to see him. I also mentioned Tucker and how everyone wants to set me up with their best friend's husband's brother or their second cousin twice removed."

Lucy clapped her hand over her mouth and made a tutting sound. "That happened to me a time or two and it's so uncomfortable. Makes me relieved to be engaged."

"So while we were commiserating, Luke had the idea that we should be a pretend couple. Since the town gossips have already paired us up, what do we have to lose?" Stella shrugged. "Personally speaking, I have everything to gain. By being Luke's boo for the summer I won't have to be thrown into the lion's den on any more blind dates. Mom and Dad will finally lay off me. Guys like Paul and Tucker will have to suck it up and face the fact that I'm off the market. Likewise, all the women who've been stalking him will have to cease and desist."

"You can't be serious." Lucy's beautiful brown eyes bulged and her mouth went slack. "Stella, have you completely lost your mind?" Stella wanted to laugh at Lucy's indignation. Judging by her expression, Lucy was suffering from a serious case of outrage.

"That's usually what I find myself saying to you," Stella responded. "My how the tables have turned." Last December Stella had been forced to counsel Lucy as she dove headfirst into a relationship with her high school sweetheart who had left Lucy brokenhearted eight years earlier. More times than not, Lucy had ignored her warnings and followed her heart. In the end, Lucy's instincts had been spot-on. She'd walked off into the sunset with Dante and soon they would be getting hitched. Stella often thought she should be taking lessons from her sister. Lucy could make a fortune selling her services. *How to land a movie star over the holidays in six easy lessons.*

Lucy rummaged around on her desk, pausing to look up at Stella. "I'm confused. Why go to all this trouble? Seems a lot easier to just tell everyone in town to leave you alone, including Tucker and Paul."

"Come on, Lucy. You know how this works. Even if I did manage to convince Tucker and Paul to beat it, there's still our parents to contend with along with a host of other town matchmakers. Do you have any idea how many blind dates Mom and Dad have tried to set me up on? They are clearly trying to get their spinster daughter off the market."

"Spinster? You sound like you're living in a Jane Austen novel." Lucy wrinkled her nose. "I didn't know they've been pressuring you so much. I'm sorry about that. Do I dare ask who with?"

Stella made a face. "Nobody special." No one who made her pulse quicken. No one who made her go weak in the knees. No one who she could picture herself sitting on the beach with, watching the stars as they lit up the night sky.

"Stella, you say that about everybody. I know you loved Rafe, but you're going to have to bend a little in order to give someone else a chance to be in your life." Lucy squeezed Stella's hand. "You deserve to be adored."

Was it such a bad thing to expect someone wonderful? She shouldn't have to settle for less to find someone decent. Sometimes her heart ached just thinking about all she'd lost. Sure, in the end, Rafe had turned out to be a huge tool, but when things were good between them it had felt like a fairy tale. Growing up in Mistletoe, Stella had always felt invisible, so to be appreciated and valued by a man like Rafe had been amazing. She'd felt like Cinderella at the ball when he'd asked her to marry him. Was it wrong to want to feel that way again?

"This gives me time to breathe," Stella explained. For so long she'd been treading water simply so she wouldn't drown. It felt as if Luke had thrown her a life preserver.

"And time to get over Rafe?" Lucy asked bluntly. Lucy knew her more intimately than anyone else in the world. Even though she and Lucy shared an unbreakable bond, Stella was a bit reluctant to dredge up painful memories.

"Come on. Fess up." Lucy playfully swatted her with a manila folder. "You know I'll get it out of you one way or another."

Stella shrugged. "Sometimes it seems that I'm over Rafe, but then I catch a glimpse of him at the market and it feels like I've been slapped in the face. I thought I'd be growing old with him. I'd already written my vows when he told me he didn't want to marry me. And still I lay awake at night and ask myself at what exact moment did he stop loving me? And why didn't I see it?" Her eyes burned with unshed tears. "I thought I'd turned a corner on all this, but then he had the baby.

For some reason it brought up all of these emotions inside of me."

Stella felt Lucy's arm around her shoulder. "I think it's all tied up in loss. You had the rug pulled out from underneath you, so you're still trying to get your balance. Give yourself a break."

Loss. What she had been going through was akin to grieving a death. There was no timetable for it, no magical moment when she could wave a wand and be healed. She honestly believed that if she didn't have the additional pressures and expectations about dating someone placed on her shoulders, she would finally be able to move on with her life. It was impossible to make progress when she felt so many eyes watching her. She kept wondering if they were waiting for her to stumble.

"Thanks for understanding, sis." Stella ran a hand through her hair. "So far Rafe has been coming out of all this smelling like a rose. He got the wedding to his childhood sweetheart. And my baby name. Not to mention he's living in the house we talked about buying for ourselves. I have to go out of my way not to drive by that sweet yellow Victorian. I can't even bear to look at it."

"He's really a creep," Lucy said, slamming her palm down on her desk. "Seriously, it's not too late for me to hunt him down and do a few Tae Kwon Do moves on him."

Stella giggled. "You don't even know martial arts. And even if you did, I can't let you do that on my behalf. We both have to uphold our professional images."

"If you say so," Lucy muttered. Stella had to laugh at

her sister. Despite her butter-wouldn't-melt-in-her-mouth demeanor, Lucy was part bulldog. Even Dante had found that out the hard way.

"Okay, so it's all making more sense now." A wicked grin appeared on Lucy's face. "The best way to get over your stinkin' ex is to get involved with a smoldering Navy SEAL."

Stella emphatically shook her head. "No! It won't be real, Lucy. It'll be a fauxmance. It's just for show."

Lucy winked at her. "Well, that's what you say now. Luke Keegan is the type of guy a girl wants to take home to Mama."

Luke's handsome face flashed before Stella's eyes. She couldn't disagree with Lucy on that point. Who wouldn't be attracted to a man like Luke? He wasn't just easy on the eyes. Luke was kind and gentle, with a huge heart that had been on full display with Miles. He was so easy to talk to and they shared a wonderful rapport. To top it off, he had a great sense of humor and a killer smile that Stella found irresistible. She just enjoyed being around him.

The whole Navy SEAL thing was swoon worthy too. She knew all about his Medal of Honor commendation, which told her he was heroic in a crisis. This man had saved lives and thwarted terrorism. Stella didn't know the details, but there had been a traumatic incident in Afghanistan that had torpedoed Luke. It made her sad to think about Luke suffering in any way. He radiated goodness.

"Oooooh!" Lucy snapped her fingers. "Imagine Rafe's reaction when he realizes you're coupled up with an actual hero." She fanned her face. "And a hot one at that. I'd love to be a fly on that wall."

Stella scoffed. "Why would he care? His life is pretty near perfect, which is annoying. Even his wife looks like he ordered her out of a catalog." Ugh. She hated the way she sounded. She didn't know Tabitha, and she didn't have any beef with her. To this day Stella had no idea whether Tabitha knew about her and Rafe's canceled wedding. Rafe was a master manipulator, and she wouldn't be surprised at all if he'd completely bamboozled her.

"No one's life is perfect," Lucy said. "Rafe is a classic narcissist. He loves the idea that you're single and sitting around on Saturday nights thinking about him." She gleefully rubbed her hands together. "It'll make him burn a little to see you out and about with Luke."

Stella rolled her eyes. "Lucy, that's not my goal." She was trying her best not to be petty in her day-to-day life. It would only serve to drag her under. If Rafe had cared for her at all, he wouldn't have treated her so horribly in the first place. She had no illusions anymore about her ex-fiancé. Stella had wanted to spend her life with Rafe because she'd believed him to be loyal, loving, and honest. She now knew he didn't possess any of these qualities.

"I know it's not your focus, but it's like having gravy on your mashed potatoes. It will be an added benefit of spending time with such a swoon-worthy man."

"I thought that I was the only man you viewed as swoon worthy." The low, rich voice came out of nowhere, surprising them both. Stella heard Lucy squeal, then watched as her sister came from behind the desk and hurled herself at the tall, gorgeous man standing there. "Dante!" she cried out as she wrapped her arms around his neck.

Stella stood back as Lucy and Dante shared a tender reunion.

This is what she hoped to find one day. A man who would love her like nobody's business. Dante regularly traveled from his home in Los Angeles to Maine in order to see Lucy and help out with their wedding plans. It was achingly romantic to see Lucy swept up in Dante's arms. She couldn't think of a single person who deserved a happy ending more than Lucy. Even though she was a bit worried that her sister would no longer have time for their impromptu meetups, movie nights, and road trips once she was Mrs. Dante West, Stella had been cheering the duo on since their Christmas engagement. The moment Stella knew for certain Dante was serious about a future with Lucy, Stella had been all in.

For the first time it hit her that she hadn't had this with Rafe. He'd never looked at her the way Dante was staring at Lucy. And she wasn't sure she'd ever lit up in Rafe's presence as Lucy did right now. Once she was able to process the thought, it felt like she'd been kicked in the gut. All this time she'd been mourning the loss of something that hadn't even existed. She started taking slow, soothing breaths to calm herself down.

Finally, she was taking steps to move on. Entering into a fake relationship with Luke would give Stella time to center herself without being pushed and prodded to date someone she wasn't interested in. And it would keep all the town matchmakers from trying to work their magic by fixing her up with a random dude who didn't make her weak in the knees. Sure, there would be wagging tongues about her and Luke, but unlike before, this time she could take the heat. Her feelings weren't on the line with Luke. She wasn't reeling from a fiancé's betrayal.

Stella was stronger now, and she was determined to take her life into her own hands. That was the only way to successfully step into her future and put the past in her rearview mirror.

CHAPTER ELEVEN

No pain, no gain. Whoever had come up with that stupid motto must've been a masochist, Luke reckoned. If his leg pain was any indication, he was gaining at a rapid pace that just might kill him. Problem was, his body was now refusing to cooperate. He felt his leg buckle underneath him right before he fell to the sand. He let out a strangled cry. Luke pressed his eyes closed as waves of pain crashed over him. Now he knew what it felt like to be seeing stars. Panic set in when he realized his leg had locked up on him.

"Luke. You're hurt." He wasn't sure if the throbbing sensations were messing with him, but he heard Stella's honeyed voice saying his name. When he opened his eyes, she was standing over him with Coco Chanel at her side. Coco Chanel began enthusiastically licking his face, which under the circumstances actually felt comforting.

"What happened? Can you get up?" Stella asked as she reined Coco Chanel in on her leash.

"I might need a little help," he admitted. Luke couldn't believe he was in this situation. He'd always been in excellent physical shape, so it was a bit humiliating to find himself unable to stand up on his own accord. Anger flowed in his veins. His injury made him feel incredibly helpless, which was the same way he'd felt after the explosion. All of the training and discipline hadn't mattered in the end. His body had still failed him.

Stella moved toward him, reaching for his arm as he tried to stand. Luke saw her eyes widen the moment she spotted the long, jagged scar on his leg where his bone and soft tissue injuries had been operated on. Clearly she hadn't seen it the day he'd rescued Coco Chanel on the beach. He was able to make it to his feet by placing most of his weight on his good leg. Worry flared in her eyes, as well as a host of questions.

"It's just a muscle spasm. It happens sometimes when I'm running." At least that's what he'd been telling anyone who asked. He let out an involuntary groan and bent over at the waist. "It flares up every now and again. I just need to walk it off," he said, knowing full well he wasn't telling the truth. The searing pain he was experiencing was from overuse, which his doctor had repeatedly warned him about. Like an idiot, he hadn't listened. For so long he'd been trained to push through...to endure pain and hardships. It was extremely difficult to ignore the loud voice in his head telling him to keep pushing.

Stella made a face. "I'm no doctor, but I don't think

that's going to work. You can't make it back to Nick's house on your own."

"You're probably right," he begrudgingly admitted. "I'm going to have to call Nick and get a lecture about how I shouldn't have been running in the first place." Nick had questioned him about putting too much strain on his bad leg. Luke had been intent on proving that he was still in impeccable shape despite the injury that had led to his early retirement. The sad part was, he was trying to convince himself more than anyone else. His pride had landed him in this predicament.

"Or you could just come to my place and rest your leg for a bit. Maybe put some ice on it and take some Tylenol," she suggested.

At the moment Stella's suggestion sounded like heaven. Relief from this agony would be a lifesaver. When he didn't respond right away, Stella leaned in and playfully hit him in the bicep. "Come on. I'm sure Patsy will be using her binoculars to spy on us. This will give us some street cred as a couple in Mistletoe."

Luke nodded his head in a gesture of surrender. He was in no position to argue with Stella. It was either go back to her beach house or call for an ambulance. His pride wouldn't accept ending up at the ER due to his own foolishness. Navy SEALs were nothing if not proud.

By the time they reached Stella's place, Luke was exhausted and numb from pain. He had leaned on Stella the entire way and hopped on his good leg. It was as if his limb had reached its tolerance level and was now frozen. She quickly led him to a couch in her living room. With an abundance of gentleness, Stella helped him swing his legs onto the couch and placed a pillow under his right leg to elevate it. Luke could tell she sensed his agony because her movements were efficient and tender. Although Luke knew Stella was an amazing teacher due to his nephew constantly singing her praises, her Florence Nightingale skills showcased her nurturing side.

As she leaned over, her dark tresses brushed against the side of his face, filling his nostrils with the scent of roses. Her nearness caused butterflies to fly around in his stomach. *Chill out*, he warned himself. Stella was in the friend zone, courtesy of their arrangement. He needed to simply play his role and not catch any romantic feelings for her.

Once he was settled, Stella said, "Let me get you something cold to drink along with an ice bag. I'll also scrounge up some pain relief pills. Not sure what I have in my medicine closet, but I know I've got something."

"I'm not picky at the moment," Luke said through clenched teeth. The pain was coming back now, and he reached out to massage his leg. The level of pain he was dealing with was off the charts.

"I'll be right back," Stella said, walking quickly out of the room and down the hall. He could hear the clinking of ice emanating from the kitchen as well as sounds of drawers opening and closing. He closed his eyes and tried to visualize something wonderful. An azure blue sea with pelican-pink sand. Chilling out in a hammock while an ocean breeze swept over him. A big juicy cheeseburger with all the trimmings. A smoldering kiss with a beautiful woman with mocha-colored skin and brown eyes he could get lost in. *Stella*. His eyes fluttered open. Whoa. He'd been fantasizing about his pretend girlfriend.

Stella was standing beside the couch, looking at him with her brows knitted together. She'd placed a tall glass of lemonade on the coffee table next to him. His mouth watered just looking at it. Beside it was a bottle of Tylenol and an ice pack.

"Here you go." She handed him the drink and two pills. Luke took the pills and gulped them down with a large swig of lemonade. It felt cool and refreshing going down his throat. More and more, Stella was beginning to look like an angel. He took the ice pack from her and placed it on his leg, wincing from the cold. After a little bit he found he could tolerate the freeze of the ice pack because it was numbing his pain. A good tradeoff, he reckoned.

Stella sat down in a big comfy love seat. She was sipping on her own glass of lemonade as she gazed at him. "I don't mean to pry, but that's a pretty gnarly scar on your leg. Is that the source of your pain?"

"Yeah," he said, pausing to take a long sip of his lemonade. He slowly placed the glass back down on the table, stalling a little bit so he could figure out what to say. It was still almost impossible for him to talk about the most nightmarish day of his life. He didn't need a therapist to tell him he was still stuck in that horrific place in time when his world had imploded. But for some reason, he didn't want to keep Stella in the dark. She'd been amazing during this crisis, and he felt an odd desire to answer her question.

"I know you've been through a lot, Luke. Nick

didn't go into detail, but I know you were injured in Afghanistan and that you received the Medal of Honor for your heroism."

He cringed at the mention of the Medal of Honor. He wasn't mad at Stella for bringing it up, but for some reason it was the one thing people seemed to remember or wanted to talk about. The medal had come about at a devastating cost—the loss of Kenneth and Aaron. He would trade it in a heartbeat to have his two friends back. If anyone asked he would tell them he was nobody's hero. All he'd ever tried to do was uphold the creed of the Navy SEALs. With honor.

He looked off into the distance, focusing on the miles of beautiful blue ocean that stretched out as far as the eye could see. "My SEAL team was doing a routine mission which we'd performed hundreds of times. We came under attack unexpectedly. All of my intel as a team leader was wrong that day." He ran a weary hand over his face. "To be honest, I don't remember much after the blast. It pretty much knocked me out. When I came to there was fire and smoke and this awful burning smell. There are so many things I can't recall about that day, but if I live to be one hundred, I'll never forget that smell. And the screams...so many wounded, others well beyond help. I later found out that two of my men were killed in the blast."

Stella gasped. "Oh, Luke. I'm so sorry. I didn't know that."

He bowed his head so he didn't have to make eye contact. It was easier this way to get out the words he wanted to say. "When I woke up in the hospital, I discovered I'd been operated on due to a bone injury in my leg. I'd lost a lot of blood, and if it hadn't been for my fast arrival at the hospital, I might have lost my leg." He let out a brittle laugh. "At times I begged for them to take it because the pain was excruciating. It wasn't until I arrived stateside at Walter Reed that I began to see the light at the end of the tunnel. I spent months learning to walk again, being operated on, and healing my bone injury."

She let out a sympathetic sound. "I can't imagine how difficult that must've been for you."

"The most agonizing part was learning about Aaron and Kenneth, my team members who didn't make it. To this day it still feels so wrong to have lost them." He bowed his head. "Neither one made it to their thirtieth birthday. Aaron has two kids who'll never know their father." It absolutely shattered him to think about Aaron's twin boys missing out on him being in their lives. It reminded him all too much of Miles's being a mother-less child. Graduations. Birthdays. Weddings. Like his nephew, Aaron's kids would have to weather all those big occasions without one of their parents. Being a support-ive presence in Miles's life was a major reason why he needed to stick around Maine.

"But you can make sure they know what kind of a man he was," Stella said. "Not just as a SEAL but as a friend, a husband, and a father."

Stella was spot on. That was something Luke intended to do when he met with the families in person. And, if allowed, he would like to be a part of the twins' lives in some capacity. Friend. Honorary uncle. He didn't care about the label as long as he could support them in their journey.

"So is your injury the reason you're not a SEAL any longer?"

Just hearing Stella say it out loud made it all too real. His life as a Navy SEAL was over. There was no going back. He would never get the chance to redeem himself.

"To make the nightmare complete, I was retired from active duty due to my physical condition. They deemed me unfit for duty and there was nothing I could do to change their decision. It was final and binding." He lifted his shoulders. "So there's a part of me that knows I shouldn't be putting stress on my leg by running, but another part of me wants to prove something."

"That you're not broken."

He swung his gaze up after hearing her unexpected response. How did she know that? Was he so easy to read? Or was she simply an intuitive and sensitive woman?

She gave him a knowing look. "I know it's different from your situation in a million ways, but I'm guilty of the same thing. Over the past two years I've done so many things just to prove that Rafe didn't break me. And none of it made me happy. It didn't help me heal. It just left me stuck."

He let out a ragged sigh. "It took me until today to realize that I'm only hurting myself and my body. I'm not going to be reinstated as a SEAL even if I managed to win the Boston Marathon and the Super Bowl."

She shot him a tender smile. "No, you're not. When Rafe's baby was born I had to face up to the fact that I needed to put all of my fantasies of us living happily ever after to rest. As crazy as it sounds, I was still holding on to some wild hope that he might come back to me begging for forgiveness." She let out a weak laugh. "It was time to dream other dreams and to make peace with it."

"And have you?" he asked, curious to know if she'd managed to put it all behind her. Luke didn't admit to her how badly he wanted to pack away his baggage, but the truth was he wasn't sure what steps he needed to take in order to make it happen.

"Not yet, but I'm getting there," she admitted. "And you will too. You just have to find your sweet spot, a place in the world that suits you just as much as being a SEAL did."

There it was. The stark, cold truth. Trying to get in peak condition again wasn't going to give him what he wanted most in the world. He was never going to be part of a Navy SEAL team again. That part of his life was over. That knowledge hit like a sledgehammer. He'd been living in denial, imagining that he could pull off a miracle with discipline and focus. And now he was sitting here with a busted-up leg praying he hadn't done anything to make it worse.

"So do you like chicken parm?" she asked, adroitly changing the subject.

Mmm. Just the thought of it made his stomach grumble in appreciation. "What's not to like? Italian food is my favorite. Why?"

"Because I'm making it for dinner and you're invited to stay. I figure by the time dinner is over you'll be back on your feet and out of my hair," she said in a teasing tone. "I'm also throwing in garlic bread and salad, so now you really can't say no."

"Honestly, there really wasn't ever a chance of me saying no," Luke admitted. "I appreciate it, Stella. Matter of fact I'm thankful for all of this," he said, gesturing toward his leg, the ice pack, and cushion. She'd made him feel like a welcomed guest, and now she would be cooking dinner for him. The last woman who'd cooked a meal for him had been his mother. And that had been ages ago. Stella surprised him. She was equal parts schoolteacher and Florence Nightingale. A caretaker. She was level-headed and a bit quirky on occasion. Vulnerable yet strong. Stella was a woman who was constantly surprising him in the best of ways.

"Good then," she said with a nod. She reached over and handed him the television remote. "Knock yourself out. By the way, you're welcome, Luke."

"Everyone is taking really good care of me in Mistletoe," Luke said. "I wasn't sure how I would fit back into the fabric of this town, but spending so much time with Nick and Miles has been amazing."

A hint of a smile played around her lips. "I need to tell you that Miles wrote an essay about you and it won first prize in a state competition. If you haven't read it yet, I wouldn't wait another day to do so. Seeing you through his eyes was wonderful. I get the sense you have a hard time embracing the hero label, which is understandable considering how you earned it, but Miles thinks you're a superhero." Her eyes teared up and she blinked them away. "With everything he's been through, that little boy needs heroes in his life. And from where he's standing, you're Superman and Black Panther all rolled up into one. I just thought you should know."

Stella left the room and Luke let out a breath. Nick had told him about the essay, but Luke hadn't read it yet. He hadn't felt worthy of the title, so he hadn't followed up with his brother about it. His chest tightened with emotion just thinking about his nephew writing an essay about him. His love for Miles was epic. Based on Stella's comment, Miles felt the same way about him. It was humbling and gratifying at the same time.

As the tangy smell of marinara sauce floated in the air, Luke heard his stomach grumble in appreciation. *I could get used to this*, he thought as he turned on the television with Coco Chanel nestled up against him. Once again he had to remind himself that none of this was real. He couldn't allow himself to get too comfortable in Stella's world. Or lean on her too much as a crutch. Even though it didn't seem like it at a moment like this, they were both playing roles. Luke needed to focus on his own future and figure out what in the world he was going to do with himself.

* * *

As Stella navigated the winding road leading to Blackberry Beach Road, she luxuriated in the wind whipping through her hair and the sun beating down on her face. There was nothing she loved more than a lazy summer day with glorious weather. This morning she'd had a few errands to run in town, such as grocery shopping, picking up dry cleaning, and making a coffee run at the Coffee

Bean. She'd allowed herself the luxury of sitting outside on the patio to drink her coffee, which allowed her to partake in one of her favorite activities—people watching. She found herself wondering if she would run into Luke. She'd been thinking about his leg pain and curious as to whether he'd made his way to a doctor's office for an assessment of the situation. By the time she'd driven him home his pain had lessened and he was able to walk, but it was still an alarming episode.

Stella's quick trip to the market had turned into a full-on interrogation from a few ladies about her and Luke's status. She had to admit it felt wonderful to see their expressions as she confirmed that they were a couple. These same women had been extremely catty to her after the wedding was called off. They'd rubbed salt in the wound by telling her "everything happens for a reason" and "the heart wants what it wants." She couldn't even feel a little bad that they seemed completely put out by the news about her and Luke. Especially when Stella had dropped a few precious breadcrumbs to make it seem as if their summer plans were epic. On her way out of the store she crossed paths with Tucker while they were both walking to their cars in the parking lot.

"Stella," he said with a nod, giving her the once-over. The way he always ogled her drove her crazy. He could never seem to keep his eyes above her neck. It always made her feel icky.

"Tucker. How's it going?" she asked, planting a smile on her face. No matter what he says, she reminded herself, it was her intention to stay pleasant. *Keep Calm and Carry On.*

"Not too bad," he responded. "Just grabbing some things on my lunch break."

"Well, enjoy this beautiful day," Stella said, moving toward her car. She didn't want to drag out a conversation with Tucker. He always had a way of throwing a curveball into any interaction they had with each other. Before she knew it Stella would be asked on yet another date that she wasn't at all interested in going on.

"I have to admit, I didn't believe you the other day," Tucker called after her.

She turned back toward him. Something about his tone didn't sit well with her. "Excuse me?"

Tucker was placing his groceries in the back of his car. When he slammed the trunk shut, he glanced over at her. "When you said you were seeing someone. I thought you were playing hard to get or just plain lying," Tucker said, twisting his mouth. "But everyone is talking about you and that military dude, so I guess it's true."

"Luke. His name is Luke," she snapped. She didn't know why she felt defensive about Luke, but it was wrong of Tucker to reduce him to his profession. He'd sounded dismissive. As she was finding out, there was so much more to Luke than met the eye. His bravery as a Navy SEAL hadn't been without consequences. Or emotional pain.

"Yeah. Luke Keegan, Nick's brother." He paused a beat, staring her down. "Just so you know, when it goes south between the two of you, I may not be around to help you pick up the pieces. You probably don't know how much of a player those SEALs can be," Tucker scoffed. "He probably has a girl in every state. It's not too late to change your mind. I'd consider giving you another chance."

Stella let out a shocked sound. "Are you being serious right now? Get over yourself, Tucker. I never once said I wanted a relationship with you. Not once. Mighty big of you to make such a generous offer, but the day I take you up on it will be when lobsters fly in Mistletoe Harbor."

Tucker held up his hands and backed away from her. "No need to go off on me like that. Or to be so sassy and rude."

Humph! He thought *this* was sassy? Tucker hadn't even scratched the surface. The women in her family were proud and well mannered, but if you pushed the wrong buttons, fireworks went off. It was maddening how Tucker couldn't see how condescending he was being. Maybe it was time she set him straight once and for all. She'd been way too considerate of his feelings ever since he began pursuing her, at the expense of her own state of mind. That ended now.

"No, Tucker, rude is the multiple times you blindsided me at places where I truly wanted to be in my own space, like that time you showed up at the hair salon when I just wanted a wash and set. Or that afternoon you just happened to be at the library when I was meeting up with Lucy. Oh, and who can forget the day you stood outside my classroom and peered through the window. That wasn't creepy or anything, was it? You frightened second graders."

Tucker's cheeks were redder than a Maine lobster. "I was trying to be spontaneous and show you that I was interested."

"In what? A restraining order?" she fired back.

At this point steam appeared to be coming out of Tucker's ears. "Don't worry, Stella Marshall. You don't have to worry about me any longer. I'm moving on. Onward and upward."

"Good. Because I already have." Right before she turned away, Stella saw his jaw go slack. Something told her that Tucker thought she was a pushover—the type of woman who never went against the grain. She'd taught him how to treat her by being way too accommodating, and he'd gone a bit over the line. Lesson to Stella— *speak up for yourself.* She didn't owe anyone her time and attention. Tucker was a jerk, but she had allowed the situation to go on for far too long due to her unwillingness to be direct with him. Somewhere deep inside of her Stella knew this was a pattern for her and one she'd played out with Rafe. Today wasn't the day to dig up those skeletons, but soon she would begin to unearth them. Her relationship with her ex-fiancé had been far from perfect. And she'd ignored way too many red flags in their relationship that had risen up to bite her in the butt.

CHAPTER TWELVE

Stella felt liberated as she wound her way down the stunning coastal road leading toward home. Telling off Tucker made her feel as if she had wings and could take flight right there and then. The people pleaser part of her felt slightly uncomfortable about it, but she knew he'd had it coming. Once she made it to her lot, Stella walked across her pebbled driveway and glanced over at the huge expanse of beach and ocean stretched out before her. It was so inviting. Maybe she would take a swim in a little bit and work out the little kinks in her shoulder.

The bouquet sitting at her front door caught her eye. She couldn't take her eye off the beautiful assortment. Yellow, pink, and white roses were interlaced with baby's breath. It wasn't even close to her birthday, so she had no idea why someone had sent her these magnificent flowers. She opened her front door, then juggled her groceries and the floral bouquet to her kitchen counter. Stella reached for the tiny envelope and opened it up with her fingernail.

Stella. Thanks for the rescue. You totally saved my bacon. We've got to stop meeting like this.

Luke

Stella felt a rush reading Luke's note, and a smile tugged at her lips. The flowers were stunning, and their heavenly aroma quickly spread through the kitchen. Luke's sweet gesture was a nice surprise. It told her a lot about the man. He was strong and loyal with a big heart. From the little she knew about what it took to become a member of the elite SEAL teams, he had to be pretty badass. No wonder Miles thought he was a superhero. Luke was an incredible man who always seemed to think of others before himself. She felt pretty lucky to be in his orbit.

A loud knock on her front door jolted her out of her thoughts about Luke and the beautiful bouquet of flowers. She wasn't expecting anybody, so perhaps it was another delivery. As she drew closer to the front door, she spotted Carolina through the panes of glass, standing on her doorstep. She had her arms folded around her chest and an impatient expression on her face.

Stella pulled open the door. "Hey, girl. I wasn't expecting to see you today."

Rather than waiting to be invited in, Carolina brushed

by Stella without even a greeting. "Alrighty then. Hello to you too. It seems someone woke up on the wrong side of the bed this morning."

Carolina turned around to face her. "I can't believe you've been holding out on me like this about tall, dark, and handsome," Carolina complained. "I thought we had a pact. Don't you remember our motto? Sisters before misters?"

"That was all yours, Carolina," Stella said, holding up her hands in protest. Carolina had a very colorful way of rewriting history. Oftentimes her friend tried to tag Stella with things she herself had done. In this instance, Carolina had come up with the sisters before misters rallying cry all on her own. There had been no pact. Not ever. It was classic Carolina. She was always adding extra sauce to situations.

"So what's up with all the intrigue? If I was carrying on with eye candy like Luke Keegan, I'd be shouting it from the rooftops." She cut her eyes at Stella. "And I'd definitely tell my bestie before she had to hear it from a ten-year-old."

"Tess?" Stella really didn't even need to ask the question. Of course it had been her sister telling her business all over Mistletoe. Honestly, she didn't understand what got into her baby sister and why she was constantly flapping her lips all over town. Her parents seriously needed to get her in check as soon as possible before she got herself into trouble. It wasn't cute at all.

Due to her mother's multiple sclerosis diagnosis and subsequent illness, Tess had been pushed a bit to the background. At that time Lucy had stepped in to provide

Tess with an extra dose of TLC and attention until Leslie's illness stabilized. But her condition had improved since then. So why was Tess still being a gossip hound?

"None other than Tess," Carolina answered with a slight smile. "I ran into her and your mom in town and she couldn't wait to tell me. But that's beside the point." Carolina perched her hand on her hip. "Why was I the last to know? Did you think I'd be upset about you landing the hottest man to ever hit Mistletoe? Other than Dante of course," she quickly added. "That's pretty much a dead even tie."

She took Carolina's hand and lightly tugged on it. "Carolina, let's go sit down and talk in the kitchen. I was about to heat up some of my mac 'n' cheese for lunch. Care to join me?"

"How can I say no? I'm still waiting for you to tell me the secret ingredient," Carolina said as she licked her lips and allowed herself to be led to the kitchen.

"Oooooh!" Carolina exclaimed as she laid eyes on the magnificent flowers. Shoot! Stella had forgotten all about them. Now Carolina would go on and on about Luke buying her flowers. "Luke has some serious good taste." She raised an eyebrow at Stella. "These are from Luke aren't they?"

"Yes, they are," she admitted, her cheeks blushing. It was insane to feel bashful, but all of a sudden it felt as if she'd been on the receiving end of a romantic gesture. She knew full well and good it hadn't been like that at all, but she couldn't stop herself from feeling some kind of way about it. Especially with Carolina gaping at her as if she were Meghan Markle marrying Prince Harry.

"You are living the dream, girl." Carolina began clapping. "Please, give me the dirt. I want to know everything. How did you snag Mistletoe's finest so quickly?" Carolina sat down at the table while Stella took the mac 'n' cheese out of the fridge and began heating it up in the microwave. She took her groceries from her shopping bag.

"Give me a second," Stella said as she emptied the bag. What was she going to say? She didn't feel good about lying to Carolina, but she knew without a shadow of a doubt that her friend would spill the beans if she told her the truth. She wouldn't do it on purpose, but Carolina had a history of blurting things out. In some ways she was the grown-up version of Tess. Stella had made a promise to Luke to keep their situation on the down low and she intended to honor her word.

"Okay, while you're doing that, I have something to tell you about your ex," Carolina said, dramatically stretching out the words. Stella turned around just in time to catch Carolina wrinkling her nose as if she'd smelled something bad.

She held up her hand. "Carolina. I thought we went over this. I don't even want to hear his name being uttered." Why did it feel as if her life would always be inextricably linked to her ex-fiancé?

"I know, but I went back and forth a million times about whether or not to tell you." Carolina bit her lip. "Knowledge can be powerful yet annoying at the same time. Tell me to shut my pie hole and I'll never speak of it again."

"Spill it," Stella demanded.

"Okay. I ran into he who shall not be named at the marina. He made a big point of seeking me out and he none too casually mentioned you." She drew a deep breath. "He said you jumped out of a window rather than come face-to-face with him at Rosie's salon. I can't believe he's such a big fat liar." Carolina was looking at her with such sincerity shimmering in her eyes. *Dang it.* Why had Rafe even mentioned it?

"I didn't exactly jump. It was more like a flop," Stella admitted. "And it was on the ground floor so there was absolutely no danger involved."

Carolina gasped and covered her mouth with her hand. "It's true?" she asked. "Oh, Stella. That is an act of pure desperation."

Stella groaned. "I know it's pathetic, but I just couldn't face him, his wife, and their precious bundle of joy. Not at the bridal salon where I'd just attended Lucy's wedding gown fitting. Not at the same salon where I handpicked my own dream wedding dress. It would have been too much, Carolina."

Carolina made a fretful sound. "Oh, sweetie. I understand. It would have been incredibly awkward."

"So what else did he say?" Stella asked. She had a feeling there was a little bit more to the story. With Rafe there always seemed to be more lurking under the surface. If only she'd known that when she first met him. She would have been spared a lot of heartache. A little voice urged her to let it go. There was absolutely nothing she could do to alter the past.

Carolina opened her mouth and then quickly closed it without saying a word. Stella knew her bestie was trying to decide whether or not to tell her the down and dirty truth. It was etched in the worry lines on her forehead. "Just tell me," she said with a sigh. "I can take it."

Carolina fidgeted with her fingers. "He said that he felt sorry for you because you were as single as a dollar bill. And he used that exact phrase." Carolina winced.

Stella sucked in a shocked breath. *Ouch.* Stella knew Carolina hadn't taken any pleasure in telling her, but it was important to Stella to know. As much as it hurt to hear, it only confirmed what Stella was beginning to suspect: Rafe wasn't the type of man she wanted to walk through life with.

When would she stop feeling gut punched by her ex-fiancé? When would she hear something like this and simply laugh it off? When would it stop hurting? Stella didn't understand Rafe at all. It almost seemed like he went out of his way to hurt and demean her. He'd been the one to call off their nuptials and marry someone else at breakneck speed. She had never done a single thing to cause him pain, yet he continued to dish it out to her like a regular meal. It wasn't a coincidence that he'd made the nasty comment to Carolina. He knew they were close friends and that Carolina would tell her.

"He's always such a class act," she muttered. Anger pricked at her like a hot poker. It was a terrible feeling to allow someone the power to keep hurting you. More than anything, Stella wanted to get to a point in her journey where these emotions weren't constantly being stirred up by memories or anything Rafe said or did.

"Rafe is a jerk. I hope you can see that you dodged a bullet with him." Carolina rolled her eyes. "He likes to imagine you sitting around pining after him as if he's the catch of the week. It feeds his ego."

"Well, little does he know I'm taken," Stella blurted out. "And Luke is all the man that I need. Nothing to feel sorry about there. Not in the slightest. Pass that along if you run into him again." Maybe that would shut him up for good. Shouldn't Rafe be so blissful with his own life and family that he wouldn't have time to poke his nose in her business?

Carolina smirked. "Oh, I won't have to say anything, Stella. I'm sure he's heard the news firsthand by now. Everyone is talking about Stuke."

"Stuke?" Stella asked, feeling confused. "You lost me."

Her friend's unbridled laughter filled the kitchen. "It's your couple name. Not sure who came up with it, but it seems to have staying power. Everyone in town is using it."

Stella had no idea how to respond to this development. *Stuke?* Her lips began twitching with mirth. It was so ridiculous it made her want to howl with laughter. She and Luke weren't even a real couple, yet the folks in Mistletoe had bestowed a name on them. The microwave dinged, lending Stella an excuse to turn away from Carolina without bursting into laughter about the silly nickname. She wasn't sure what Carolina would think about that. She was walking a little bit of a tightrope at the moment since she wasn't really part of a couple. Like Rafe said . . . she was achingly single.

Stella took the mac 'n' cheese from the microwave and

placed two portions into bowls. She grabbed two slices of naan and put them on a larger plate. "Here you go. Nice and hot," Stella said. "Let me grab two waters." Once she was settled in her own chair across from Carolina, Stella tucked into her meal. Several times Carolina looked at her with questions looming in her eyes, but she left them unasked while they ate. Once she was finished, Stella began to talk.

"This ... thing between Luke and me happened very suddenly," Stella explained. Well, that part was definitely the truth, so she didn't have to feel guilty about lying. For the rest, she was just twisting the truth a little bit. "I didn't want to make too much of it. You know how this town thrives on gossip. After the Rafe fiasco I'm always going to be a little bit wary of going public with anyone."

Carolina put her fork down and let out a sympathetic sound. "Oh, Stella. That makes perfect sense. I'm sorry if I sounded needy, but to be honest, I was a little hurt. I consider you one of my best friends and I hope you know that you can confide in me. I know you have Lucy, but you also have me."

Hearing Carolina speak so poignantly about their friendship stirred up a host of emotions inside of Stella. Because of her tight relationship with Lucy, Stella hadn't always had a group of close friends surrounding her. Carolina had turned out to be a true friend and ally. Guilt threatened to consume her. Maybe she needed to tell Carolina the truth about her fake relationship with Luke.

"So are the two of you going to the Chowder Fest this

weekend?" Carolina asked. "You know all the couples in town turn out for it. It's a great date night." She groaned. "Not that I would know anything about that."

Chowder Fest. Stella had honestly forgotten all about it. It was an annual event in Mistletoe where locals participated in a competition to see who made the best clam chowder. Restaurants participated as well as chefs from neighboring communities. The winner received a cash prize and bragging rights. Vendors sold clothing, artwork, crafts, baked goods, and apparel.

"Umm...yeah. Of course we are. We wouldn't miss it for the world." Eeek. Why did she say that? For all she knew Luke had other plans. But then again, this entire plot had been his idea. He needed to commit to it just as much as she did.

"Yay! Then I'll finally get to see Luke up close and personal and meet him. If you weren't a dear friend, I'd hate you for scooping up the finest man in town."

Stella laughed but it sounded hollow to her own ears. This was getting stickier by the minute. In order to look like a legit couple, they would have to attend town events together. If they didn't, Stella knew tongues would be wagging.

They've broken up already?
Stella can't hold a man to save her life.
Poor Luke. She's still stuck on Rafe.

After saying her goodbyes to Carolina, Stella grabbed her cell phone and dialed Luke's number. She tapped her foot impatiently as she waited for him to pick up the call. Her stomach clenched at the sound of his rich, deep voice as he said hello.

"Luke. It's Stella. I don't know what you're doing on Saturday night, but we need to attend the Chowder Fest." She gulped past her nervousness and continued to speak. "As a couple."

CHAPTER THIRTEEN

Luke looked around the town green with complete and utter awe. He was still surprised that Stella had reached out to him about attending this event as a couple. He'd been trying to figure out if she intended to follow through with their plan or bail on him. After all, she hadn't seemed too keen on the plan in the beginning. Her phone call had let him know that she was fully on board. It had been a relief to know that she'd taken the initiative and contacted him. It reinforced the idea that they were a team working together.

He couldn't remember the last time he'd attended Chowder Fest, but it had come a long way since then. The organizers had worked really hard to make it a festive event with all the trimmings. A multitude of white tents had been set up along the lawn with gaily decorated banners and flags, lending a festive vibe to the event. The smell of seafood drifted in the air, making his stomach clench and his mouth water. A great number of people had shown up for the event, and it was nice to see old friends and acquaintances, all of whom greeted him warmly. It was the Mistletoe way.

Nick and Miles would be making an appearance later this afternoon, and he couldn't wait to treat his nephew to whatever he wanted. His parents used to take him and Nick to the festival as a fun family outing. One year he'd eaten so much chowder and cotton candy that he'd gotten sick later that evening. His ten-year-old self had figured it was worth it to indulge in such amazing food. Nostalgia washed over him. His childhood had been wonderful, and this town had been at the center of so many magical moments. Although he knew his nephew's situation was deeply affected by the loss of his mother, it was a good thing Miles was growing up right here in Mistletoe.

Stella was standing beside him in line as they waited for Kyle's lobster chowder. As the owner of one of Mistletoe's most celebrated seafood restaurants, Kyle knew his way around a kitchen like no other. If Luke had to select a last meal on earth, he would pick something from the Lobster Shack's menu and die a happy man.

"If the length of this line means anything, we're about to be treated to something wonderful," Luke said to Stella. He glanced over at her, fully appreciating her skinny jeans that fit her in all the right places. She'd paired them with a floral top and a pink lightweight sweater that skimmed her waist. He still found it impossible to believe that her ex had dumped her and that she was currently single. There should be a line longer than the one he was standing in to go out with a stunner like Stella.

"It's one of my absolute favorites. As you know, once you've gotten a taste of it, you're hooked," Stella gushed, her face becoming animated right before his eyes. He loved the tiny freckles on the bridge of her nose and the way her eyes turned different shades of brown depending on her mood. Her mocha-colored complexion glowed. Being in her company was as easy and relaxed as a summer's day, like he'd known her for way longer than he had. He felt stupid for not taking time to get to know her when they had been younger. He'd been too tied up in Friday night lights and the popular crew.

"By the way, I've been wondering about your leg. Did you reach out to any orthopedic specialists?" Her tone radiated concern while her eyes burned a hole through him.

"I haven't made contact yet," he hedged, "but I plan to." Luke didn't know why he was avoiding it so much. Maybe a part of him was afraid of finding out he'd done more damage. He was supposed to be in the healing process, not making his injury worse.

"You really should," she said with a firm, no-nonsense nod of her head. He imagined some of her students got the same look. Stella was right though. He couldn't keep putting it off. One of his surgeons at Walter Reed had given him the names of two orthopedic surgeons in the Mistletoe area who could help him out. He just needed to suck it up and do it.

Once they got their bowls of chowder, they headed toward the patio area and sat down to eat. Many eyes were focused on them, as they'd both expected. Although there were plenty of stares, there were also smiles. He'd forgotten how many residents had been praying for him during his stint in Afghanistan. And he knew from Nick how beloved Stella was. He couldn't help but feel that folks wanted the best for both of them. Mistletoe had given him so much through the years. He hadn't always appreciated it, but being in a war zone had taught him to value his hometown. It wasn't perfect, but it belonged to him.

"Luke Keegan. I thought that was you!" a voice exclaimed. It came from a petite white-haired woman who Luke instantly recognized.

He jumped to his feet. "Miss Botts!" He quickly closed the distance between them and gently wrapped his arms around her. Given her age and her small frame, Luke didn't want to break her. With her full rosy cheeks and classic features, Miss Botts had always reminded him of a doll. Florence Botts had been Luke's nursery school teacher and a huge influence in his young life. When he was five she'd encouraged him to reach for his dreams and never settle for less. Her wisdom and belief in him had stuck with him over the years, adding to the confidence instilled in him by his parents.

"Luke, you're a sight for an old lady's sore eyes," she remarked, eyes twinkling like stars in a midnight sky.

He reached for her hand and held on to it. "It's great seeing you again. It brings back a lot of good memories."

"You've made this town proud," Miss Botts said. "I always knew you were going to do great things. You had an adventurous spirit and a loving heart. If you remember, you used to share your lunch every day with another student whose family was struggling. No one told you to do it, Luke. It simply came from the goodness inside of you. That still warms my heart to this day."

"He was my friend, and it didn't seem right not to share," Luke said. "But it's nice to hear I was a good kid." He chuckled. "By the time I reached high school I may have been ready to shed that image." Although he hadn't been a bad kid by any means, he hadn't exactly been a choir boy. Alongside Nick, Dante, and Dante's younger brother, Troy, he'd engaged in his fair share of mischief.

Miss Botts shook her head. "I don't believe a word of it. You were always as good as gold." She peered behind him. "Hi there, Stella. Nice to see you. As a former teacher, I still have close ties to the Mistletoe school district." She gifted Stella with a beatific smile. "I hear tremendous things about you. It makes me so proud to see you teaching the next generation."

"It's great to see you as well, Miss Botts," Stella said with a grin that lit up her face. "You've always been a great inspiration to me. You were my favorite teacher, bar none."

Miss Botts smiled, and Luke could tell she was pleased by Stella's praise. It probably wasn't every day one of her students went full circle and became an educator.

"Would you like to join us?" Luke asked, gesturing toward the table. "We'd love to have you."

Miss Botts couldn't contain her huge grin. "Thanks for asking, but I wouldn't dare intrude on your date." She winked at them. "The two of you make such a charming couple. Don't forget to invite me to the wedding." With a wave, Miss Botts walked away from them, leaving Luke with his mouth open.

"Seriously?" Luke muttered. "Folks are already walking us down the aisle." It was laughable. He'd barely been back in town two weeks. Miss Botts meant well and clearly adored both of them, so he wasn't bothered by her comment.

When Stella didn't respond, he swung his attention toward her. Her pinched features and the grim set of her mouth spoke volumes.

"Are you all right? Your face looks a little funny." Yikes. He instantly wanted to take back what he'd just said. It sounded like an insult. "I don't mean strange," he said, correcting himself. "You look upset."

"It's nothing," she said in a clipped tone. She continued eating the chowder without looking at him. *Uh oh.* Usually when women said it was nothing it was a whole lot of something. And unless he fixed it, the rest of the night was going to be awkward, which was the last thing he wanted. So far, being in Stella's presence had been a breath of fresh air even when she'd been in the throes of a minor meltdown outside Rosie's shop.

"Is it me?" Luke pressed. "Because if I did something or said something to make you uncomfortable, I'm sorry. I know that I was the one who twisted your arm about this situation, so—"

"I don't want a bunch of speculation about us getting married." She blew out a huff of air. "I've already been the subject of ditched-at-the-altar whispers." She shuddered. "I can only imagine how they'll spin this when our romance ends. And I know it's just one comment from the sweetest woman in Mistletoe, but it brings up a lot of bad memories."

Luke pushed his empty bowl away from him. He'd enjoyed every last spoonful. If he wasn't on a "date" with Stella, he would definitely line up for seconds. But at the moment he needed to clear up something. "I can't say that I know how you feel about that period in your life, but I can empathize with you. And I won't bother telling you that people won't put your name in their mouths again, but I'm going to make you a promise." He placed his arms on the table and leaned forward, making sure his voice was low. "When we stage our breakup at the end of the summer, I'll make sure everyone in Mistletoe knows that I was the one who got dumped. That way you won't have to hear any *poor Stella* talk. We'll have control over the narrative. How does that sound?"

"You would do that for me?" Stella asked, disbelief shimmering in her eyes. She reached out and touched his forearm, and he sucked in a deep breath at the skin-on-skin contact. He tried to shake off his reaction, but it was as if an electric current were passing through him. It was impossible to concentrate with Stella caressing his arm with such tenderness.

For a wild moment Luke wanted to make a believer out of Stella. He wanted to show her that he was a man of his word, and she would never have to question it. He bit down hard on the inside of his cheek. Her ex really had done a number on her, so much so that she didn't seem to know her own worth. She was the type of woman who men brought home to their mothers. Stella Marshall was a babe—beautiful, articulate, bright, and eye catching. What more could Rafe have wanted in a woman?

As his friend Brando liked to say, Stella was wifey material. Just because her stupid ex hadn't appreciated her special brand of wonderful didn't mean the rest of the world couldn't. Or wouldn't.

"Yes, I would, Stella. In a heartbeat." Their eyes locked and held for several beats. Luke couldn't have looked away from the intensity radiating from Stella's eyes for anything in this world. When Stella was happy, she simply glowed. It shimmered like the sun. Something in the air shifted and he could feel an electric pulse thrumming around them. He hadn't felt anything quite like this in his life, so much so that he wondered if he was imagining it. Luke's throat went tight, and he found himself unable to utter a single word. What was wrong with him?

Loud cries went up in the crowd, cutting through the tension that hovered in the air between them. It brought him out of the haze he'd been in. Stella seemed just as off-kilter. Maybe she'd felt it too.

"What's going on?" he asked as he craned his neck to see what had caused the commotion. All he saw was a group of people milling around the gazebo area. Stella scrambled up on the table bench and looked out over the crowd. Luke moved quickly to her side of the table so he could spot her in case she stumbled. "It's Dante and Lucy," she said with a smile. "Even though he's a hometown boy, the townsfolk still tend to treat him like a celebrity. He's in town for a few weeks helping out with the wedding plans."

Luke wondered if it was hard for Stella to see Lucy get married after her own wedding fiasco. All he could see on her face was happiness for the engaged couple. It said a lot about Stella that she was so supportive of her sister's plans. He didn't imagine it was easy though. If her ex hadn't called things off, Stella would be a married woman right now. And he wouldn't have the pleasure of her sweet company, getting up close and personal with the stunning teacher. Rafe's loss was definitely his gain. Even though he and Stella were only pretending to be involved, Luke was feeling a deeper connection with her as each day passed.

When Stella moved to get down from the bench, Luke stepped forward and picked her up by the waist, then gently deposited her on the ground. Stella's eyes were filled with surprise as she looked up at him. Just having her in such close proximity caused all of his senses to be on high alert. Stella fit perfectly in his arms. "Can't have you falling, can we?" he asked.

"That wouldn't be good," she acknowledged with a nervous laugh. "I certainly don't want to spend my summer vacation in a cast." Avoiding eye contact with him, she turned toward the commotion. Stella called out to her sister and beckoned her to their table. Looking relieved, Lucy headed right toward them with Dante following behind her. "I can't wait till Mistletoe gets sick of my famous fiancé," Lucy said the moment she reached them, sounding out of breath.

"If it isn't Lucy Marshall," Luke said in an upbeat tone that matched his ear-to-ear grin.

A smile lit up her face the moment Lucy spotted him.

"Luke! I can't believe you're back in Mistletoe. It's so great to see you," she said, reaching out for a hug. With her heart-shaped face and striking features, Lucy hadn't changed all that much. "Nick has been filling us in on all your exploits. Not to mention your adorable nephew who can't stop talking about Uncle Luke. He's taken out a few library books on Navy SEALs."

The idea of Miles conducting this type of research hit him smack dab in the center of his heart. "That kid is something else. I'm not sure I deserve his hero worship, but he's the president of my fan club," Luke said. "It makes me feel ten feet tall."

Dante reached out and clapped Luke on the shoulder. "Luke Keegan. You're a sight for sore eyes."

"Dante. It's been a long time, man," Luke said as they went in for a hug. Frankly, he couldn't remember the last time they'd seen each other. Probably right around the time he'd enlisted and Dante headed off to Hollywood. Many years stood between them. The memories they'd shared had been epic. From Friday night lights on the football field to double dating at the drive-in, they'd spent endless hours in each other's company.

Dante stepped back. "Look at you. You're ripped. Must be all that Navy SEAL training. You put the Rock and Jason Statham to shame. If you ever want to get into the stunt double business give me a call."

Luke laughed. He wasn't sure he was cut out to be a stuntman, but he appreciated the compliment from his old friend. "Congratulations on your engagement. Nick told me all about it." As one of Dante's closest friends, Nick knew all the intimate details of the reunion romance between Lucy and Dante. From what Luke had been told the couple had been put through a few challenges on their road to a happy ending. "And you've gotten famous since we were trying to win state championships," he said with a chuckle. Back then they'd been all about girls and football. "It's pretty amazing."

"Thanks," Dante said, looking over at his fiancée with an expression Luke could only describe as lovestruck. "I came back home to film my movie and to make amends with my family...and Lucy." He chuckled. "I ended up reconnecting with the love of my life. All during the Christmas holidays."

Luke couldn't imagine how everything had fallen in place so perfectly for Lucy and Dante since life usually didn't work that way, but he was happy for them. Although he'd never been lucky in love himself, he believed in it. He'd seen it up close and personal with his parents and with Nick and Kara. He could only hope that one day it found him, although he wasn't banking on it. However his love life worked out in the long run, he would be content simply being Uncle Luke.

"I'm happy for you, Dante. Sounds like you're living the dream." What must it be like, he wondered, to have your life tied up in a neat little bow? He envied Dante having such a certain future while his own seemed so unsettled. *Dig deep.* His own words to his SEAL team surfaced, reminding him that he needed to work on himself so he could get his life in order. A new life wasn't just going to materialize for him.

"I heard about you and Stella," Dante said, arching his eyebrows. Luke wasn't sure if Dante knew they were fake dating or if he thought they were the real deal. Dante wasn't giving away any clues. "Watch yourself. These Marshall women are a handful." Dante began chuckling and Luke joined along with him. Stella had definitely showed him her unpredictable side. Never could he have pictured her fleeing a bridal salon by way of vaulting herself out of a window.

"Our ears are burning," Lucy said, looping her arm around her fiancé's waist and leaning into him. "What were you saying about us?"

"Nothing but good things," Dante said, dipping his head down and placing his lips on Lucy's. It wasn't long before they were full-on smooching. It had been a long time since Luke had been in the presence of a couple like Dante and Lucy. The sparks between them could start a blazing fire.

"Save some of this mushy stuff for later," Stella said, tugging her sister's arm and breaking up the kiss. "Unless you want to be on TMZ by tomorrow morning."

"No thanks," Lucy said. "That is literally the only downside to being engaged to a celebrity. Everyone wants a piece of him."

Dante grabbed her hand. "But you're the only one who has me."

Luke made eye contact with Stella, who was rolling her eyes. "In case you're wondering, yes they're always this lovey-dovey."

"We're just making up for lost time," Dante said. It was truly a testament to their love that they'd reunited after such a long time.

"We're going to head over to Troy and Noelle's

chowder booth," Dante said. "I promised to take some pics with a few of the hardware store's customers."

Troy was a few years younger than Luke, but they'd all hung out together and played on the same football team. He imagined Noelle was his wife or girlfriend, although he couldn't recall Nick mentioning he'd gotten married.

"I'd love to say hello," Luke said. He swung his gaze toward Stella. "Do you want to head over with them?" Meeting up with old friends was something he would never get tired of. He was beginning to realize that being back in his hometown grounded him in a way nothing else ever could. These folks reminded him that he'd had other dreams before he had become a Navy SEAL. That there was more to him than his years of service. Even though he still had a lot of things to figure out, Luke sensed he was in the right spot to begin putting those pieces together. Mistletoe might just be a place to plant roots after all.

"Sounds good to me," Stella said. As they all began to walk together, Luke clasped Stella's hand in his. At this point it simply felt like a reflex, which was a bit confusing. All he knew was that he wasn't solely doing it for appearances. He couldn't really put into words how he felt, but it was nice holding hands with Stella.

"By the way, Troy just got married to Noelle," Stella explained. "She has a son named Jimmy from another relationship that they're raising together. They make a really sweet couple."

"It sounds like the whole town is getting hitched," Luke said, shaking his head at how much things had changed over the years. He'd missed out on so many joyous occasions, and although he was proud of his service, it had cost him a lot. There hadn't been much time spent with Miles, Kara, and Nick. His parents weren't getting any younger either.

"Not the whole town," she said in a soft voice. Immediately, Luke regretted his choice of words. It was like rubbing salt in a wound.

He stopped walking and slightly tugged on her hand. "I shouldn't have said that. I'm sorry, Stella. I wasn't thinking."

"You have nothing to apologize for. I'm just being overly sensitive. Believe it or not, I'm really happy for my sister and Dante and everyone else who's found their path. It's just that..."

"Sometimes you wish it was you." He wanted to reach out and smooth away the worry lines on her forehead. He wished he could make her believe that everything would work out for her in the end. But he didn't have a crystal ball and he knew she might not want to hear it from him.

Stella nodded. "I do. And I wish that I didn't want the wedding and the white dress and the promise of forever, but if I'm being completely honest, I do. It's right there in the deepest regions of my heart." She pressed her palm against her chest.

"That's nothing to be ashamed of, Stella. You deserve it all." He tapped his finger to his chin. "Okay, so let's think about this for a minute. I'm guessing it's not too late to call up Rosie's nephew. What was his name again? Teller? Tuttle?"

Stella burst out laughing. "Tucker." He loved making her laugh. Just seeing her beautiful face crinkling up with joy caused a tightening sensation in his chest.

Luke snapped his fingers. "Oh yes, Tucker." He quirked his mouth. "I'm guessing the ladies here in town aren't lining up to couple up with him."

"I highly doubt it," she said, vigorously shaking her head.

"Well, Stella, in my humble opinion you deserve the very best." He reached out for her hand, stroking her thumb with his own. "Waiting for the right man to become your other half is a smart move. Someone like you should never settle."

Just putting on the white dress and getting married wouldn't be enough for a woman like Stella. She wanted the whole thing—an authentic love story. And he didn't blame her one bit. She deserved the very best this world had to offer.

CHAPTER FOURTEEN

A few minutes later they caught up to Lucy and Dante at Troy's booth, and Luke was able to meet Troy's wife, Noelle, and reminisce about old times. He also bought a cup of corn and clam chowder from their booth, which he shared with Stella. At this rate, Luke would be stuffed when they left the event. But he certainly wasn't going to pass up the opportunity to taste as many chowders as his stomach would allow.

As they walked around the grounds, Luke was treated like a bona fide superstar. Although the word *hero* still made him cringe, he had to admit it felt good to be welcomed back home with such love and enthusiasm. For so long he'd been MIA from this Maine haven. But now, he had to decide whether or not he could plant roots here and make a new life for himself. Could Mistletoe be his home base? Would he be happy here long-term?

He spotted a few members of his high school football team, and they reminisced about the glory days for a few minutes. Everyone seemed to know Stella and it was clear to him that she was beloved by all. Several of her students excitedly approached her and she handled each interaction with kindness and grace.

"There's a cool jazz band playing—" Stella stopped midsentence.

All of a sudden she slid her hand in his and squeezed. It felt as if she was clinging to him like a lifeline. Luke had no idea what was going on, but he felt her stiffen up. "Rafe." The name slipped past Stella's lips. She was as frozen as a statue. Luke swung his gaze to where Stella was looking. A tall, dark-haired man was standing by the cotton candy booth with a woman. A baby stroller sat in front of them. They looked a little too perfect if you asked him, but he supposed some folks liked that granola vibe.

"You're all right," he reassured her in a low voice. "Hold my hand as tightly as you need to. I'm not going anywhere."

Something about holding Stella's hand made him feel protective of her. He wanted to slay all of her dragons, especially a fire-breathing one named Rafe. He could sense she wanted to turn on her heel and leave, but it wouldn't solve the issue at hand. Mistletoe was a small town, and she and her ex were bound to run into each other again. Stella needed to face this down and let Rafe know that she'd moved on. *This isn't real*, he reminded himself. *The two of you are a pretend couple.* But Rafe didn't need to know that.

It did feel good to be connected to Stella in this way, real or not. Luke hadn't held hands with a woman in years. He'd almost forgotten how it felt.

"Oh, good grief. He's looking over here." She clenched her teeth. "Why is he staring at us?"

"Because we're the best-looking couple here," Luke quipped. "That's why." He puffed his chest out for good measure and stood up a little straighter.

The corners of Stella's mouth curved upward into a smile. Aaaah. He'd lifted her mood with his corny comment. He liked seeing Stella happy. It bothered him to see her unraveling due to the presence of her ex-fiancé. He wondered if she was still in love with Rafe. He hoped not because she was a million times better than him.

"Maybe we should walk over to the stage area," Stella suggested, shifting from one foot to the other. She glanced nervously in her ex's direction. Who was this woman standing next to him? She'd shrunken down to a smaller version of herself. It made Luke angry to know that this joker still had a hold on her.

Luke shook his head. "We're not going anywhere. The days of you running away from him are over."

Stella looked at him with big eyes. "They are?" she asked in a low voice.

"Yes," he said firmly. He moved a step closer toward her so that only an inch or so remained between them. He was going to seize the moment and build up some couple cred for the two of them. "Don't hate me, Stella, but I'm going to kiss you."

Stella's lips parted as if she was about to say something, but no words came out. Her eyes closed as he dipped his head down and placed his mouth on hers. His nostrils filled with the sweet scent of her—roses. Her lips were soft and inviting. At first Stella seemed hesitant, but after a few moments she began kissing him back. Within seconds, their embrace shifted from obligatory to intoxicating. He hadn't expected the kiss to escalate into one filled with so much depth and heat and fire.

As the kiss deepened and blossomed, Luke felt something awakening inside of him. Stella's hands were wrapped around his neck, anchoring them together. Her skin was achingly soft as her fingers brushed against the hairs on the back of his neck.

The feelings being stirred up within him weren't ones he was used to experiencing. The lines between reality and make-believe were blurring. The more he tried to convince himself that this kiss was for Rafe's benefit, the harder it became to stay grounded in that reality. How could he remain in character when his lips were ablaze? Everything around them faded away until it was just the two of them kissing up a storm. He didn't want this to end even though he knew it couldn't last forever.

This kiss was one for the ages. Best kiss ever, bar none. It left him weak in the knees. He'd kissed Stella to put the pressure off her married ex-fiancé staring at them as if they were exhibits at the zoo. Hearing from Stella how badly he'd treated her made him instantly dislike the guy. He'd known several men like Rafe in his lifetime, and Luke had a hunch that he enjoyed seeing Stella as single and unattached. At least now he'd seen with his own eyes that she wasn't sitting around playing Scrabble.

He just hoped Stella wouldn't be upset with him for going rogue and staging an out-of-this-world kiss. Even if she was, Luke could honestly say he didn't regret it. And it wasn't likely he ever would.

* * *

Stella clung to Luke's shirt as the pulse-pounding kiss ended. She needed something to steady her quivering legs. Had she ever had a kiss like the one Luke had just laid on her? It was doubtful. Her lips were tingling and her limbs felt jittery. Her body had a mind of its own, especially her lips. Not only had she enthusiastically kissed Luke back, but she'd wanted it to go on and on. Luke had been the one to pull away while every instinct had told her to keep on smooching him.

When she opened her eyes, Luke was peering down at her with an intense expression etched on his perfect features. For the first time she noticed a little scar by his eye. It only served to make him look more ruggedly handsome. *No fair!* This man was achingly sexy, flaws and all.

He knit his brows together. "Are you all right? You seem a little bit wobbly." He was grinning at her, showcasing straight pearl-colored teeth.

Yeah, she was definitely wobbly, which was totally understandable. Who could blame her after a kiss like that? Maybe he was clueless about the way his kiss was affecting her? But Luke was looking a little too pleased with himself, as if he'd single-handedly cured cancer or eradicated hunger. Yep. He knew all too well that he'd left her completely flustered. She hoped the kiss had left him feeling a little bit woozy as well.

"I'm fine," she said, smoothing back her hair. "W-what did you do that for?" she asked. "Now people are really going to talk about us."

Luke shook his head. "Isn't that a good thing? It'll serve both of our purposes." He seemed slightly put out by her comment. "I did it because of Rafe. He was staring at us like he'd never seen a couple hold hands before. We gave him a good show, Stella."

Rafe. She'd completely forgotten about her ex. It was amazing what havoc a good kiss could wreak on one's mind. Satisfaction surged inside her. She didn't want to be petty, but it felt good knowing that Rafe had to watch her making out with another man. Rafe might not have wanted to marry her, but Stella knew him well enough to know it probably burned him to see her with someone else. He would much prefer her to be single and dateless, which is why he'd made the ridiculous comment to Carolina. *Humph. Single as a dollar bill.* It was quite satisfying to realize that if nothing else, Rafe would feel like a fool for running his mouth. And judging by the way the kiss had made her feel, she was certain it had looked like the real deal. No one would ever suspect that they weren't a couple.

"So much for a heads-up," she murmured, knowing she didn't have a whole lot to complain about. Luke was an amazing kisser and he'd knocked her socks off.

"That would have spoiled it. You would have tensed up too much. This was perfect. Come on, Stella. Admit it." Luke looked around them. "And no ex in sight. You're welcome."

He wasn't lying. Stella didn't want to embarrass herself by telling Luke how sensational their kiss had been. Granted, she hadn't been kissed in a very long time, but by any standard it had been amazing. It had left her tingling from her head down to her toes. She'd killed a few birds with one stone. Word would buzz around town about their blazing hot kiss, which would effectively register them as a couple in the town's eyes. It would take the pressure off Stella in so many different ways. It provided her with great cover.

"Okay. Thank you for thinking so fast on your feet," she said, batting her eyelashes at him in an exaggerated fashion that imitated a damsel in distress. It immediately brought a smile to his face. "And for coming to my rescue once again."

"It was my pleasure," Luke said, bowing at the waist and reaching for her hand. He pressed his lips to it. "Might as well give them an eyeful."

It was strange how in the moment Stella hadn't given a single thought to Rafe or the townsfolk. It had been all about Luke and his red-hot kisses.

"By the way, I've been meaning to tell you something." He waited a beat before continuing, his dark eyes twinkling. "I signed up for PT sessions at the suggestion of a doctor. I've only had two so far, but it's a step in the right direction. Literally."

Stella let out a whoop of excitement and threw her arms around Luke. A few seconds later she let go of him, fearing that her reaction had been over the top. At least it added credibility to their ruse. Anyone who'd just witnessed her throwing herself against Luke's chest wouldn't have a hard time believing they were a couple. He was grinning down at her as if he didn't mind a bit.

"That's wonderful news. I'm thrilled for you." Stella could feel a gigantic smile stretching across her face. There was no way of reining it in at this point. Good things happening in Luke's world made her happy.

"Uncle Luke!" Stella and Luke turned just in time to see Miles running full tilt in their direction. He crashed into Luke's chest with all the enthusiasm of an eight-year-old boy. Luke steadied Miles by placing his arms on his little shoulders. "Whoa there. Where's the fire?"

"There's a three-legged race competition over by the gazebo. I want you to be my partner." Miles pressed his hands in front of him in prayerlike fashion. "Please. Please. The winner gets a gift card from the toy store."

"What about your dad?" Luke asked. "I don't want to hurt his feelings. Maybe he wants to partner with you."

Stella wasn't sure what was going on, but she had the strangest feeling that Luke didn't want to partner with his nephew, which made absolutely no sense. Luke was absolutely crazy about Miles, and there didn't seem to be a single thing he wouldn't do for him. She would bet her last dollar that no one in Mistletoe could outdo this very fit Navy SEAL in a three-legged race. It would be an easy win for Miles. Unless of course Luke's leg was bothering him. Stella hadn't noticed him limping, but she sensed Luke could tolerate a high level of pain without flinching.

"Dad won't care," Miles insisted. "He wants us to

spend quality time together. That's what I heard him telling Gram and Pops on the phone this morning."

Stella resisted the urge to chuckle. It seemed that Miles, like her baby sister, enjoyed eavesdropping on conversations. She was happy to know Tess wasn't the only ear hustler in town.

Miles tugged at Luke's hand. "Let's go, Uncle Luke. It's about to start. We don't want to be disqualified."

"Okay. Let's do this!" Luke looked over at Stella, sending her a pleading look. "Are you coming, Stella? We need a cheering squad."

"I wouldn't miss it for the world," Stella said as she trailed after them. As they raced toward the gazebo with Miles in between them, Stella felt a jolt of happiness wash over her that she hadn't felt in a really long time. It seemed as if all was right with her world. A foreign concept after the last few years of turmoil. She was beginning to think it had everything to do with Luke...and it scared the life out of her.

CHAPTER FIFTEEN

For the next few days Luke kept a low profile in Mistletoe. He spent quality time with Miles, made a few stops at the library, and pursued some job leads. He'd been asked by his childhood friend, Lamont Green, to work at his construction site and oversee some of his crews. Luke was considering it, purely out of boredom. There was only so much he could occupy his time with before he started feeling useless. He hadn't seen Stella since the Chowder Fest event, which had been by design.

He was still feeling stunned by the kiss they'd shared. It had been strategic on his part, but he hadn't expected fireworks and sparklers to go off. And the feelings of protectiveness she stirred up within him were slightly alarming. He'd wanted to protect her from Rafe even though he hadn't approached or even come within thirty feet of Stella.

Luke got behind the wheel of his truck and made his way to the downtown area. He was meeting up with one of his closest friends and SEAL team buddies, Brandon Wong. Most days Luke didn't even want to admit to himself how much he missed his team members. It was like a huge chunk of his heart had been cut out when he'd been sidelined.

Along the way to the Coffee Bean he passed by Mistletoe High, catching a glimpse of the football field where he'd spent so much of his time. Glory days. Back then he'd never dreamed where his life would take him. He'd pursued the path of becoming a Navy SEAL as a lark, never imagining it would become his heart and soul. As he drove past the marina, the lure of the ocean and the magnificent boats drew him in. He wondered if Stella might want to head out with him on the open seas for an afternoon of sailing. Did she enjoy boating? Who was he kidding? Going sailing with her would be purely for his own enjoyment and not simply for the town's benefit.

He liked spending time with her. *A lot.*

He liked Stella. *A lot.*

Luke felt comfortable being around her. Something just clicked between them.

And it had absolutely nothing to do with convincing the females in town that he was off the market. It had to do with how she made him feel. Luke wanted to be around when she managed to put the past in her rearview mirror. He thought a lot about doing regular, everyday activities with her. Going clamming at the beach. Seeing classic movies at Casablanca's. It was confusing to feel these emotions when he'd convinced himself he didn't want or need romance in his life. But Stella inspired him to want more for himself. And part of that was being with her.

Once Luke arrived at the coffee house, the aroma of freshly brewed coffee led him to the counter where he ordered two cold brews and a few pastries. Minutes after Luke sat down at a table outside, he spotted his buddy striding toward the establishment from the parking lot.

Brandon Wong, otherwise known as Brando by their SEAL team, was a welcome sight. With spiky dark hair and a compact physique, Brando was an exceptional SEAL and a wonderful human being and friend. As Brando drew closer, Luke waved him over to the patio and stood up to greet him when he reached the table.

"You have no idea how good it is to see you, man." Luke clapped him on the shoulder as they went in for a hug.

"Likewise. The whole team misses you something fierce."

"That means a lot. I miss being over there with you guys, although I'm coming to terms with the Navy's decision to take me off of active duty." It was hard for Luke to admit it, but he wasn't in top shape anymore. If he'd had a flare-up during a mission, it might compromise their objectives and safety protocols. He couldn't live with himself if anyone else died because of him.

"I know it might sound corny," Brando said, "but you went out like a champ. If it hadn't been for your actions, we would have sustained more losses. You were in superhero mode that day."

On some level Luke knew that Brando was dropping

truth bombs, but he couldn't focus on those aspects. It was so much easier for him to dwell on the things that hadn't gone according to plan.

"How's your leg?" Brando asked. "You're looking good. I bet that I can still do more pull-ups than you can."

"In your dreams, Brando." Luke shrugged. "The leg hasn't been doing too well. Two steps forward, five steps back. I'm getting these attacks where it seizes up and I'm racked with pain."

Brando narrowed his gaze as he looked at him. "Your body is trying to tell you something. Are you doing physical therapy?"

"I just started," he admitted. "I should have signed up as soon as I got home, but I thought I could handle it on my own." Just saying it out loud made him realize how stupid it sounded. As a SEAL, Luke had always treated his body like a temple and committed himself to working out and healthy living. Neglecting his physical condition had been foolish. At least now he was doing something to improve his situation.

Brando shook his head. "Why are you so stubborn?"

Luke shrugged. "I was just born this way. Blame it on my mama."

"Oh no!" Brando said, tilting his head back as he laughed. "Not throwing your mom under the bus."

For a few moments they chuckled just like old times. Being around Brando reminded Luke of all the good things that came with being a part of a band of brothers. He'd missed being a part of something greater than himself. His SEAL team had always operated like family members—standing together through thick and thin. If he ended up sticking around Mistletoe, Luke needed to tap into the aspects of the community that made him feel as if he was using his talents for the greater good. He loved helping people and serving the needs of others. It was one of the reasons he'd sought a career in the military. Search and rescue would allow him to be employed in a career that made an impact.

Luke didn't want to kill the mood, but he needed to ask Brando something. He'd already put it off for way too long. It was gnawing at him.

"Have you talked to either of the families lately?" Luke didn't have to reference them by name. Brando knew exactly who he was referring to. They'd talked numerous times about the families of both Kenneth and Aaron over the last six months. Recently, they'd set up a fund site for Aaron's kids to help his wife, Winona, with expenses. Luke had also been sending the twins gifts and cards over the past few months.

Brando scratched his chin. "Yeah. Kenneth's mom is in a bad way. Winona seems to be holding it together from what I hear. She's got the twins to keep her busy and focused. I'm sure it's difficult, but she seems to be moving forward."

"And Kenny's mom? Dorothea?" Luke asked. "What's going on there?"

His friend sighed. "I don't know the specifics, but she's been depressed according to Zach. She quit her job and can't seem to get out of bed most days. Who can blame her? Kenny was her only child." Zach Navarro was another member of their SEAL team who'd been with them on the day of the bomb blast.

He'd been best friends with Kenny, so he knew the Smith family well.

Luke ran a hand over his face and blew out a ragged breath. "That's terrible. I really want to reach out to her and the rest of the family. I've been trying to give them space so they could grieve, but I want to let them know I'm thinking about them. They might have questions that only I can answer. Do you have her information?" Luke had intended to touch base with Kenny's parents on many occasions, but he'd been held back by trepidation. But, after witnessing the way Stella had been open and honest about her emotions, he was inspired to connect in person with the Smiths. Bottling up his feelings was gnawing away at him. He needed to man up.

"Sure, Luke. I'll text it to you. I would wait a bit before contacting her though. I don't think it's a good time." He ducked his head and took a lengthy sip of his coffee.

"What aren't you saying?" Luke asked. His gut told him that Brando knew something more specific about Dorothea's situation. Luke wanted to know everything, no matter how damaging it might be to hear.

Brando fiddled with his coffee cup and looked away from Luke's gaze. "She blames the team for Kenny's death."

Luke's heart constricted. "The team? Or me?"

Brando shrugged. "I don't know all the details, but it sounds like she's very anti-SEAL at the moment. It's understandable though. If you remember, she was never a big fan of Kenny being a Navy SEAL. She never gave him a moment's peace about it."

Luke did remember. Kenny used to tell them all the time about how his mother feared that he would never make it home in one piece. On several occasions she'd tried to get him to find another, more predictable profession. Each time Kenny had explained to her his reality— he was meant to be a SEAL. "There's nothing else I'd rather be doing." If he'd said it once, Kenny had said it a hundred times. As a mother, Dorothea had feared something awful would happen to her son, and she'd been right. Everything she'd feared had come to pass. And it had to be weighing heavily on her heart.

"Hey, Luke. How's it going?" His heart did somersaults at the sound of Stella's voice. She was standing by their table holding a foam tray with two drinks in it. He didn't know how he'd missed seeing her enter the coffee shop, although he and Brando were sitting on the far end of the patio engrossed in a heavy conversation. With her bright yellow sundress, Stella resembled a burst of pure sunshine. The realization hit him smack dab in the center of his chest. That's how she made him feel.

At the sight of her, Luke jumped to his feet, as did Brando. "Stella," he said, immediately going in for a hug. He told himself it would look strange not to hug the woman everyone thought he was dating, but the reality was Luke enjoyed hugging her. She fit perfectly against him, and she always smelled like flowers.

"Stella, I'd like you to meet Brandon Wong, one of the members of my SEAL team and a close friend. We call him Brando," Luke said. "Brando's the guy you want on your side when trouble comes calling. He's visiting for a few days."

"Nice to meet you, Stella," Brando said, offering up his hand.

"Likewise," Stella said as she shook hands with Brando. "Welcome to Mistletoe."

"Stella is a schoolteacher. She's on summer vacation and really kicking up her heels," Luke explained, his tone teasing.

Brando and Stella exchanged pleasantries for a few minutes. It wasn't long before his buddy was pulling out pictures of Jolene and their baby, David. Stella oohed and aahed over the pictures, her eyes lingering with longing on the child. Luke enjoyed the easy rapport between Stella and his close friend. She was going out of her way to make Brando feel welcome in Mistletoe, and it meant a lot to Luke.

"If you have time while you're in town, have Luke give you a tour of the Holly Hill Lighthouse and the glass-making shop," Stella suggested. "And you have to try a Maine lobster. Once you've eaten a Maine lobster, you'll be spoiled for anything else." She pointed across the street. "You can't go wrong at the Lobster Shack. Kyle will hook you up. He's a big fan of Luke's."

"I'm only in Mistletoe until tomorrow, but we'll see what we can fit in. That lobster is at the top of my list," Brando said. "I can't leave town without tasting it."

"Give me a call later," she said, turning toward Luke. "There's a clambake and fireworks next week at Blackberry Beach in honor of the Fourth of July. I'm probably going to have some people over to my house to hang out before the festivities."

Luke had been thinking about the annual Fourth of

July bash for some time now. It was his favorite holiday to commemorate, bar none. There was something so heartwarming and special about celebrating the country he loved so much. Stars and stripes. The smell of hot-dogs and hamburgers emanating from the grill. The night sky turning into a rainbow of vibrant colors. Family and friends gathering.

What he'd learned as a member of the military was that freedom could never be taken for granted, mainly because so many people around the world didn't have it. He'd seen it firsthand in many of the hotspots around the globe. Being able to celebrate the Fourth of July back in his hometown cemented the fact that he was fortunate.

What a difference it would be to spend the Fourth here in Maine rather than overseas. Just the thought of it caused him to get choked up. He'd missed the familiar rituals of home and the people who'd known him all of his life. Mistletoe was made up of folks who wanted the best for him. Sure there were gossips and folks who loved to meddle, but it was a tight-knit town full of people who cared about one another.

"That sounds great," Luke said. "Fourth of July and Mistletoe go hand in hand."

Stella smiled. "Okay then. It's a date." She lifted her tray up and said, "I hate to run but I'm dropping off coffee for a friend. It was nice meeting you, Brando. Talk to you soon, Luke."

"I'll call you later," he said. For a second he wondered if they would have talked about the kiss if Brando hadn't been present. He'd been thinking about it a lot, way more than he would have if it hadn't affected him. Luke needed to think of a way to bring it up casually without freaking Stella out. He wasn't even sure that he knew what he wanted to say. *How about that kiss, Stella?*

"So the two of you are an item?" Brando asked after Stella walked away. He was sitting on the edge of his seat waiting for Luke to answer. "I felt a vibe between you. She's gorgeous by the way."

"It's complicated, although we are spending a lot of time together and figuring things out," Luke admitted. He wasn't trying to be evasive, but he didn't want to mislead Brando. They'd been through the fire together as Navy SEALs—life and death missions that had made them blood brothers for life. And if he was being completely honest with himself, after the kiss he and Stella had shared the other night, he was beginning to catch real feelings.

The joke was on him. He'd devised this fake romance plot and now he was so tangled up in it he didn't know if he was coming or going.

A huge grin threatened to overtake Brando's face. "From where I'm sitting it doesn't look too complicated. You were beaming just now. And the way you were looking at each other..." Brando let out a low whistle. "Hot stuff there."

Brando's enthusiasm made him grin. "You know I'm not great at relationships. This is uncharted waters for me." And he meant it. He was swimming in the deep end. Stella was the type of woman who was complex and multifaceted. After what she'd endured with Rafe, he knew she wouldn't settle for less. Nor should she. He wasn't close to being whole, not physically or emotionally. *Do I even deserve to be with her?*

"Hey, don't count yourself out based on past relationships. I had a terrible record until I met Jolene. She sorted me out by making it clear that if I didn't fly right, she was gone." Brando dragged his hand through his short hair. "She was too important to me to run the risk of losing her."

Brando and Jolene had gotten married two years ago. Their son David had been born last year. Brando had changed from a hard-partying bachelor into a devoted husband and father in a very short period of time. Luke barely remembered the pre-Jolene version of Brando. He'd changed into a man who valued commitment and family.

"I'm so happy for you guys. You're really living your best life." Luke drained the rest of his coffee from the cup. "I've still got some things to sort out," he admitted, pushing the empty cup away from him. "I haven't fully processed what happened on my last mission. I have these nightmares where I try to stop the explosive devices from going off, but each and every time I'm too late. I wake up drenched with sweat every time."

"It's okay to struggle with those memories, Luke, but it's also all right to talk to someone if they keep getting worse." Brando steepled his fingers in front of him. "And it doesn't mean you can't create something wonderful with Stella. Being back home means you get to start a whole new chapter of your life. Without feeling guilty about surviving when others didn't. You deserve to be here."

Survivor's guilt. He'd been wondering if he was grappling with it, but now his best friend had put it out there. It made it all the more real for him. It was hard to move forward when he felt guilty about surviving the blast. About being called a hero. About being honored with the Medal of Honor. He wanted to pursue something authentic with Stella, but he had to wonder if he deserved a woman like her. He was carrying a lot of emotional burdens that might just pull her under.

Brando was right. If he waited for his life to be sorted out, Luke might never try to build something real with anyone. And Stella wasn't just anyone as far as he was concerned. She was everything he'd ever wanted in a partner. Smart. Beautiful. Caring. Kind. But he had no idea if she had feelings for him. What if his feelings were one-sided?

Years ago he'd wanted so badly to make things work with his ex-girlfriend, Allison, but the feelings hadn't been there on his side. She'd wanted the wedding and the white dress and a lifelong commitment, but Luke hadn't been in love with her. Hurting her with his indecisiveness had been one of the worst things he'd ever done. Luke had vowed to never go down that road again. Maybe that was one of the big reasons he'd avoided relationships. He couldn't bear the idea of crushing someone's dreams again. Or not living up to their expectations.

Kissing Stella had shown him that even though he'd hatched a plan for a pretend relationship, what he'd felt the other night had been anything but fake. Just being with her made him want to be a better man, one who wasn't tethered to the past. He hadn't planned on a relationship upon his return to Mistletoe. His goals were to support Nick and Miles, find gainful employment, and meet face-to-face with Kenny's and Aaron's families. But Stella was becoming more important to him each and every day, which could become a huge distraction.

He was in as much danger with Stella as he'd ever been while being on active duty in Afghanistan.

CHAPTER SIXTEEN

Kneeling in the dirt planting teacup roses wasn't exactly Stella's idea of summer fun. She hadn't been given the gift of a green thumb like her mother, although she adored flowers. The previous occupants of her house had planted glorious flowers—roses, hyacinths, and azaleas that kept blooming year after year, providing Stella with an abundance of joy. Now it was her turn to add to the beauty of her property.

Stella hadn't spoken to Luke since the other day at the Coffee Bean, and she couldn't help but wonder if he was avoiding her. Was she just being paranoid? Things had seemed fine between them then. Maybe he was busy with PT and trying to find a job. It was a relief to know he was under a doctor's care and engaged in physical therapy a few times a week. It was the type of self-care she didn't think Luke made time for in his life. After suffering a trauma, he needed to focus on healing.

She sighed. Luke had a lot on his plate these days in addition to trying to keep up with a fake romance. What if he'd decided to end their showmance to make room for everything else? She wasn't ready for it to end, which was a bit shocking considering he'd had to convince her to be a part of the ploy in the first place. The truth was she enjoyed the time she'd been spending with Luke. He made her feel valued and smart and wanted. She couldn't really say Rafe had ever made her feel all those things. How had she ever thought they were going to last a lifetime together?

The ping of her cell phone had her digging in her back pocket for her phone. She glanced down at the screen and saw Luke's name. It caused pure adrenaline to race through her veins.

What are you doing?

Several dots appeared on the screen, so she knew he was still texting.

Can you meet me at the lighthouse?

After days of silence he wanted her to meet up with him at the drop of a dime? How annoying! She tapped out a single word.

Now?

Yes. It's important.

I can be there in twenty minutes.

A thumbs-up sign flashed on the screen. Stella jammed the phone back in her pocket.

Important? Ugh. She had a sick feeling roiling around in her stomach. Was this it? The moment he told her that their fake courtship was over? Stella headed inside to get cleaned up. If Luke was going to break up with her, she wanted to at least look good while he was doing it. She ended up wearing a pair of jean Capri pants that flattered her figure and a loose-fitting tunic top. It was always breezy at Holly Hill, considering the lighthouse sat on a cliff above the ocean. Sunglasses and a pair of sneakers finished her outfit.

Approximately twenty minutes later she pulled into the pebbled driveway, driving under the stone archway with the bronze-and-green sign welcoming her to Holly Hill Lighthouse. After parking her car, Stella walked up the small hill toward the lighthouse. The chatter of voices carried on the breeze let her know she wasn't alone. Luke and Miles were tossing a football and running in all directions.

As soon as Luke saw her he called out to her. "Hey, Stella."

"Miss Marshall. Catch!" Before Stella knew it, Miles was lobbing the football in her direction. Stella's quick reflexes saved the day as she expertly caught the toss. Luke and Miles ran over.

"Nice catch," Luke said, his voice full of praise. "You think fast on your feet."

"I'm a second-grade teacher. We're ready for anything." She looked down at Miles. "Isn't that right?"

"Yep. That's why you're my favorite teacher I've ever had." Miles beamed at her.

She reached out and ruffled the top of his head with her hand. Miles hadn't had many teachers in his young lifetime, but Stella still appreciated the sentiment. It always made her feel good to know she was making an impact on her students. "I love hearing that."

"Can we go to the top of the lighthouse, Uncle Luke? I really want to look out of the telescope and see all of Mistletoe from the parapet."

Luke chuckled. "I'm not sure you can see the entire town, but it'll give you a fantastic view." He turned toward Stella. "Is it okay with you?"

"Of course," Stella agreed. "Climbing those stairs will be my exercise for the day." She couldn't remember the last time she'd climbed to the top and looked out across the shores of Blackberry Beach.

"Let's do it!" Luke said. Miles threw his fist in the air in celebration and raced ahead.

Once Miles was gone, Luke made a face. "Sorry about Miles tagging along. Nick asked me to watch him for a bit while he dealt with a work emergency."

"No need to apologize. Miles is awesome. And it looks like he's found some friends." Stella jerked her chin toward the base of the lighthouse where Miles was chatting with a few kids. Stella didn't mind climbing to the top of the lighthouse, but she was burning up with curiosity about why Luke had wanted to meet. "I'm wondering what's going on. Your text was pretty cryptic."

Luke stuffed his hands in his pockets as they walked toward the lighthouse. "I've been a bit MIA since we saw each other at the Coffee Bean."

"So I wasn't imagining it?" Stella asked, keeping her tone light.

He quirked his mouth. "No, you weren't. I've been staying away from you on purpose."

They were now within a few feet of Miles. Stella felt a little jolt at hearing Luke admit that he'd been avoiding her on purpose. It was silly to feel hurt, but the familiar emotion pricked at her. She needed to take a deep breath and suck it up. She'd been through way worse than this.

"Let's continue this conversation later," Stella suggested. She didn't want to risk Miles hearing anything about their arrangement. As soon as they reached his side, Miles and his friends couldn't wait to head to the top. Stella took up the rear, preferring to climb the steep, spiral staircase at a more leisurely pace. Once they reached the top, she and Luke headed toward the gallery. Stepping into the outer viewing area left Stella breathless...and not just from climbing the steps. The view was awe-inspiring.

The lighthouse was a magnificent structure built back in the late 1800s by a beloved sea captain, Jarvis Whitten. After ending his seafaring career, Jarvis built the lighthouse and dedicated his life to steering other vessels safely to their destinations. According to town lore, Jarvis loved his lighthouse but he hated being lonely. After seeking out a bride in Mistletoe and striking out, he ordered a bride through a catalog. Much to the town's surprise, Jarvis and Sophia were a love match who produced five children. The lighthouse stood as a testament to their love story. Although minor repairs had been made over the years, it still had its original design and structure.

Miles and his pals took turns looking out through the periscope and marveling at what they could see of their town. After a short period of time, Miles asked if he could go back downstairs with his friends and their father. Luke agreed but told Miles to stay close to the base of the lighthouse and not wander off.

"That kid never stops moving. It's like he can't sit still for a moment," Luke said, shaking his head as Miles raced off.

"Tell me about it. I have a classroom full of kids with that type of energy." Stella leaned over the edge and flung her arms wide open. "There's something so freeing about being up here. It's like we're on top of the world."

"I've always loved the view from here," Luke said as they gazed out over the town of Mistletoe. "When I was a kid I used to look out over the ocean and imagine myself traveling all over the world."

"And you did it," Stella said. "Good for you. Dreams are important."

"I did, but not exactly in the way I envisioned. I'm proud of my service, but lately I've been thinking about everything I missed out on."

"That's probably because you went through some traumatic things that you're still trying to process. Your mind is working overtime trying to sort things out."

Luke leaned against the railing. "I did love being a SEAL, but it's strange knowing I have to start over."

"I know you went through a life-and-death situation, Luke. I can't imagine the strength it takes to recover from losing your friends and suffering a serious injury that ended your career." She held her hands up. "Don't get me wrong. I'm not trying to compare our situations at all, but I've struggled with rebuilding my life ever since things fell apart," Stella admitted. "It's not easy picking up the pieces. And frankly, some days are harder than others."

She turned toward him, feeling the heat of his stare.

"From where I'm standing, Stella, your life is pretty wonderful. You have a great family, you're a beloved teacher...and you're beautiful." Luke reached out and stroked Stella's cheek. Their gazes locked and held. Something flickered between them. It felt like a flame growing hotter and brighter.

"You're pretty eye-catching yourself, Keegan," Stella said. What did she have to lose by being honest? She might never get this chance again with Mistletoe's finest. He took a step closer so that their arms were touching. She sensed he was going to kiss her just before he dipped his head.

Stella met him halfway, eagerly placing her lips on his. She hadn't expected this at all, and she felt a thrill knowing it wasn't for anyone's benefit. The kiss was spontaneous...and only for the two of them. Not a single soul could see or hear them. Luke's lips tasted sweet, and he was kissing her with aching tenderness. She let out a sigh as she parted her lips, intensifying the kiss.

When Luke stepped away, Stella immediately felt the loss of his nearness. The kiss had been so unexpected and scorching hot. But still a bit confusing. They'd both agreed to pretend date to make their lives less complicated. Now, thanks to this smooch, their fake situation had become muddled.

"This doesn't feel fake anymore," Stella whispered. It was a huge risk to be so honest and vulnerable with Luke. Maybe kissing didn't mean anything to him. What if he didn't feel the same way as she did? The thought of being hurt again made her want to crawl back inside of her shell, where it was safe.

"I know," Luke said, his thumb grazing her cheek tenderly. "I've been feeling the same way since Chowder Fest. It was hard to remember that we were faking it. It's why I wanted to meet up today. To talk about how to proceed going forward."

Her mouth went dry. "What should we do?" Stella asked. "This is definitely a curveball."

"There's only one thing we can do," Luke said. "When life throws you a curveball, you knock it out of the park." Luke reached out for Stella's chin, tilting it upward. Before she knew what was happening, he was kissing her again. His hands at the base of her spine pulled her closer until their bodies were pressed together and the kiss turned into pure molten lava. Stella felt as if every bone in her body was melting. She clutched Luke's shirt collar so she didn't lose her balance. She was literally being swept off her feet.

When he stopped kissing her, Stella wanted to cry out in protest.

"I'm officially calling off our agreement," Luke said, his voice husky. "From now on, you're my girl. And I'm your guy. How does that sound?"

Joy unfurled inside of her. She felt as if hummingbirds

were flying around inside her chest. Luke wanted to be with her as much as she wanted to be with him. With just a few words he'd validated her feelings and given her a heaping dose of happiness.

She could feel a gigantic smile stretching from ear to ear. Stella hoped she didn't look like an idiot. "That sounds wonderful." Who was she kidding? She couldn't play it cool even if she tried. If she were on solid ground, she might even do a cartwheel.

"It is, isn't it?" Luke asked. "It'll be nice to not have to pretend to be a couple. I kept feeling that I was messing up."

"It was kind of fun though," Stella admitted. "I was really in my head about it. When you texted me, I thought you wanted to call off our showmance. It made me realize how much I like spending time with you."

"The feeling is very mutual, Miss Marshall," Luke said, placing his arm around her waist and drawing her close. "I don't know where this thing is going with us, but I'm really happy with where we are right now. My life is far from being sorted out, but you make me feel as if I can figure everything out." He held out his hand and Stella intertwined hers with his. It felt solid and steady.

"I'm happy too, Luke." And she was. Soul stirringly, unbelievably, ecstatically happy. Luke made her feel as if she could still hope for things she'd buried in the past. She'd given up on the idea of having a romantic partner, but thanks to Luke, she was now seeing things differently.

Luke held her hand tightly as they made their way back down the winding steps to the ground floor. Stella appreciated Luke's firm grip since she still felt a little shaky about the turn things had taken between them. Stella had honestly never dreamed that Luke's feelings would mirror her own. Back when she'd first seen him walking into the school gymnasium to surprise Miles, she'd never imagined that he would be a romantic partner for her. At the time she'd been adamantly opposed to being in a relationship. The thought of falling for someone had been about as appealing as having her teeth pulled with no Novocaine.

But now, a few short weeks later, everything had changed. Luke had come into her life with the force of a tropical storm, infusing her with a whole new outlook on life and love. She didn't want to get ahead of herself, but for the first time in a very long time she felt hopeful.

* * *

On the drive back to Nick's house, Miles talked a mile a minute about the lighthouse and how he wanted to write his summer report about Captain Jarvis and his life in Mistletoe in the 1800s. Luke tried his best to pay attention to his nephew, but his mind kept wandering back to Stella. The last kiss they'd shared before going their separate ways had been just as toe curling as the others.

If someone had asked Luke how he'd come back to Mistletoe as a retired Navy SEAL and ended up getting a girlfriend when it was the very last thing he'd wanted, he wouldn't even know how to start to explain it. Being around Miles and Nick had convinced him that they were in a good place. His nephew was resilient. Luke was committed to supporting them, but he knew Nick was navigating the situation with grace and finesse.

All he knew for certain was that he wanted to be with Stella.

Stella had burrowed herself inside of him, reaching a place that was normally off-limits. He'd opened up to her in a way he had never done before. In return, he wanted to know everything about her—her favorite color, what she ate for breakfast, if she liked knock-knock jokes and Double Stuf Oreos. It hurt to imagine she was still in love with Rafe, because it was obvious to Luke that he had never been worthy of a woman like Stella. Most of all, Luke wanted to know the secret to winning her heart. Planting roots in Mistletoe was looking more appealing by the moment. Relationships weren't his strong suit, but Luke wanted to try and build something solid with Stella.

He felt relieved that they were on the same wavelength. He planned to take things slow and steady with her. The fastest way to ruin a budding romance would be to rush things, and he still had so much to learn about Stella. Did Rafe still own a piece of her heart? He hoped not. Maybe now that he and Stella were together, any feelings for her ex would be extinguished.

He shrugged off his concerns about Rafe, choosing instead to focus on where things were going between him and Stella. Luke hadn't been imagining the romantic tension hovering in the air between them. It was electric. He'd never felt anything so powerful before. Their chemistry was off the charts.

"Uncle Luke. Are you listening to me?" Luke cast a quick sideways glance at Miles. The look on his face was priceless—a mixture between confusion and humor. It was in moments like this that Luke felt grateful to be back in Mistletoe spending precious time with his nephew. As he'd learned time and again over the past few years, tomorrow wasn't promised.

"Yeah, buddy. Of course I am. Your project will be amazing. And if you need any help, I'm your guy." Back in the day Luke had done a few projects on Holly Hill Lighthouse and Captain Jarvis. As a kid he'd been fascinated by sea captains, lighthouses, and pirates. From the looks of it, so was Miles.

Miles giggled. "You have a goofy look on your face. It's the same look you have when you're with Miss Marshall."

Luke shook his head. Miles was way more observant than he'd been as an eight-year-old. Nothing much escaped his notice. "I guess I'm just a huge goofball," he said, sticking out his tongue and making a funny face. Miles's laughter filled the truck and lifted Luke's spirits to the stratosphere. Today had been one fine day. It had shown him that good things were right around the corner. He just had to be willing to embrace them.

It scared him senseless to feel this way. After so many years of avoiding relationships, Luke was finally stepping into one. It was nerve-racking. His stomach had been all tied up in knots during his conversation with Stella. He would have been gutted if she'd wanted to keep him in the friend zone. For the first time in his life Luke was imagining what life might be like with a woman by his side. Not just any woman, he realized. *Only Stella.* And he knew that he was getting way ahead of himself. He wasn't even fully settled here in Mistletoe, and he was still jobless. He hadn't spoken to the Smiths face-to-face yet, and it was high time he corrected that situation. A phone call just wouldn't do.

Luke needed to sit down with Kenny's family and tell them about the day their beloved son died. Only then could he truly move on with his life.

CHAPTER SEVENTEEN

Several days had passed since Luke and Stella made their relationship official. They'd seen each other every single day in the interim, meeting up for lunches, walks at the marina, and clamming at Blackberry Beach. Today was a beautiful day to celebrate the Fourth of July. Temperatures were set to soar into the high eighties today with no rain in the evening forecast. It boded well for a spectacular fireworks display. On several occasions when Luke was a kid the fireworks had been cancelled due to inclement weather. He still remembered the disappointment he and Nick felt every time the announcement had been made. Luke would bet not a single kid in Mistletoe would be let down this year.

He was in the middle of making a batch of cookies to bring over to Stella's house. He wasn't much of a baker, but it was almost impossible to mess up chocolate chip cookies. Or so Kara had always told him. Just making these brought her to mind—his beautiful, fun-loving, sarcastic sister-in-law. A true sister of the heart. Yet another devastating loss he'd endured. He wasn't sure he'd ever fully processed it. Right after the funeral he'd flown back to Afghanistan and plunged himself into life-and-death missions. Just as he'd done with most of the emotions he hadn't been able to face, Luke had stuffed them down into a big black hole. Problem was, they kept rearing up when he least expected it.

A knock sounded on the front door and Luke went to answer it. He didn't have time for a social call, so he hoped it wasn't anybody looking for him. Unfortunately, there were still a few women in town who hadn't gotten the message that he wasn't available. At least now he didn't have to pretend to be coupled up. The reality of his newfound situation caused him to grin like he'd just won the lottery.

When he pulled the door open, a young girl—no more than ten or eleven years old—was standing at Nick's doorstep. Her big brown eyes were the color of mahogany while her old-fashioned pigtails hung past her shoulder. She was adorable.

"Hey there, short stuff. Miles isn't at home. He won't be back for a half hour or so," Luke said, glancing at his watch. "Maybe you can give him a call later."

"I'm not here to see Miles," the girl said, brushing past him to enter the house.

"Hey. Wait a minute," he called out. This kid was pushy. "Where do you think you're going?"

What was it with kids these days? The voice in his

head sounded exactly like his father. It made Luke feel old. Pretty soon he'd be wearing comfortable shoes and suspenders.

The little girl turned toward him. "I'm Tess. Stella's sister." She stuck out her hand. Taken aback, Luke took a few moments to reach out and shake her hand. He'd heard all about Tess. But what was she doing here?

"I'm here to talk to you, Luke. But before we chat, I'd like to thank you for your service to this country, especially today of all days." She bowed her head in his direction.

"Umm. You're very welcome," he stammered. He'd never had anyone bow to him, let alone a child. Tess was a bit unnerving. He couldn't remember ever feeling quite so flummoxed by someone her age. Stella had told him stories about her precocious little sister. He was well aware that she wasn't your average run-of-the-mill kid. At this very moment she might be plotting world domination.

"Can we sit down?" Tess asked. "I wouldn't complain if you offered me a glass of ice-cold water." He felt a smile tugging at the corners of his mouth. Tess was something else. He could easily imagine her being a CEO or a high-powered attorney. She was definitely going to run the world.

"Sure thing. Let's head toward the kitchen," Luke said, leading the way down the hall. For the life of him he couldn't figure out what had brought Stella's little sister in search of him.

"Make yourself comfortable," he said, gesturing toward the kitchen table.

Once they were both seated and settled with ice-cold waters in front of them, Luke decided to get down to brass tacks. "So, Tess, what brings you here?"

"I wanted to talk to you about my sister." She crossed her hands in front of her and met his gaze head-on. "What are your intentions?"

Luke sputtered on his water, sending liquid all over the table. "My what?" he asked, his voice incredulous. Was he being pranked? Maybe Stella was hiding outside in the bushes waiting to jump out at him and say "Gotcha."

"Intentions." Tess repeated the word for him. "Stella has already had her heart smashed to kingdom come by a good-looking, sweet-talking man like yourself."

"Thanks. I think," he muttered. He took a long swig of his water. Something told him he would need it to sustain himself.

"I'm here to warn you not to go down that road with Stella." Tess's tone was steely.

Luke frowned. "You're warning me?"

"Yes," Tess said, her chin quivering ever so slightly. He suddenly realized that she wasn't quite as tough as she liked to project. At the end of the day, she was still ten years old. And at the moment she appeared quite vulnerable. *Go easy on her*, he reminded himself. *She's protecting Stella.*

"If you're not in this for the right reasons, then you should just walk away." A sheen of tears glistened in Tess's eyes. "My sister has a ginormous heart and she deserves to be happy. I think she likes you a lot. And I hope that you like her too."

"I do, Tess. I really do." It was a big step for him to say it out loud.

Tess looked up at him with hope etched on her face. "So you're not going to do anything to hurt her, are you? Promise me."

"I don't *ever* want to do anything to hurt Stella."

"So you're not going to promise me?" His heart broke a little at the crestfallen expression stamped on her face.

"I can't make a promise like that, Tess. No one can. It would be a lie. The last thing I want to do is lie to you." He splayed his hands on the table, searching for the right words. "Sometimes things happen in relationships and even if two people want the very best it doesn't work out in their favor."

Tess buried her face in her glass as she took huge sips. When she finally lifted her head up and put her glass down, she said, "Stella is amazing and from what I've been hearing around town, so are you. She's the type of big sister who doesn't just tell me what I want to hear. Everything she tells me and does for me is for my own good. She gives to everyone in our family and never asks for anything in return. I want Stella to have the same happy ending that Lucy got."

Luke thought his heart might be melting. "I know you do, Tess. That makes you an awesome sister."

She knit her brows together. "It does?"

"One hundred percent. You're protecting her the way she's always cared for you. I think that's pretty amazing."

Tess began sniffing the air. "Luke, I smell something burning."

Luke let out a groan and jumped to his feet. "My cookies." He grabbed an oven mitt, then wrenched open the oven, yanking the tray out. Not a single cookie had been spared. "Looks like they're burnt city," he said to Tess. "And here I thought you couldn't mess up chocolate chip cookies."

"I'm sorry for distracting you, Luke," Tess apologized. "It's all my fault."

"No worries, Tess. I'll just make another batch. Trust me, this isn't the first time this has happened." Luke had a history of burning dinner, appetizers, desserts, and more. One of these days he was going to get it right.

She grinned at him, bearing an uncanny resemblance to Stella. "Well, I can't wait to taste them later on. I need to get going before my family sends out a search party."

Luke walked Tess to the door. He patted her on the shoulder as she stood on the threshold. "Thanks for stopping by, Tess. It was a pleasure to chat with you." And he meant it. How often did adults get the chance to have a heart-to-heart with a ten-year-old girl? It was obvious Tess loved Stella to the moon and back.

Luke stood in the doorway and watched as Tess skipped down the walkway. A part of him had wanted to make a promise to Tess about not hurting Stella, but the rational side of him couldn't do it. There were no guarantees in relationships. More than anything else in this world, he didn't want Stella to be hurt. Especially by him. Stella was burrowing herself deeper and deeper into his life and the innermost regions of his heart. He could barely go an hour without thinking about her. It was both nerve-racking and exciting.

He'd never been the type of guy to believe in the idea of soul mates. Or finding your forever in another person. He'd believed in it for others like Nick and Kara, but never for himself. Perhaps on some level he'd never felt worthy of that type of love. But lately, because of Stella, he was opening up to the possibility of something much bigger than he'd ever dared to dream. Perhaps this time the stars would be aligned in their favor.

Maybe, just maybe, Stella really was the one.

* * *

Stella buzzed around her kitchen, balancing a tray on her right hip while clutching a pitcher of lemonade in her left hand. Lucy and Dante were sitting out on the patio debating wedding cake designs and flavors. Stella liked watching them interact with each other. Even when they disagreed on something they still treated each other with love and respect. It hadn't been that way with her and Rafe. He'd been domineering about all aspects of wedding planning. Several times he'd reduced Stella to tears with his unrealistic demands. *And for what?* In the end he'd walked away from her and their wedding.

The patio door slid open, and Lucy stepped back into the house with a pleased expression on her face. "You look like someone who got her way," Stella teased. Lucy hadn't changed since they were kids. She'd worn that same look of satisfaction throughout their lives. "So did you pick the chocolate crème cake?"

"Not exactly," Lucy said, reaching into the fridge for

a cold soda. "We compromised. Half is the chocolate crème and the other half is caramel de leche."

"Now that's a sweet concession," Stella said. Lucy groaned at her corny joke. "It's going to be wonderful just like everything else about your wedding. You must be counting the days."

"I am," Lucy admitted. "Don't tell anyone, but I'm still pinching myself that I get to marry my first and only love."

"You deserve every bit of happiness that comes your way. I want to be you when I grow up." Stella meant it. Lucy had really stepped out on a leap of faith to rebuild her relationship with Dante after he'd shattered her heart and left Mistletoe, only to return eight and a half years later as a megastar. She was way braver than Stella ever could be. And now she was reaping the rewards.

"I admit that I was a little salty when he came back to town," Lucy said.

Stella snorted. "A little? You were acting like a one-woman wrecking crew for a while there. And then the two of you fell in love all over again." She sighed.

Lucy sniffled. "If we don't change the subject, I'm going to get weepy. How can I help set up?" Lucy asked. "Are we eating outside?"

"I thought it would be nice to set up the food inside then everyone can head to the patio to eat after they make their plates." Stella gestured to her refrigerator. "I'm keeping everything chilled for now. Luke agreed to man the grill." Just saying it out loud made her happy. It was the little things that some women took for granted when they were coupled up. Even when Stella was with Rafe, he hadn't ever lifted a finger to help out. Having Luke serve as the grill master meant something to Stella.

"So you're actually dating Luke for real now?" Lucy's eyes were practically bugging out of her head. "You're a genuine couple?"

She'd explained it to Lucy several times over the past few days, but her sister didn't seem to fully grasp the notion that she and Luke were now in an authentic romantic relationship. Maybe she thought Stella was punking her since they'd been fake dating for weeks. She tried her best to tamp down her slight irritation. "Yes, Lucy. Like I told you, spending so much time together allowed us to develop real feelings for each other. It's all very fresh and shiny, but we're both enjoying this new phase." Stella felt a huge smile sweeping across her face. She couldn't even put into words how blissful she felt at the moment. There was no telling where things were headed, but she felt optimistic.

"Don't get me wrong," Lucy said, "I definitely saw sparks between you, but I thought both of you didn't want a relationship."

"I didn't want to be pressured into one. There's a difference. And I think Luke felt the same way," Stella explained. "No one forced us together. We just gravitated toward one another after spending so much time pretending to be a couple."

Lucy narrowed her gaze as she regarded Stella. She could see the wheels turning in her sister's head.

"What's wrong?" Stella asked. She could tell Lucy

wanted to get something off her chest. She knew her sister like the back of her hand.

Lucy put a finger to her lips. "I didn't say a word."

"Well it's written all over your face, so just come out with it." Stella heard the impatience in her voice. She wanted Lucy to be honest with her, but at the same time she didn't want her sister to say anything to dampen her spirits. What she was experiencing with Luke was soul stirring and exciting and real. Stella knew all too well how things could turn on a dime. Nothing was written in stone.

Lucy closed the space between them and reached for Stella's hands. "This is coming from a place of love, first and foremost. Luke seems like a good guy. I mean, come on, he's a Navy SEAL. It doesn't get more honorable than that."

"But?" Stella had seen a *but* coming from a mile away. Lucy's eyes were full of concern. It was funny to be on this side of it since it had always been Stella watching out for Lucy. When she'd reunited with Dante, Stella had been like a mama bear protecting her cub. She imagined Lucy felt the same way about Stella's heart.

"I'm worried that you're rushing things with Luke and that you're going to get hurt again." Stella opened her mouth to speak, but Lucy held her hand up. "Just hear me out. Luke is back from a war zone after going through a traumatic incident. You've had your own pain and suffering due to your narcissistic ex-fiancé. I'm just saying to be careful. Don't jump in feet first."

Stella took a few moments to absorb Lucy's comments. Nothing she'd said surprised Stella. The same thoughts had rolled around in her own head a time or two. But the truth was she'd come to a huge realization about her feelings for Rafe, and they were nothing like what she felt for Luke.

"There were a lot of things that weren't right about me and Rafe. It's taken me a long time to put the pieces together, but looking back I may have loved him, but I didn't like him." Stella saw Lucy's eyes widen. "He wasn't always nice to me and for a very long time I ignored the red flags." She took a steadying breath. "All this time I've focused on losing him when in reality I was mourning the things I wanted—a life partner, a home, a family." A tear ran down her face as reality settled in. "I don't love Rafe, Lucy. And I'm not on the rebound. Because of Luke I faced some hard truths about what I was settling for by agreeing to marry Rafe in the first place. He used to be extremely passive aggressive toward me and I made excuses for it. His behavior took a toll on me, so I've really had to take a good look in the mirror to figure out why I said yes to his proposal in the first place."

"Oh, Stella," Lucy cried. "I knew from our conversations that Rafe could be difficult at times. When you got engaged I figured he'd sorted himself out."

"He did briefly, but it didn't last long. And I should have walked away well before he did." Stella bowed her head. She still felt ashamed at how much she'd tolerated.

She swung her gaze up to look at Lucy. "So you see, I know Luke and I didn't have the perfect setup for a romance, but it's real. It feels right. We have a connection that's genuine. It was nothing either of us ever expected or wanted. I honestly never thought I'd ever feel this way for someone again...not after what Rafe put me through." She shrugged. "I kind of accepted that I'd be alone, but then Luke came along. I'm not saying we're walking off into the sunset together, but it feels nice to have someone in my life who cares about me."

"Are you looking for something serious?" Lucy asked. The question was an overwhelming one for Stella. Her only experience with love had been with Rafe, and it hadn't been a healthy relationship. What did she know about relationships?

"I don't know, Lucy. Each and every day my feelings are growing. My stomach does butterflies when he's nearby, and I can't stop thinking about him. I know it sounds crazy, but I feel like we've known each other for a lifetime."

"That sounds pretty intense. It's how I feel about Dante." Lucy shot her a knowing look. "I'm not going to press you on it, but it sounds to me like you may already have fallen."

Stella busied herself with stirring the potato salad. She didn't make eye contact with Lucy out of fear she would see all her emotions resting on the surface. Love was such a big word. It was something she'd vowed to avoid at all costs. And now she was dating a man who made her feel vulnerable to all the possibilities.

As much as she was excited about being coupled up with Luke, Stella knew he still had issues to wade through. Getting closure with Kenny's family might never happen. She worried that Luke was more wrapped up in resolving the Smiths' issues than taking a look at his own. He didn't talk a lot about the mission that had ended his military tenure and cost him the lives of Kenny and Aaron. It was way more complex than bridging the gap between himself and Kenny's mother.

As much as she knew Luke wanted to give others closure, Stella had the feeling he needed it just as badly.

CHAPTER EIGHTEEN

By the time Luke arrived at Stella's house with Nick and Miles, a few other guests had already trickled in. Stella's parents, Tess, and Carolina were relaxing on the patio with Dante and Lucy. She was still waiting for a few members of Dante's family and some of her work friends. A festive vibe hung in the air. Stella was incredibly excited to be around family and friends and celebrating the Fourth of July. Every time the door opened or she heard footsteps, Stella's mind went to Luke. She was counting down the minutes until he arrived. It was a sure sign she was crazy about the man.

"I come bearing chocolate chip cookies," Luke said as he entered the kitchen holding up a tray of mouth-watering cookies covered in Saran Wrap. "Where should I put them?"

"Over on the table," Stella said, gesturing behind her.

"If you can find a spot." Thanks to all of her guests bringing contributions, the table was laden with fruit, salad, chips, brownies, and a variety of other treats.

Luke placed the cookies on the table and turned toward Stella. "How's it going? You look festive." Stella had decked herself out in a pair of jean shorts and a red, white, and blue T-shirt. On her arms she was wearing red, white, and blue bangles.

"Thank you. I like your shirt." He was wearing a vibrant red shirt paired with a pair of denim shorts. A pair of Havaianas sandals perfected the outfit.

"Thanks." He tapped his chin as a thoughtful expression appeared on his face. "I had a visit earlier from someone who looks a little bit like you, except she's a lot shorter and way sassier." The glint in Luke's soulful brown eyes broadcast his amusement.

Stella covered her face with her hands. "Oh no. She didn't! I wish that I could say I'm shocked, but I'm actually mortified."

"Don't be," Luke said, pulling her hands away from her face. "She loves you, Stella." He looked down at her, a sweet smile gracing his face. "It's pretty obvious to me that everyone in your orbit does. That's a testament to who you are as a person. She's just watching out for you, which is pretty amazing for a kid her age."

"Watching out for me? Uh oh. What did she say to you?" Dread swept over her. When it came to Tess all bets were off. As cute as she was, Tess had a problem with boundaries. Anything was possible considering she'd once kicked Dante in a misguided attempt at defending Lucy's honor.

"Don't worry," Luke said, drawing closer to her and pressing a kiss on her temple. "If anything, it only enhanced my opinion of you. According to Tess, you're wearing a Superwoman costume under that tank top." Luke reached out and tugged at her shirt.

She loved this playful side of him. It made her feel lighthearted in a way she hadn't experienced in a long time. It felt good to laugh and joke with Luke. There hadn't been enough of this in her life in the last few years. Someday she wouldn't be shocked by her little sister's antics, but at the moment all she could do was shake her head.

"Tess is ten years old. She tends to put her older sisters on a pedestal. Lucy and I try not to let her down, even when she makes outrageous requests." Like last Christmas when she'd asked Lucy to see if Dante would be her special guest at school. At the time, Lucy and Dante hadn't yet reconciled. Somehow, Lucy had found a way to make it happen.

Luke scoffed. "Tess? Outrageous? I'm having a hard time picturing that." His laughter brought adorable crinkles to the corners of his eyes.

"Are you talking about me? 'Cause my ears are burning." Tess was standing by the sliding glass door with their father by her side. Walt Marshall was a good-looking man with salt-and-pepper close-cropped hair framing a handsome, russet-colored face.

"Daddy. Have you met Luke? He's Stella's hot Navy SEAL boyfriend," Tess said with a wide smile.

"Tess!" Stella said in a scolding tone. She didn't know where Tess got the nerve. Luke had a huge smirk on his face. Clearly, he thought Tess was charming. Fast forward six years and her parents really needed to be on their toes with Tess and the boys in town.

Tess shrugged. "What? I'm only repeating what everyone else in town is saying."

"Well maybe you should stop repeating everything you hear and knock off the eavesdropping," Walt said, shaking his head as he looked down at his daughter. He took a few steps toward Luke. "Hey there, Luke. It's nice to see you again. It's been a long time." Walt shook hands with Luke and added, "Word on the street is that you're dating my beautiful daughter." He looked Luke up and down with a somber expression stamped on his face, then folded his arms across his chest.

"Dad!" Stella said with a groan. "Are you really doing this?" What in the world was going on with her dad? He was normally easygoing and sweet. Was this a result of Rafe treating her so poorly? Was he now being overly protective?

Luke chuckled. "It's okay, Stella. It's fine. Hi, Mr. Marshall. It's great to see you again."

Walt clapped Luke on the shoulder. "I'm just pulling Stella's leg." He leaned in and said in a loud whisper, "She can be a little uptight sometimes."

Stella swatted in the direction of her dad, who grabbed her forearms and pulled her into a hug. "I'm just having a little fun, sweetie."

The patio door opened, and Nick stuck his head in. "How about we fire up the grill, guys? I'm not naming any names, but a few people out here are getting hungry for burgers and dogs."

"That's my cue," Luke said, rubbing his hands together. "I'm about to get my grill on."

"Why doesn't everybody grab some food to take outside for the grill master?" Stella asked, grinning at Luke. Why did it feel that she'd grinned more in the past few weeks than she had in her entire life?

Tess and Walt headed outside with platters in their hands while Luke reached for another tray to carry.

"Oh, wait. I have something for you," Stella said, holding up a finger. She dug around in the kitchen counter drawer, letting out a cry of triumph when she located what she'd been searching for. "Ta-dah!" She held up the red, white, and blue apron with the words GRILL MASTER emblazoned on the front.

Luke let out a hearty laugh and took the apron from Stella. He put it on as Stella went behind him to tie it in the back. "Thanks. This is great," Luke said, turning around to face her.

"You're welcome," she said, her eyes moving over him from head to toe. "You look pretty good for a hot Navy SEAL."

"Oh, really?" Luke asked. "I never get tired of hearing you call me hot."

"You know there's a grilling tradition you have to uphold, right? In order to ensure grilling success someone has to kiss the grill master."

"That tradition sounds right up my alley," Luke said as she reached up on her tiptoes and pulled his head down toward her. Stella placed a tender kiss on his lips, one that came straight from her heart. She really liked kissing him. And she hoped there would be many more kisses in their future.

Luke placed another peck on her lips. "More of this

later on, okay? I need to start grilling the food before there's a rebellion out there." Luke reached over and picked up a tray of burger patties from the counter.

"I'll be right out," she said, shooing him away. "I need to put some ice in a bin for the drinks."

Stella watched as Luke headed outside. She peeked through the window and saw him laughing and joking with Nick and Dante. He fired up the grill and playfully wielded the spatula like a sword. Tess and Miles were enthralled by his every move. Her heart was filled almost to overflowing. If she could, Stella would capture this moment in a bottle and tuck it away as a forever memory. Happiness—true joy—wasn't something she would ever take for granted again. She just hoped she could hold on to this feeling and that it didn't slip through her fingers like sand through her toes.

* * *

As night fell, everyone headed to the beach with blankets and flashlights. The sky was perfectly clear with a scattering of stars twinkling brightly above them. Luke and Stella had both put on sweatshirts due to the cool breeze that always settled in by the water, and Stella had liberally sprayed bug repellant on all of them as they walked out the door. The mosquitoes in Mistletoe were vicious this time of year.

Luke led Stella to a secluded area where they would have a clear view of the fireworks. Although the rest of the group was nearby, Luke wanted to spend some private time with his girlfriend. The emotions bubbling up inside of him took him completely by surprise, like a random thunderstorm in summer. His feelings for Stella were epic. He knew it was far too late to backtrack. Everything between them now was genuine. And his feelings weren't like anything he'd ever felt for any other woman.

Stella Marshall was in a league of her own. And despite his best intentions not to date anyone until he'd sorted his life out, Luke had been irresistibly drawn to her. Just like right now. He couldn't seem to take his eyes off her. Her natural beauty was illuminated by the soft glow of the moonlight. He placed his arm around her, and she nestled into him with her head against his chest.

A buzz of exhilaration filled the air as an announcement came over a loudspeaker that the fireworks would begin shortly. The crowd clapped and cries of excitement rang out across the beach. Luke hadn't felt such a thrill since he was a youngster sitting on this very beach awaiting the holiday festivities. There hadn't been a single thing about this night he hadn't enjoyed.

"Oooh, this never gets old," Stella said, rubbing her hands together and grinning. She looked like a little kid at the moment, full of excitement and pure joy. She was the living breathing embodiment of what the fireworks display always made him feel like on the inside.

A hissing sound emanated as the first of the fireworks burst into the air and lit up the sky. The moment he heard the fireworks and the sounds filled his ears, Luke flinched. He shifted his body so that Stella was no longer resting against him. His immediate reaction was to recoil from the intense noise and retreat. It sounded like an explosion. Suddenly his breathing became shallow and it felt as if he couldn't get any air. Growing up, Luke had always loved Fourth of July fireworks. The popping sounds. The myriad colors bursting to life in the heavens. Now it felt like he was under attack. As burst after burst turned the sky into a rainbow of colors, Luke felt as if his world was crumbling around him. For the life of him he couldn't get his bearings.

"Luke! Are you okay?" He heard his name being called through a haze. Stella reached out and touched his arm. He lightly shrugged her off as she made contact. Luke couldn't have her touching him right now. He couldn't bear the contact, which made no sense since he loved Stella's touch.

Her shock and confusion were illuminated on her face with each explosion of color lighting up the sky. And with each flash of fireworks Luke was catapulted back into a hellish nightmare. Fire. Ash. The smell of burnt flesh. Agonizing screams. With every crack, pop, and hissing sound Luke thought he might be dying. His chest felt as if someone were sitting on it. Was he having a panic attack? He opened his mouth to respond to Stella, but nothing came out.

Just power through it, he told himself. *All in. All the time.* His Navy SEAL creed. He needed to tether himself to something in order to make it past this moment. He was strong. He was brave. He'd endured worse than this. He'd been through the fire time after time. How many times had he made the impossible possible? What was wrong with him?

"I-I'm all right," he finally said through clenched teeth. He bowed his head and did his best to breathe. His chest was tight. He needed to get away from all this noise and chaos, but he felt like a marble statue, incapable of moving. In an ideal world he would be miles and miles away from this Fourth of July fireworks extravaganza.

"Obviously, something's wrong. Tell me, Luke." The concern emanating from her eyes gutted him. She was kind and compassionate and Luke knew she genuinely cared about him. While a part of him wanted to tell her about his panic attacks, another part of him didn't want her to see him as weak. As a member of the Navy it had been drilled into him that strength was his greatest attribute. Weakness had never been an option. Who was he if he couldn't be strong and hold himself together?

"I'm sorry, Stella. I need to get out of here." He pushed the words out of his mouth almost against his will. This evening had been so perfect…until all this stuff got dredged up. He hated to end the night this way, but he was falling apart at the seams, and he didn't want Stella to see him like this. Luke cared way more than he'd realized about what she thought of him.

"I'll pack up my things so we can go," she said, reaching for the picnic basket. He held up his hand to stop her. The last thing he needed right now was company. Luke wanted to lick his wounds in private. He wanted to scream about his pain and vent about the loss of his friends. Stella wouldn't understand any of it, and he didn't blame her. She was a small-town schoolteacher who thankfully would never experience what he'd endured.

"I don't want to put a damper on your evening. I'd rather end things on a high note in the hopes you'll forget you saw me like this."

"Are you sure? What's going on? Please. Talk to me, Luke." She was pleading with him, and for a moment he considered telling her everything. He could ask to go back to her place and talk. Could explain that the fireworks brought him back to the moment six months ago when his entire life imploded. *You have nothing to be ashamed of.* Her cozy house was just a stone's throw down the beach. What he wouldn't give to be inside that bungalow with Stella. With a silent groan he stood up, compensating for his bad leg by leaning his weight on the left one.

"Night, Stella. Will you be okay getting home?" He had to ask, even though he knew the walk would take mere minutes. And with the crowd of revelers at the beach, she wouldn't be alone. Embarrassment hit him squarely in the gut. He couldn't even walk Stella to her door without unraveling. He just needed to get as far away as possible from the noise and the brightness and the bangs.

"I'll be fine. Goodnight, Luke." Stella's voice was filled with bewilderment. She knew something was wrong, but she couldn't put her finger on it. He also detected a hint of disappointment riding under the surface. He couldn't blame her. Tonight had been absolutely perfect until he'd ruined everything.

Luke walked off into the darkness, enveloped by shame. His body had betrayed him in every way tonight. He was battling so many emotions. Stuffing things down into a big black hole wasn't working anymore. It was all bubbling to the surface and it felt overwhelming.

Stella Marshall deserved so much more than Luke could ever give her. He'd seen the hurt in her eyes, and he hated himself for bringing her pain. They'd shared a beautiful kiss tonight. It had been a romantic evening. For the first time in forever Luke had started to believe that he could make a life here in Mistletoe with Stella at his side. For a few hours he'd allowed himself to forget that he was broken. If a few fireworks sent him spiraling into a dark place, what hope did he have for a normal life?

CHAPTER NINETEEN

What in the world was happening? One moment she and Luke had been cuddling underneath a blanket and enjoying a glorious fireworks display, and then the next everything fell apart. Stella didn't leave the beach until all the fireworks were extinguished from the sky. Part of her was in shock while another part simply felt sad. She hadn't known how to answer Lucy's questions about Luke's whereabouts. Her sister had looked as confused as Stella felt. By the time she'd said her good-byes to her family and friends before heading home, Stella was on the verge of tears. It was hard not to blame herself for Luke's departure. Had she done something to send him running? Nothing about the situation made sense to her. He'd told her on several occasions how much he loved fireworks. But the look on his face said otherwise.

Finally, after such a long time of feeling at loose ends, Stella had been happy. Tonight had felt like a new beginning, full of promise. But what did she know? Hadn't she once thought Rafe was her Prince Charming? There was no comparison between the two men. Luke was a man of honor while Rafe lacked scruples. Even though she was annoyed with Luke, there was truly no question as to who was the better man.

She still wasn't about to let Luke off the hook for bailing on her. It dredged up a lot of the feelings she'd harbored for years since Rafe walked away from her.

A petty feeling took hold. If Luke wasn't feeling this relationship, she should just cut things off before she got any deeper. He'd wounded her tonight with his odd behavior and sudden departure. It was as if he'd picked at a scab that was almost healed and left the cut open and vulnerable. She didn't want to feel rejected, but it felt so personal. She'd been looking forward to tonight, believing it would be special due to their recent decision to pursue a romantic relationship. And yet, something had gone terribly wrong.

Stella opened up her freezer and pulled out a carton of Ben and Jerry's. She was sitting here all alone trying to numb the pain with mint chocolate chip ice cream. Normally she would call up Lucy to come over and commiserate with her, but with Dante in town, Stella didn't want to bother her. Was this her new normal with Lucy? Would she always be stepping on eggshells and afraid to claim her sister time?

"At least I still have you, Coco Chanel," she said, bending down and patting her poodle on the head. If it was possible for a dog to roll their eyes, Coco Chanel was doing it at this very moment. She trotted away from Stella and settled into her plush doggy bed. Humph! "I can't believe you. After all I've done for you."

Okay, Stella. It's time to put your big-girl panties on. Take a deep breath and keep it moving. This too shall pass.

She was wallowing. Lucy was always available to her. Being engaged to Dante hadn't changed that one bit. If Stella called her right now, Lucy would move heaven and earth to get to her. She reached over and grabbed her cell phone from the table. Nothing could ever separate the sisters. Not marriage or kids or a Hollywood movie star.

A loud knock on her back door startled her and brought her out of her thoughts. A glance at the wall clock showed it was almost eleven o'clock, and she couldn't imagine who would be stopping by at this hour. Stella reluctantly put down the carton of ice cream and made her way to the door. A quick look through the glass pane revealed Luke standing there. He'd changed into a pair of jeans and an oatmeal-colored shirt that fit his tall, rugged body to perfection. Stella's heart beat fast at the sight of him. Why did he have to look so scrumptious? Especially right now when she was annoyed with him. She slowly turned the handle and opened the door.

"You don't have to ask why I'm here," Luke blurted out. "I know it's late. Can I just have a few minutes of your time?"

Stella nodded and flung the door wide open. The fact that Luke had made his way back to her house hours after they'd parted ways made her curious, and she was still open to listening to him. As soon as Luke stepped inside, Stella felt his energy fill the space. She folded her arms around her middle in a self-protective gesture. Even though she welcomed Luke back into her home with open arms, she still needed to protect herself against getting hurt. Tonight had shown her that because of the way she felt about him, Luke possessed the power to wound her.

Neither one of them made a move to sit down. Luke leaned against the kitchen island while Stella propped herself against the counter. A heaviness hung in the space between them.

"I should have explained things earlier at the beach and I'm sorry that I didn't. My only excuse is that I was embarrassed and I couldn't find the words."

"You? Embarrassed about what?" She couldn't hide her surprise. Stella found it hard to believe that a man like Luke would ever feel this way. He radiated confidence and swagger.

A tremor was racing around in his jaw. "My reaction to the fireworks. It took me straight back to Afghanistan. All the noise sounded like the explosions that day. And my body reacted. It was fight or flight...and I had to get away because in that moment it felt like I was dying. Like I couldn't get a breath.

"I've been dealing with nightmares and flashbacks for the last six months. Certain things trigger them. It's not as if I could even remember everything that happened, but it seems as if I'm recalling more details as time goes by." He idly fiddled with a glass on the counter. "I was having a great night with you, Stella. Probably the best time I've had in years. It's frustrating that I ruined it."

Stella walked over to Luke, swiftly closing the distance between them. Guilt enveloped her. She'd made his behavior personal and it hadn't been at all. "It's not your fault, Luke. You didn't do anything wrong. I can't believe that I didn't connect the dots or do anything to help you."

"Please don't blame yourself. I hate that I confused you. Stella, I never want to do anything to make you doubt me." Luke reached for her hands and they laced their fingers together. It was such an odd sensation to feel so connected to Luke in this moment when just a short time ago she'd been bereft. His honesty and vulnerability rocked her to the core.

"It's not about me," Stella insisted. "Yes, I had no idea what was going on with you and it threw me. But knowing you're going through this type of turmoil is the bigger issue. I'm so sorry that you're suffering."

When she looked into his eyes, Stella could see shame infused in their brown depths. "I'm supposed to be stronger than this." He let out a ragged sigh. "Strength is what got me through SEAL training and all my years of service. It's something I've always had in abundance."

"You're human, Luke. And what you went through was traumatic. Being affected by it doesn't mean you're not strong. But you're not Superman. Unless of course you're hiding something from me." To lighten the mood, Stella reached out and lifted up his shirt as if she were trying to find his superhero costume. All she saw was a washboard stomach and abs of steel that made her suck in a deep breath.

"I always wanted to be Spider-Man, anyway," he teased with a slight smile. It was good to see Luke joking with her despite their heavy conversation.

"Well, if you know your Spider-Man lore, Peter Parker went through some hard times, especially when his uncle was killed. That's how he transformed into Spider-Man." She squeezed Luke's shoulder, wanting to comfort him. "Not even superheroes are unscathed by life."

"Waking up in that hospital and finding out that Kenny and Aaron had been killed still haunts me. Maybe it always will. And I made a vow that I would see their families face-to-face and offer my condolences and answer any questions they might have about our mission and what happened. It's only right."

"If that's what you want to do, then I think you should make it happen," Stella said. "It might give you closure. And that doesn't mean you won't still grieve the loss of them," she added, "but it might help you move forward."

Luke nodded his agreement. "I think it would do a world of good to see their families and talk about all the amazing things they accomplished."

"Why don't I make some tea and we can chat? I'd really like to hear about your friends, Luke. Sometimes when we lose people it helps to talk about them."

Luke nodded. "I haven't really been able to do that much, but I'd like to try."

While Stella made the tea, Luke took out teacups and saucers. He asked her where the sugar was and she pointed him toward the pantry. Luke went into the fridge and pulled out some milk, depositing it on the table.

"Are you hungry at all?" she asked. "I have some of your chocolate chip cookies over in that tin and some zucchini muffins my mom made, not to mention a variety of chips."

"A muffin sounds good. I'm always hungry," Luke said with a shake of his head. "My mother still worries that I'll eat her out of house and home when I come over."

"It sure doesn't show," Stella said, her eyes zooming in on his sculpted frame. "You're in great shape." Stella tried her best not to stare, but Luke made it hard not to admire his finely honed body.

"Running has always helped," he admitted. "I need to get back to the gym, because running is off the table for the foreseeable future. It's jarring for my injury. I'm really working on strengthening this leg through physical therapy." Luke wrinkled his brow. "I'm learning about all kinds of things that will help my knee, like the benefits of swimming and certain stretches to help improve movement. Don't be surprised if you see me taking a dip in the waters on Blackberry Beach."

Hearing that Luke had committed himself to a regular physical therapy program was wonderful news. The idea of Luke pushing his body past its breaking point had worried her. Spending so much time with Luke over the past month had shown her that he was a man who demanded excellence of himself. His standards were so incredibly high that he sometimes failed to see that his expectations were beyond reason.

"Why don't we go in the sitting room, where it's more

comfortable?" Stella asked. She loved her cozy kitchen, but she wanted Luke to feel comfortable and completely at ease. The sitting room was one of the most inviting rooms in her home and it would be a perfect spot to talk about Luke's SEAL team members. She knew it wouldn't be easy for him to discuss the two men who'd passed away, but keeping his pain locked up inside him was tearing him apart.

Stella poured the tea, then placed the cups, saucers, a creamer jug, and a bowl of assorted sweeteners on a beautiful rattan tray. Stella then laid out a few muffins and grabbed some napkins. "I think this will tide us over for a bit."

"Let me carry that," Luke said, reaching out and taking the tray off her hands. Grateful for the gesture, Stella led the way to the sitting room and showed Luke where to place the tray. They ended up next to each other on her plush salmon-colored couch. A housewarming present from her parents, it had always been her favorite piece of furniture in the house. The color made her smile, and more times than not it reminded her of her parents and home.

Luke sat back on the couch and they both drank their orange tea while avoiding what they were supposed to be discussing. Stella tucked her legs underneath her then leaned forward to place her empty teacup down on the coffee table.

Stella decided to dive right in. As much as she wanted to help Luke, her curiosity had been piqued about the two men. "So what was Kenny like? Tell me about him. I want to feel that I knew him."

He put his cup down and looked over at Stella. "Kenny was the heart of our team. He was a romantic, always talking about one day meeting the girl of his dreams." Luke chuckled. "He liked to say she would be a mixture of Beyoncé and Misty Copeland. His idea of a perfect meal was a lobster roll and handcrafted chips with a hard cider to wash it down." He drew in a deep breath. "We were supposed to meet up here in Maine for a meal in Bar Harbor. That'll never happen now." His voice was thick with emotion. "I'd give anything to see Kenny fall in love, to be a guest at his wedding and to see him with silver at his temples. But none of that's going to happen."

Luke shifted his position on the couch, moving his body forward and leaning over with his hands crossed in front of him. The expression on his face was one of deep contemplation.

"Aaron was the single most competitive person I've ever known. He would routinely organize a game night for the team members and pretty much dominate every game. No matter what it was, Bingo or Monopoly or Old Maid, this guy had to win or else." Luke let out a deep-throated laugh. "He had the most extensive repertoire of knock-knock jokes I'd ever heard. And each one was cornier than the next." Luke rolled his eyes. "He always kept us laughing though. Aaron said it was his job to keep us smiling despite the stress of being deployed in the Middle East.

"When his twins were born, I don't think I've ever seen a happier man. I'm so glad he was able to be a part of the delivery via Skype. Then he got to spend some time stateside and see them in person. They'll always know that their dad moved heaven and earth to meet them."

"That's a beautiful legacy they left behind. Both of them will always be remembered for the joy they brought to those who loved them." She reached over and touched Luke's arm. She sensed that he needed some physical contact in this emotional moment. "I can tell how much you adored them, Luke."

He steepled his fingers in front of him and placed his chin on top of them. "I did. We all did. The fact that they're gone...taken in an instant—"

"It isn't something you can wrap your head around." She bobbed her head. "That's how I felt when Kara died. We'd just made plans for a girls' night out the following week. When I got the call about the accident, I was in such shock that I raced over to the hospital because I couldn't believe she was gone." Stella shut her eyes tightly as the memories of that horrible day came back to her in painful waves. "I still have moments when I pick up the phone to call her before remembering that I can't." She tried to blink away the tears, but they ran unchecked down her cheeks.

As soon as he saw her tears, Luke reached for her, enveloping her in his arms. The scent of old-fashioned soap rose to her nostrils—a sweet, comforting smell. Stella felt so safe in his embrace, as if nothing in the world could hurt her with Luke holding her so tightly. A huge part of her wished the hug would never end. She might just be content staying like this for the rest of her days.

"I'm sorry for getting so emotional," Stella apologized.

"I'm supposed to be supporting you right now, not falling apart."

Luke brushed a few strands of her hair away from her face. "You have nothing to feel sorry for. Nick told me how close you and Kara were. I'm just beginning to realize that all these losses piled up for me like dominoes falling on top of each other." He twisted his mouth. "I haven't handled them very well."

"Cut yourself some slack, Luke. It was all bound to take a toll on you," Stella said. Luke was a strong man, but he wasn't a machine. He needed to give himself some grace and not be so hard on himself. It sounded like he was just beginning to turn a corner with his mindset. Perhaps this newfound knowledge would take some of the pressure off.

"I can't, because it's my fault, Stella. I bear full responsibility," Luke said, his voice raspy and full of pain. "Because of decisions I made that day, two of my SEAL team members didn't make it home. And that's something I'm going to have to live with for the rest of my life."

CHAPTER TWENTY

Stella let out a startled gasp. Just hearing Luke say he blamed himself for Kenny's and Aaron's deaths sent a chill straight through her body. She'd sensed that Luke had been holding this guilt inside of him for a long time now. She guessed it was the reason behind him not wanting the hero label and his downplaying the Medal of Honor distinction. He didn't feel worthy of any of it.

"Luke, that's not true," she said. "That's just the grief talking. You've got to get that idea out of your head."

Luke began clenching and unclenching his hands. He wasn't even looking at her, staring straight ahead at the wall. "No, Stella. I'm right. I made a mistake that day. As team leader it was my job to make sure the intel was right before we headed into that area. The Afghan man who gave me the information was someone I'd been working with for over a year. I paid him regularly for intel and up until that point he'd always been reliable. But that time the information he gave me didn't pan out." He ran a shaky hand over his face. "The moment we entered the building I knew something was off. I gave the order for my men to fall back just before the bomb went off. Things could have been so much worse." Luke's breath became ragged, his chest heaving up and down.

"I was flung into the air and I remember fire and agonizing screams. I was in so much pain I must've lost consciousness. I don't remember anything else about the explosion. Sometimes details come back to me, but they're shadowy and I have no idea if they're real or not. I still have nightmares about it."

"Oh, Luke." Stella acutely felt his pain. She wished that she could absorb some of it for him so he didn't have to hurt so much. "You must have been gutted when you woke up in the hospital."

"I couldn't believe what I was hearing from Brando. He was the one who broke the news to me. Thankfully, he hadn't suffered any major injuries in the blast. Just some scrapes and bruises." He gritted his teeth. "It was like one of those nightmares where you can't wake up and you're frozen. All I knew was that two of the finest men I'd ever known were gone. All because I'd gotten things wrong."

Stella reached out and grazed his cheek with her palm. "It's not good for you to think this way. You were heroic that day and you saved countless lives. Focus on that aspect. You can't blame yourself for what someone else put in motion."

"It's not that simple. I was the leader of my team. I

called the shots on our missions. Ultimately it was my job to keep everyone safe. We had a no-fail mindset that we operated by." He shuddered. "Failure meant lost lives, which is what ended up happening. I own that."

Stella didn't want to try to convince Luke how wrong he was. She wanted to gently support him the way he'd always lifted her up. Beating him over the head wasn't going to work. "It makes sense that you're assigning blame to yourself because you were in a leadership role. You came out of that day alive and still in one piece despite your injuries while others died. I'm sure you've heard of survivor's guilt. A lot of people have it after suffering trauma. I'm no expert, but I think you might have it."

"Brando mentioned it when he came to visit. I'd thought about it before but not seriously. It's one of the reasons I think it would be good to talk to the Smiths and Aaron's family. Maybe giving them answers would help me as well."

"My advice is to seek out whatever will help you heal. I support you, Luke. And I'm here for you," she said, knowing she would stand beside him through this emotional journey. It was good knowing he trusted her enough to talk about such a sensitive subject. She hoped it meant their relationship was headed in a good direction. Everything was pretty new between them, but it felt as if she'd known this adult version of Luke for a very long while. She believed in him. And little by little, Stella was beginning to believe in the possibility of them.

* * *

The following morning Luke woke up to Stella nestled against his chest. Of all the mornings he'd awoken in his life, this had to be the best so far. No nightmares had plagued him. They'd talked until the stars were stamped out of the sky, and then Stella had slept like an angel in his arms. For once in his life he hadn't sought out a physical connection with a woman. Been there done that. This time it was all about the emotional connection he felt with Stella. He was deeply attracted to her, but he didn't want to mess things up by taking things too fast.

It was amazing how comfortably he'd slept last night. Although it didn't make any sense, the couch had been roomy enough for a man of his size, as well as Stella. It had felt as if they'd been sleeping on a cloud. Luke figured it had more to do with Stella than the couch itself. Buoyed by the time they'd spent together, Luke felt as if he had a new outlook on so many things.

Going back to Stella's place to clear the air had been one of the wisest decisions he'd ever made. He'd laid his heart bare and put into words the thing he was most ashamed of. Talking to Stella had been a freeing experience. She was right. Both men deserved to be memorialized. It was one of the reasons he felt honor bound to talk to their families. The fact that Stella had encouraged him to meet with the families made him feel as if he was on the right track. Even though Brando had discouraged him from going to see the Smiths, Luke didn't see a reason to wait any longer. Maybe he could help Dorothea through the grieving process by answering questions she had about her son's death. Luke didn't remember all the details from that horrific day, but he was eager to disclose everything he knew.

When Stella woke up, she scooted away from him. Unsurprisingly, she looked just as beautiful as always. "Good morning," he said, unable to resist pressing a kiss on her temple.

"Morning. How was your sleep?" she asked, raising her arms over her head in a stretch.

"I slept like a baby," he answered. "Thanks for letting me crash here last night. And for being so supportive. I know I unleashed a lot on you last night."

Stella grinned at him, sending him into orbit. "Of course. Thank you for being so open with me. I know it couldn't have been easy to tell me about Afghanistan."

Stella was right. Allowing himself to be vulnerable wasn't the Navy SEAL way. He'd learned to be stoic over the years in order to survive grueling training and difficult missions. It was almost as if he had to learn all over again how to be in the world as a regular person. He knew not everyone would be as understanding and patient. Which simply drove home the point that this woman was special. Like the rarest of diamonds, Stella sparkled and shimmered. And he felt extremely fortunate that they'd found each other. He didn't know where things were going between them, but he knew it felt right being with her.

"Honestly, you made it so easy, Stella," he confessed. "You just listened without judgment or trying to tell me how to handle things. You heard me." Last night had shown him exactly how compassionate and soothing

Stella was. If a storm was headed their way, she would weather it with grace and composure.

"In case you didn't know, I'm very invested in your happiness. I want the best for you," Stella said, locking gazes with him. For Stella it was a bold statement. She was letting him know she cared about him. As someone who'd been hurt in the recent past, this was a huge step for her. That knowledge sat between them, and Luke wanted to let her know she wasn't in this thing alone. He cared deeply about her as well.

"I feel the same way about you, Stella," he acknowledged. "I never expected to meet anyone when I came back to town. But you turned out to be the biggest surprise of all."

"Bigger than all the women in town trying to date you?" she asked with a chuckle. Stella's laughter was contagious and he joined in along with her. Her face was lit up with happiness, and he hoped it had a little bit to do with him. Because he knew she was making his life richer and fuller, and he hoped he gave the same to her. He was falling like a ton of bricks and there really wasn't anything he could do to stop these feelings from blossoming.

"You've got jokes," Luke said. For a moment they simply stared at each other, both of them basking in their appreciation of each other.

"How about some breakfast?" Stella asked. "I can whip up some omelettes and grits for us. Some sausage too if you like."

His stomach grumbled at the mention of food. Luke was a firm believer in starting the day off with a full meal. For him, the more carbs the better. "It all sounds amazing. I'm starving."

"Good." She looked down at her clothes and tugged at her top. "I really should change into fresh clothes, but if I'm cooking I might as well just keep this on, right? We can just pretend I didn't sleep in my clothes." Her tinkling laughter made him smile.

He winked at her. "I won't tell if you won't."

Once they were in the kitchen, Stella started taking items out of the fridge and placing pans on the stove. She brought out a cutting board and began dicing an assortment of vegetables and ham.

"Do you have any orange juice and champagne? I make a mean mimosa." He winked at her. "I might not be able to cook, but I can do that."

"I definitely have orange juice," Stella said. "And I might have some champagne in the cupboard. During the holidays I always buy some for gatherings and I think there's one still sitting on the shelf." Luke let out a cry of triumph when he spotted a bottle of prosecco where Stella said it would be. "Jackpot!" he called out, holding up the bottle.

"Yay!" Stella said as she gave him a thumbs-up then turned back to her cooking. As mouthwatering aromas filled the air, Luke busied himself making the mimosas and setting a table for two. For a moment he toyed with the idea of setting up at the patio table just to give Stella's nosy neighbor a thrill and something to flap her jaw about. He reined in his desire to have a little fun with her, realizing he preferred an intimate breakfast with Stella with no curious gazes trained on them.

By the time breakfast was ready, Luke could honestly say he would have eaten just about anything. He sat down across from Stella and eagerly helped himself to generous portions of sausage and grits. The omelettes Stella made were masterpieces—nice and fluffy and perfect.

"These are yummy," Stella said, sipping her mimosa. "You've got skills."

"Cheers," Luke said, holding his glass up and clinking it against Stella's. "To breaking all the rules." Just being with Stella constituted rule breaking. They'd broken their arrangement in order to pursue something real. He considered it one of the best decisions he'd ever made.

"I hear that," Stella said. "To summer...and all of its possibilities." They clinked glasses again and Luke wondered if she was referring to their relationship with her toast. He hoped she was.

Stella made him feel that his possibilities were unlimited. Despite everything, life was ripe with promise. He was back home with Miles and Nick, who he could be a support system for as they continued to adjust to life without Kara. His parents were getting older and once they returned home from their cruise, there were dozens of ways he could help them out around their home. Just because he wasn't a SEAL any longer didn't mean his life couldn't have an impact on other people. Being around Stella drove the point home.

There was so much to look forward to in the coming weeks and months. Even though he'd felt as if his life had come to a crashing halt six months ago, the truth was, it was only just beginning. And he couldn't deny that Stella Marshall was a big part of it.

* * *

A few days had passed since the Fourth of July and Stella's heart-to-heart discussion with Luke. Above all else, it stuck in her mind that he was a good man trying to find his way in the world. She hoped he would stay in Mistletoe and that their relationship would grow into something that would make both of them content. She didn't want to assume anything since her past had taught her what happened when you make assumptions. This time around Stella was going to try to enjoy the journey without putting too much pressure on herself or Luke.

Tonight they'd made plans to see a movie at Casablanca's. *Stormy Weather*, starring Lena Horne—one of the most beautiful and talented actresses from Hollywood's Golden Age—had been one of her grand-mother's favorites. Stella was excited that Luke was open to seeing a classic film and not the adrenaline-pumping action movies most men favored.

Not that there was anything wrong with them, she thought with a chuckle. Action flicks were Dante's bread and butter.

Stella inhaled the salty sea air as she looked out across the shores of Mistletoe Bay. It was a gorgeous day for an outing with her sister. Weeks ago she'd convinced Lucy to sign up for a painting class with her at the marina. They were both painting the Maine landscape stretched out in front of them—sparkling blue waters, seagulls soaring in the air, and a harbor full of boats. This was the type of serenity Stella enjoyed during summer break.

No students calling out to her, no papers to grade, and no stale coffee in the teachers' lounge. For at least another month she was footloose and fancy-free. She'd created a list of a dozen things she wanted to do with Luke this summer. While some of them involved leaving the local area, others were things they could do right here in Mistletoe. Crabbing at the beach. Riding the Ferris wheel at the summer carnival. Taking a cruise out on Mistletoe Bay.

And for a walk on the wild side, skinny-dipping at the lake. That would be a good way for her to step out of her comfort zone and do something different. Hadn't that been one of her vows for this summer? To be bolder and more settled in her own skin. Engaging in a fake dating relationship with Luke had definitely been daring, but she wanted to keep stretching and growing.

Her mind kept going back to the Fourth of July when she and Luke had gotten closer on an emotional level. They'd held each other all through the night and he'd peeled back the layers and revealed his vulnerabilities. She now felt more connected to him than she'd ever imagined possible. Her feelings for him were growing stronger with every passing day.

Being around Luke had changed Stella's way of thinking about her relationship with Rafe. Now, she was able to see so much of what had been missing between them. She'd never had an intense discussion with her ex. Not like the ones she and Luke had shared. It had always been very superficial. She couldn't recall a single time either one of them had shown their vulnerabilities or revealed the deepest parts of themselves. It hadn't been a solid foundation for a future. She'd been blinded by her desire to settle down and be paired off with someone.

But maybe Rafe had known something wasn't as it should have been between them. He'd still been a big huge jerk to her, but perhaps he'd ended things because he just couldn't imagine them being together for the long haul. Lately, thinking about him didn't hurt as much. It simply felt as if he belonged to another life and another time.

"So what's going on with you and Luke?" Lucy asked with wide eyes. "Any updates?"

"It's going well. We had a little hiccup at the fireworks, but he came over later that night and really opened up to me about some of the issues he's been dealing with."

"Yeah, I knew something was up when he disappeared that night," Lucy said. "I'm glad you smoothed things out. I really like him. Dante told me a few stories about their high school antics, and those boys were a handful."

Just remembering how Luke had been so vulnerable with her caused a little shiver to run through Stella. "He's been through a lot, Lucy. I admire him so much for being such a good person and caring about others the way he does. He could have come back from Afghanistan hardened and embittered, but he's trying to help others even though he's hurting. He's going to New Hampshire to speak to the family of one of his SEAL team members who died on one of their missions."

"Oh, wow. That's bound to be emotional." Lucy bit her lip and looked at her canvas with a critical eye before adding a flourish of blue to her painting. "Is he prepared for a meeting like that?"

Stella thought about Luke a moment before saying, "I think he can handle it. He's such a wonderful mix of kindness and compassion. Luke is strong. And he's determined to see this through."

Stella wanted Luke to achieve closure. If he needed this face-to-face meetup with Kenny's family in order to move forward, then she supported him doing it. Perhaps it would end his nightmares and feelings of guilt. And maybe it would help Kenny's family process what had happened to their beloved son. "I can't think of anyone who's more deserving of something good happening to them than Luke."

Lucy leaned over and peered closely at her face. "Stella! Are you in love with Luke?"

The question came at her like a fastball. She opened her mouth to shut her sister down, but she found herself struggling to speak. A few other painters looked over at them. Why had Lucy been talking so loudly?

"Shhh. You're practically screaming. Do I have to remind you that gossip never sleeps in this town?" Stella slightly jerked her chin in the direction of the other patrons.

"Oh, I'm sorry," Lucy apologized. "You know how I can't control my volume when I get excited." She narrowed her gaze as she stared at Stella. "You didn't answer my question. Are you in love with Luke?"

The question settled over Stella like a warm, cozy blanket. For so long the word *love* had made her feel afraid and insecure and uncertain. Now, it made her think of all the possibilities stretched out before her. Loving Luke felt as natural as the waves crashing to the shore on Blackberry Beach. He made her believe that anything was possible. And suddenly it was near impossible to imagine her life without him.

"I-I think I am," Lucy said in a halting voice. She felt a bit tentative to voice her feelings out loud, as if she might be jinxing things. Not so long ago she'd vowed to never go down this road again, and yet, miraculously, she was here. She'd fallen head over heels for the most amazing man in the world. Sweet, tender Luke. Her own very special Navy SEAL.

Lucy let out a little squeal. "You *think*? Girl, that is not something you think...it's something you know in the deepest regions of your heart."

Stella rolled her eyes. "Okay. I *know* that I'm in love with him." Saying the words out loud made her soul soar into the stratosphere. She felt as if she had wings.

"Crazy in love?" she asked, referencing their favorite Beyoncé song.

Stella threw back her head and let out a hearty laugh. "Yes! If you must know that's exactly how I feel. Crazy, madly, deeply, passionately in love with the man."

"Oh, Stella. I'm so happy for you." Lucy closed the distance between them and enveloped her in a huge bear hug. Six pairs of eyes were focused on them like laser beams.

"It's nice to know we're never truly alone in Mistletoe. There's always someone watching," Stella quipped as she turned her focus away from the curious glances and back on her masterpiece in progress.

"Nothing to see here, people. Nothing to see here," Lucy said in a gruff voice before turning back toward Stella and grinning.

For once, Stella didn't really care about the stares and whispers. No one could take away this amazing feeling fluttering around inside of her. She was in love. And it was a magical, surreal, and wonderful state of being. She hoped this feeling wouldn't ever fade away.

CHAPTER TWENTY-ONE

Later that evening, Luke picked Stella up for their movie date. He couldn't think of the last time he'd sat down and watched a film in an actual theater, so the very idea of doing so filled him with excitement. After grabbing some lobster rolls and fries from the Lobster Shack, they headed over to the marina for a preshow picnic. After settling down on a blanket, they dug into their food and Luke pulled out the bottle of sparkling cider and plastic flutes they'd been given at the restaurant.

"Funny how I'd almost forgotten how special this town is," Luke remarked as he bit into his lobster roll and watched the boats drift by. "I've really missed being here. For so long I tried not to think about it, but it's been glaringly obvious ever since I came back."

"I always hated the saying that you can't go home again," Stella said, making a disgruntled face. "Because it's really not true. Look at Dante. He stayed away for almost nine years, yet he was welcomed back with open arms. Coming home to Mistletoe was the perfect decision for you, Luke. I can't even express how happy I am that you're here. It's hard for me to imagine a world where we didn't get the chance to reconnect."

"I feel the same way. Now I have to admit, I wasn't totally sold on living here permanently," he said with a grin, "but it's really growing on me. Where else can I get the best lobster roll in New England and watch classic movies on the big screen?" He tapped his chin. "Oh, and I can't forget about the infamous Holly Hill Lighthouse and Blackberry Beach and the Chowder Fest."

"Is that all?" Stella asked with a mischievous look stamped on her face.

"Not a chance," he drawled, moving closer so he could give her a kiss. He only intended for it to be a little peck, but once his lips were on hers it went from light and leisurely to a full-on blaze in seconds. Luke placed both of his hands on either side of her face to anchor her to him. He brushed her hair away from her face with one hand, enjoying the feeling of her silky strands between his fingers. Stella returned his kisses with equal measure.

As the kiss ended, Luke placed his forehead against hers. They stayed like that for a few moments, neither of them wanting to break apart. Was this it? he wondered. That feeling of all being right with the world simply because you were with a certain someone. He just knew he'd never felt this way before. As much as it scared him senseless, he found himself wanting to dig in and build something solid with Stella so he could go on feeling this way. *For a lifetime?*

"You're the biggest draw this town has by far, Stella Marshall," he said in a husky voice. "Don't you ever forget that." And he meant it. Stella was by far Mistletoe's star attraction.

"Now that's what I like to hear," she responded with a smile.

Luke threaded his fingers through hers, loving the sensation of their hands and skin touching. He couldn't recall experiencing all these euphoric emotions before. Not even as a teenager.

"I need to ask you something." He'd been waiting to clear the air with Stella on a certain subject, but he'd been putting it off. Frankly, there was no time like the present.

"Okay. You can ask me anything," she answered, her brown eyes wide with curiosity. He wondered if Stella would change her mind once he asked his question.

"Are you still in love with Rafe?" he asked, spitting the question out before he chickened out. It was a difficult thing to ask, but he was falling for Stella, and he needed to know what he was up against.

Stella hesitated and his heart twisted as he awaited her answer. So much was riding on her reply. It was hard to build something solid if her heart rested with someone else. But the way he felt for Stella was so powerful he knew he would do whatever it took to win her heart. His own heart was beating a mile a minute and his palms were moist. He had it bad.

"No, Luke, I fell out of love with Rafe a long time ago." She met his gaze head-on without wavering. "I think most of my feelings that have lingered were based on my own dreams that got crushed. I always thought at this point in my life I'd be settled down, but life has a way of throwing you curveballs. Lately I've been working hard to learn from what I went through, and I think I've acquired some invaluable lessons. Not just about love and commitment, but about myself."

Luke exhaled a deep breath that instantly caused his tension to dissipate. "I can't pretend that I'm not relieved."

Stella reached out and tickled him near his collarbone. "Did you think you had some competition?" Luke tried to ward off Stella's hands. It was one of his deep dark secrets that he was very ticklish. Stella found all of his vulnerable tickle spots and wouldn't let up until he surrendered.

"Okay, okay. I give up," he said, holding up his hands. "I'm really glad that Rafe is firmly in the past."

"He is," Stella acknowledged with a nod. "Your being in my life showed me that I'm truly over him. I'm not stuck in that awful limbo anymore."

Luke knew all about being stuck in the past. For him, it was as if he were standing in quicksand and unable to move forward. His PT sessions had shown him that it was much easier to work on physical injuries than emotional ones. He was ready to work harder on resolving those issues. Meeting with Kenny's folks would be a huge step in the healing process.

"I think we should walk over to Casablanca's now," Stella suggested. Luke jumped to his feet and offered his hands to pull Stella up. They quickly packed up the blanket and deposited their trash in the garbage and recycling bins. Stella reached for his hand as they walked back toward Main Street, admiring the art installations that had been strategically placed all over the downtown area. This year's theme was "Under the Sea" and it included sculptures of mermaids, dolphins, lobsters, whales, and other aquatic sea creatures. It was a fantastic way to feature local up-and-coming artists and make the town's landscape even more vibrant.

Although they were full from dinner, Luke insisted on buying a big tub of popcorn, M&M's, and two sodas once they were inside the theater. "Can't watch a flick without treats," he said to Stella, who gave him a nod of approval. For the next hour and a half, Luke was transported into the musical love story featuring dazzling actors Lena Horne and Bill Robinson. At the end of the movie, everyone in the audience clapped and cheered, highlighting the intimate nature of Casablanca's.

When they came out of the movie theater, Luke reached for her hand as they walked across the town green to his truck. "Okay, so I have to admit that I'm not very knowledgeable about old movies. I grew up on *Star Wars* and *Fast and the Furious*. But I really liked the movie. It was cool. And different."

"Hey, I loved those movies too, but I also had

grandparents who adored old movies. My granny, Lula, especially loved them."

"Lula, huh?" Luke asked, smirking.

Stella grinned as she said, "Yep. If you merge Lucy and Stella it kind of gets you Lula. At least that's what my mom thought."

"Sort of, kind of," he teased.

She laughed along with him. "So Granny Lula used to host Lucy and me every month at her house for classic movie night. Popcorn. Candy. Soda pop. The whole nine yards. I learned so much about the old film studios like MGM and Warner Brothers. The whole studio system was fascinating. Bette Davis and Joan Crawford were legendary. Lena Horne was one of the most beautiful women in her day but because she was African American she didn't get as many opportunities to star in major films."

"That's a shame. She was a triple threat from what I just saw. Singing. Acting. Dancing. The whole package as far as I'm concerned."

"She sure was. I love seeing all the clothes and the cars from this time period. I'm not saying I would have enjoyed living then, but they sure had style."

They reached Luke's vehicle, and he moved to open the door for Stella and helped her in, firmly closing the door after she was inside. Once he was behind the driver's seat and revved the truck, Stella didn't hesitate to commandeer the radio. She loved powerful ballads by Celine Dion and Mariah Carey. He tried his best to hide the smirk tugging at his lips. It was wonderful how she didn't have the best singing voice, but she kept on belting out songs with all the confidence of a balladeer. Seeing her happy made him ecstatic. She'd changed since the day they'd met at her school. She'd always been sweet and kind, but now she was more centered and confident. She didn't seem as stuck in the past as before. Now, it was just him trying to wrestle with the past and make sense of his future.

"I'm thinking more and more about visiting Kenny's family," Luke admitted. "It's been gnawing at me that I need to see them face-to-face."

"If it's weighing on you so heavily, you need to listen to your gut," Stella said. "Trust your instincts."

"I'll keep you posted on what I decide," he promised. He was definitely going to update Stella. Being out on the town with Stella felt like a declaration of sorts. They were no longer hiding behind a fake relationship. It was all out in the open for all to see. For both of them, it was progress.

"Great." Her gaze was intense as she looked at him. "Just remember that this one meeting doesn't determine your future."

Although he nodded his head, Luke wasn't sure he totally agreed with Stella. Being able to talk to the Smiths and connect with them was monumental for him. As much as he truly believed they needed to hear about their son's heroism, Luke knew he needed something from them as well. He needed to know that they were navigating their way through the grieving process. Luke owed it to Kenny. And he genuinely cared about what they were going through. How many nights had he lain awake thinking about them? How many times had he wondered if he'd failed in his duty as team leader by not seeing them in person?

Touching base with the Smith family could be mutually beneficial. Looking into their eyes as he offered them his condolences would be powerful. Maybe then he would be able to stop blaming himself.

CHAPTER TWENTY-TWO

The rainy, gray weather caused Luke to scrap plans for a beach day with Stella. He'd been looking forward to his first dip in the waters of Blackberry Beach. Instead, she was coming by to pick him up so they could grab lunch in town and hit up a few stores. Luke needed some summer reading, so they were going to browse at the library and the Bookworm shop. All he really cared about was spending time with Stella. For all he cared they could be doing laundry or painting Nick's fence. His world lit up every time she entered the room.

A little while ago he'd received a text from Winona, Aaron's widow, inviting him to Skype with her. He'd been calling and leaving messages for several weeks but hadn't heard back until now. She was visiting her parents in Colorado and unable to meet up with him in person. Winona apologized for not getting back to him earlier.

Just knowing she was receptive to speaking with him made all the difference in the world. He was getting tired of carrying the weight of Kenny's and Aaron's deaths around his neck. When the time came for the Skype call, Luke's nervousness evaporated the moment Winona's smiling face appeared on-screen. Having met her a few times in person, he was struck by how great she looked despite everything she was going through. She'd cut her long red hair into a short bob that suited her oval-shaped face. He felt a twinge of disappointment in not seeing the boys in the background.

"I have to apologize in advance if I cut the call short. These boys are quite a handful and they might wake up at any time," Winona said with a chuckle. "They're both doing well and growing like weeds."

"That's good to hear. I've been wanting to talk to you since Aaron passed away," Luke acknowledged. "Thanks for arranging this. It's really comforting seeing you looking so well."

Winona crossed her hands in front of her. "Luke, I've so appreciated your cards and messages. And the stuffed animals you sent the boys are their favorites." She let out a beleaguered sigh. "For a long time, I wasn't ready to talk to anybody. Losing Aaron was just so devastating. And the idea of raising twin boys without him seemed impossible. But in the last two months I turned a corner and things are looking up. Being in Colorado with my parents and siblings helps. I have so much support on a daily basis."

He let out the deep breath he'd been holding. "I'm so happy the three of you are doing so well. Honestly, you look wonderful," Luke said. "You've all been in my thoughts and prayers." And he meant it. Not a day went by when he didn't offer up a prayer for their well-being and comfort. Aaron would be so proud of Winona holding down his family.

"We are, Luke. The twins are growing and thriving. They're content. I wish they'd gotten more time with their dad, but I'll be able to tell them all about his heroism and show them pictures of him holding them. They'll always know how much he loved them."

"Well, if you ever need me to step in for any reason, I'll be happy to tell them how he bragged about them to the whole team." Luke teared up at the memory. "You would've thought those babies were made of solid gold. He adored them... and you."

Winona brushed a tear away and chuckled. "He sure did. Any time the subject of kids came up he was the first one to whip out pictures of the twins. I really miss him. We weren't together for all that long, but I'll cherish those memories for the rest of my life."

It would never feel right that Aaron had been taken away from his family in such a premature way. He should've died peacefully in his sleep at 102 years old. He should've had so much more time with his loved ones. Luke couldn't wrap his head around the unfairness of it all. But, all things considered, it was pretty fantastic to be face-to-face with Winona and seeing for himself that she was doing all right.

The sound of high-pitched cries rang out in the distance. Winona made a face. "Let me just grab whoever is making that racket and we'll come back to wave goodbye." Winona stood up and vanished from the screen. A few minutes later she was back with a baby cradled in each arm.

"Double trouble," she said with a chuckle. "This is Matteo and this one here is Quincy. Boys, meet your uncle Luke."

Luke felt a groundswell of emotion bubbling up inside of him. "T-they're adorable." Somehow he managed to get the words out. "They're both mini-me's of Aaron." The resemblance was uncanny. He only wished his buddy was still around to bear witness to the lives he'd created.

An ear-splitting cry drowned out Winona's reply. She rocked both of her arms. "I'm so sorry. They won't settle down until I give them something to eat. It was so great to chat with you."

"No worries. I completely understand. Let's talk again soon." Although Winona and the twins vanished from the screen and the call ended, Luke didn't immediately get up from the table.

He was still grinning from ear to ear when he opened the door to Stella a few minutes later. She was standing on his doorstep with a basket in her hands. Luke sniffed the air as a delectable aroma wafted around the entryway.

"I come bearing gifts," she said, holding the basket up in the air. He deftly took the basket and held it in his hand as he swooped in for a kiss. He pulled her in so that she rested against his chest. After kissing her, Luke grinned down at her.

"You look like you just won the lottery," Stella said,

her eyes skimming over his face. "Did you get good news or something?"

"I kind of feel like I did win the lottery," Luke admitted. The heavy sensation that had been sitting on his chest had eased up substantially since speaking with Winona. His greatest fear had been that she would be depressed or unable to function in her daily life. Their conversation had turned out better than he'd ever imagined.

He quickly got Stella up to speed by telling her all about his heartfelt Skype session with Winona. He knew that he was talking a mile a minute, but things had gone so well and he was bursting with excitement. He couldn't seem to stop grinning for anything in this world. His soul felt so much lighter now.

"Oh, that's incredible news," Stella said, appearing just as thrilled as he was. "I know you must feel on top of the world. Aaron would be so happy that the two of you connected."

"And I got a glimpse of the babies. Stella, they look just like Aaron." Just hearing Winona refer to him as Uncle Luke made him feel ten feet tall. And it let him know that she wanted him in the boys' lives, which was huge.

"Oh, I wish that I could've been a fly on the wall to see them," Stella said. Her face was flushed while her eyes were glossy.

He was discovering that Stella loved babies. The way she'd gushed over Brando's pictures and how she'd been keeping a baby name for her future child all pointed toward one thing. Stella was the type of woman who wanted babies in her future. Her expression was soft and open, and it felt as if he was getting a glimpse into the most intimate part of her. Would he be a good father? Could he handle a crying baby? Just knowing one might be in their future caused goose bumps to pop up on his arm. There were so many exciting moments ahead of them, but he needed to do something first.

"I've decided to take a drive to New Hampshire tomorrow to see Kenny's family. I think the time is right."

"Tomorrow?" she asked, surprise registering on her face and in her tone. "Did you just decide to do this right now?"

"Yes. I don't want to keep putting this off. Now that I've spoken to Winona I have a really good feeling about seeing the Smiths. She's in such a good place and she was warm and positive. It's been seven months since Kenny was laid to rest. It's time for healing."

"Don't you think maybe you should call them first? Surprise visitors aren't always welcome, especially under these circumstances."

Luke frowned at the doubt he heard in her voice. "You don't think they'll want to see me, do you?"

She reached out and touched his face. Her hand was soothing. "No, babe, that's not it. I'm just worried that your timetable for healing might not match up with theirs. I don't want to see you get hurt. I know your heart is in the right place."

He took her hand and kissed it. "I'll be fine. This makes sense to me. Talking to Winona made me think about the fact that none of us knows how long we're going to be around. I've been thinking about it ever since the bomb blast. Tomorrow isn't promised to any of us, so it's important for me not to put off doing things that I can do today. Does that make sense?"

"Oh, Luke, it makes all the sense in the world."

"When things fell apart after the attack, I had a lot of time to think when I was recuperating in the hospital. I thought a lot about life and loss and what I could do moving forward to make a difference. I've been exploring job opportunities online, but nothing so far has been a good fit. Until I talked to Nick's boss in the search and rescue unit." Luke shrugged. "She wants me to come in for an interview."

"That's incredible," Stella said in an excited voice.

"I haven't really said anything to Nick yet," he admitted sheepishly. "I didn't want to get his hopes up in case it doesn't work out."

"Tell him," Stella encouraged him. "He's going to love working with you."

Luke crossed his fingers. "Nothing's official yet so I'll keep it under wraps for a bit. I still have to ace the interview, and if they want me, undergo training."

"Well, you have certification in search and rescue, so it's a no-brainer. They'd have to be out of their minds to say no to you."

Luke drew her close and looked deeply into her eyes. "Has anyone ever told you that your brand of positivity is contagious. If we could bottle it, we'd make a small fortune."

Stella shook her head. "Oh, I've had my moments of negativity, especially in the last few years. But all in all, I know I'm blessed. Life really is good. I've learned to make lemonade out of my lemons."

"I like your style, Stella Marshall." He looked her up and down approvingly, his eyes lingering on her curves. "Matter of fact, I like pretty much everything about you. The way you kiss me. The way I catch you checking me out sometimes when you don't think I'm watching you." He stood back and openly admired her. "The way you look in those jeans." He let out a low whistle of approval.

Stella waved her hand in front of her face. "You sure know how to make a girl blush."

"Oh, babe, I'm just getting started," Luke drawled as he pulled her into his arms and began kissing her like nobody's business.

* * *

Bright and early, Luke woke up and grabbed a quick breakfast of eggs and toast in preparation for his trip to New Hampshire. After putting the Smiths' address into his GPS, Luke was ready to hit the road. He'd purchased a few audiobooks and a gritty voice filled the car as he listened to *Murder on the Orient Express* by Agatha Christie. As the miles passed by, Luke found himself relaxing as he tried to put himself in the shoes of Hercule Poirot and catch a killer. It had been a long time since he'd enjoyed a full-fledged mystery written by the grande dame of suspense. He was enjoying it way more than he'd anticipated.

It was a three-and-a-half-hour drive to Renfrew. In addition to his audiobook, Luke enjoyed the beautiful New England landscape—lots of greenery and trees.

Before he knew it, he was a half hour from his destination and filled with a mixture of excitement and nervousness. He had so much to say to the Smiths. So many words he'd bottled up inside of him for the last seven months. Luke hadn't told Brando he was visiting the Smiths out of fear that his friend might try to dissuade him from going. He'd managed to find their address from an old email the Navy had sent out for sending condolences to Kenny's family.

One hundred and twenty-six Silver Hill Road. The house was a white clapboard structure with navy shutters. A white picket fence surrounded the property. A profusion of flowers graced the side yard. A vintage baby blue Ford sat in the driveway. It brought a smile to Luke's face. Kenny had always talked about his grandpop's old car and how he and his father had worked countless hours to overhaul the vehicle so it would be drivable.

"Somebody has a green thumb," Luke said out loud as he stepped out of his truck and surveyed the place. The front porch looked inviting with brightly colored Adirondack chairs and a big basket of sunflowers gracing a table. As he opened the gate and proceeded toward the house, a rustling noise gained his attention. A woman was digging in her garden, resting on a kneeler as she went about the business of tending to her flowers and vegetables. She was wearing a sun visor and a pair of faded overalls.

"Hi there. Mrs. Smith?" he called out as he advanced in her direction.

"Not looking to buy anything," she answered in a brisk tone as she cut her eyes at him. With sepia-colored skin and big brown eyes, she was an attractive woman. Luke's chest tightened. Her resemblance to her son was striking. There was no question that she was Kenny's mom.

He took off his Red Sox cap and placed it in front of him. "Ma'am, I'm not trying to sell you anything. I'm here to talk to you about your son, Kenneth."

She reared back so that she was sitting up. Her eyes were full of suspicion. "Who are you?"

"My name is Luke Keegan. And I was your son's SEAL team leader," he said, introducing himself. "I've been wanting to talk to you ever since Kenny passed away, but I wanted to give your family some space and time to properly grieve. I know it might seem a bit odd for me to just show up, but Kenny and your family have been on my heart and mind lately."

"I know who you are. My son used to talk about you all the time." Dorothea was staring at him with a shuttered expression. "He thought you were the model Navy SEAL. My Kenny wanted to be just like you." Her lip curled upward. "Only now he's dead. All because you wanted to be a hero."

"Mrs. Smith, I never wanted—"

"Save it!" Dorothea called out, cutting him off. She scrambled to her feet and faced him. "You got your Medal of Honor and lots of media coverage, all at my boy's expense. He thought your word was bond and it got him killed." She let out a brittle laugh. "He once said the SEAL team would follow you through fire if you asked them to. And that's exactly what they did!" She let out a sob as tears streamed down her face.

Dorothea's pain was palpable. It was an explosive

thing, pulsating in the air around them. It gutted him to see her like this, so broken and filled with rage. He knew it was grief, but it hurt to know she thought so poorly of him. He'd loved Kenny like a brother. In a million years Luke would never have done anything to jeopardize his safety. And, if it were possible, he would switch places with him in a heartbeat. So many nights Luke had lain awake wondering why he hadn't been taken instead of Aaron and Kenny.

"I understand your anger," he said in a gentle tone. "I'm heartbroken too. Your son was one of the finest men I've ever known. What he achieved in his service to this country was outstanding. I wanted to see you face-to-face so I could tell you about the things he accomplished and how much we all loved him. Staying away didn't seem like the right decision to make." Over the years the importance of honor had been drilled into his head. For Luke, this was his way of living up to the Navy SEAL code.

Luke was speaking to Dorothea from the heart, but he couldn't shake the feeling that his words were falling on deaf ears.

"Get off my property! I don't need anything from you." By this point her voice was raised to near shouting. A portly man with light brown skin and graying hair rushed to Dorothea's side. Luke hadn't even seen him coming, he was moving so fast.

"Dorothea. Take it easy. What's going on out here? I could hear you hollering all the way inside the house." He looked at Luke with a bewildered expression.

"I'm sorry, Mr. Smith. Your wife is upset on account

of me," he explained. "I'm Luke Keegan, a friend of your son's. We were on the same SEAL team. I came by to pay my respects. I realize now I should have called first," he said, ruefully shaking his head.

"Luke. Yes, I recognize your name. I'm Neal Smith." Neal didn't smile or extend a hand to Luke, but he got a kindly feeling from him. "Kenneth thought the world of you," he added.

Just then Dorothea let out a wail that raised the hairs on the back of Luke's neck. "My son is gone, Mr. Keegan, so I don't understand what you're doing here. Go home! You've got things waiting for you…things our boy will never be able to have now. You shouldn't have come here."

Luke sucked in a ragged breath. His chest tightened. This was way worse than he'd envisioned.

Neal placed his hands on his wife's shoulders. "He doesn't mean any harm, Dottie. He was a friend of our Kenny."

"If it hadn't been for him, Kenny would still be alive. Our baby won't be getting married or having kids. We won't ever get to see him again or watch him fall in love." She glared at Luke. "You don't deserve any of those things if my boy can't have them." Her body seemed to give way, and Neal reached out to catch her before she slumped to the ground.

Luke stepped forward to help support Dorothea, but Neal brushed him away. It was a sucker punch to his gut, and nausea rose up in his throat. He struggled to catch his breath. All of his good intentions had gone up in smoke.

"I think you should leave, Luke. It's for the best. I'm sorry, but my wife isn't up to this type of visit." He locked eyes with Luke, imploring him to heed his advice and go.

Knowing he'd done more harm than good with his visit, Luke immediately retreated and walked back to his truck on trembling legs. By the time he got in the driver's seat, he was a wreck. As he revved the engine, he took one last look in the side yard at Dorothea. She was sitting on the lawn sobbing as Neal cradled her in his arms. Luke pressed his foot on the gas and drove as fast as he could away from Silver Hill Road. A few minutes later he pulled over to the side of the road and leaned forward so his face was pressed against the steering wheel.

You don't deserve any of those things. Dorothea's words repeated over and over in his head, highlighting his worst fears. He wasn't worthy. He didn't merit a happy ending. The miscalculation he'd made had robbed Aaron and Kenny of their futures. Kenny's mother's words had been cutting and blunt, but she was right. He didn't deserve to walk off into the sunset and enjoy a happy life when Kenny wasn't able to.

* * *

Stella tried to keep herself occupied while she waited for word from Luke. She didn't want to pester him since she knew he might still be on the road back from New Hampshire, but at the same time she was dying of curiosity about his visit with the Smiths. Perhaps he was simply taking some time to soak it all in. Or maybe things had gone so well that he'd been invited to stay over with the family. Just the thought of it made Stella smile.

But what if it hadn't gone well? She pushed the thought out of her head. Luke would be heartbroken. And he would continue to beat himself up about it. No! Luke was an amazing man and his sincerity radiated from him like a beacon. Surely the Smiths would see his intentions were good. He'd suffered too as a result of the explosion. Not only had he lost two close friends but his entire world had turned upside down with his injury and forced retirement.

She tried to keep herself busy, but thoughts of Luke kept intruding. *Do something to keep your mind occupied!* For the next half hour, she vacuumed, swept her hardwood floors, emptied the dishwasher, and began going through her closet for unwanted items to donate. Coco Chanel watched from Stella's comfy queen-sized bed as she amassed a huge pile. She turned toward her poodle and held up a funky orange top that she hadn't worn since college. "I'm not sure anyone would want this, Coco Chanel." In response, her pooch haughtily lifted her nose in the air, giving Stella a case of the giggles. Stella tossed the top to the trash pile and reached back into her closet.

Stella felt the item before she saw it. Stuffed in the back was the vintage bridal gown she'd planned to get married in. She grabbed it, slowly pulling it out with an equal measure of reverence and trepidation. Stella let out a relieved breath when she was able to look at the gown without falling apart. She lightly stroked the luxurious fabric, admiring the way the silk slid elegantly through her fingers.

It was amazing to look at the gown and simply be able to admire it for its design and style. She no longer mourned the wedding that wasn't, the future that had crashed and burned. Right now, the dress was just a gorgeous garment she would never wear. Stella knew what she was going to do with it. The wedding gown would no longer take up space in her closet. The dress was going places. She put it back inside its garment bag and draped it across her bed. Later on she would take the dress to Rosie and arrange for her to gift it to one of her upcoming brides. That way someone else could find joy in wearing it on their special day.

A walk on the beach right about now would do her a world of good, Stella realized. She was tired of looking at her phone and waiting on word from Luke. It was humbling to realize how deeply she cared about the things that mattered to him. "Come on, Coco Chanel. Let's get our steps in for the day," she called out to her dog. In response, her pampered pooch jumped off her bed, then wagged her little tail as she ran to the back door. Stella snapped her leash on to her collar and headed outside into the sunny afternoon. She stuck her phone in her back pocket just in case she got a call or text from Luke.

An hour later and Stella had walked the entire length of the beach and back without a single ping on her cell phone. Try as she might to rationalize not getting any updates from Luke, she couldn't make sense of it. They had been in each other's pockets for weeks now. It was rare that they went hours without any contact. Finally, she texted him saying she was going to reach out to Nick if he didn't let her know he was all right. Moments later her phone buzzed, and two words jumped out at her.

I'm okay.

Stella stared at the words on her screen, waiting for Luke to say more. Her heart sank at the realization that those two words were it. He wasn't giving her anything more than a terse response. Despite the heat, goose bumps popped up on the nape of her neck. Luke's words didn't reassure her one bit. Something was wrong. She could feel it in her bones. Even though she'd been over the moon about her relationship with Luke, she was suddenly reminded of the fact that things could always turn on a dime at any time. Isn't that what she'd learned from her ex-fiancé? Relationships fizzled. Connections were severed. Hearts broke.

Being in love with Luke didn't guarantee they would walk off into the sunset together or that he would love her back. Being in love didn't promise anything at all. And that realization terrified her.

CHAPTER TWENTY-THREE

It was nighttime before Stella heard from Luke again. He called her, saying he wanted to come over to talk. Stella felt relieved at the idea that he wanted to see her. Judging by the sound of his voice, Luke needed to talk to her, which finally allowed her to breathe normally. His disappearing act and silence had been confusing and alarming. Now, at least, he'd reached out to her. Her emotions went to the stratosphere in seconds. This, she thought, was what it felt like to love someone. Everything she felt was tied up in Luke.

Stella was at the door the moment she heard the crunch of his tires in her pebbled driveway. It seemed like forever until he was standing at her doorstep. She flung the door wide open and threw herself against his chest. Immediately, she knew something had shifted with Luke. He didn't place his arms around her the way he usually did. He wasn't hugging her back. Her mind worked quickly to justify it. He was tired, she imagined, after his trip to New Hampshire.

When she let go of him, Stella ushered Luke inside and toward her bright and airy kitchen. She'd put on a pot of coffee for them and the heavenly aroma of it wafted around the room.

"Coffee?" she asked. "You look like you could use some."

"Sure," he replied, sinking down into one of her chairs as if his legs might give out. His hands were clenched tightly at his sides. Stella didn't want to come right out and ask him what was wrong, but as the seconds ticked by, she knew it couldn't be avoided.

She poured coffee into each of the cups she'd placed on the table next to the cream and sugar. Stella sat down next to him, close enough so that she could reach out to him if necessary. She sensed that something was weighing heavily on his mind. Although he was still achingly handsome, Luke looked as if he hadn't slept in days. The bright glare of her kitchen lighting showed every worry line on his face. Although it felt good to lay eyes on him, Stella wasn't reassured by seeing him. Every nerve ending in her body tingled with heightened awareness. He placed both hands on either side of the coffee mug and raised it to his lips. He drank in huge gulps as if he needed it for sustenance.

"What happened in New Hampshire?" she asked as the silence between them dragged out. "Where have you been this whole time?"

"I've been driving around...thinking. It didn't go

well," he said in a clipped tone, his eyes downcast. "The minute I introduced myself to Kenny's mom she began railing against me. Told me I was to blame for his death and that I wasn't worthy of a happy life." He massaged the bridge of his nose and looked down. "I never got the chance to say much of anything."

Stella gasped. "Oh no. That's terrible. I'm so sorry, Luke."

He let out a brittle laugh. "I should have seen it coming. Brando tried to warn me. He told me to give it some time and not go there, but I couldn't let go of the idea of going to see them."

"I know you must be heartbroken." And she was heartsick for him. He'd been counting so much on this meeting. From the sounds of it, things had gone terribly wrong.

Luke fiddled with his mug. "It's not about me. The Smiths are the ones who are really suffering." Anger bounced off him in waves. She reached out for his hand. He pulled it away and reached for his mug, draining the remaining brew.

She blinked past the moisture in her eyes. He'd rebuffed her and she had no idea if he'd even been aware of it. It hurt to feel so disconnected from him. Luke was a million miles away, and it felt like she couldn't reach him, no matter how hard she tried.

"Look at me," Stella commanded. There was a sharpness in her voice that she hated. But she felt him detaching.

He swung his gaze up. His expression was still shuttered, while there was nothing welcoming in the depths of his eyes. This wasn't *her* Luke. It hurt so much to see this cold version of the man she'd fallen in love with.

"You're pulling away from me. From us. I can see it in your eyes," Stella said, hoping Luke would contradict her. Maybe she had this all wrong. Perhaps he was just wounded by his encounter with Kenny's parents.

"I don't want to hurt you, Stella. Matter of fact, it's the very last thing I ever want to do. That's why this is so hard."

Her heart muscles constricted. *Hard?* What was so hard? Seeing her? Talking to her?

"Your heart needs to be kept safe with someone. Protected. I can't be that person. I don't know why I ever thought I could be." He met her gaze without blinking. His tone was rife with resignation. It took her a moment to realize he was ending things with her. Luke's words served as a body blow. She wrapped her arms around her waist. Her face felt flushed and her palms were moist.

Feeling numb, she said, "I'm in love with you, Luke. It's too late for safety."

Shock registered on his face as soon as the words tumbled out of her mouth. He groaned. "I never meant—" He stumbled over his words. Stella saw the confusion swirling around him. Even though she was in pain, she recognized that he was as well. Going to New Hampshire, seeking approval from the Smiths, had sent him into a tailspin of guilt and grief.

He abruptly stood up. "I'm sorry for all of this, Stella. I wish that I could be the type of man worthy of a woman like you. I'm just not."

"Don't, Luke. Please don't give up on us." She hated

the pleading tone in her voice, but if it would get him to reverse course, she would say anything...do anything.

He turned back toward her. "I'm not giving up on you, Stella. I'm just not in a place to be with anyone right now. Least of all you. You want commitment and picket fences and babies. I-I can barely get out of my own way these days without being a human wrecking ball."

Anyone. Was that what she was to him? Just anyone?

She opened her mouth to say something, but it felt like cotton was stuck in her throat. Luke moved toward the front door and quietly let himself out without saying another word. She stood in the hallway, her gaze focused on the door. Her entire body felt cold, as if a storm had swept through her house and engulfed her. This wasn't her first heartbreak, but she couldn't ever remember feeling as if someone had ripped her heart out of her chest cavity. This felt...different from last time.

Once she felt certain Luke had driven away, she let out a plaintive wail, one that came from a place deep inside of her that she hadn't even known existed.

* * *

Luke snuck into Nick's house as quietly as he could manage. Ending things with Stella had been way more agonizing than he'd ever imagined was possible. Even though he knew it was in her best interest, it still gutted him. *I'm in love with you, Luke.* He hadn't seen it coming. Those words would haunt him for a long time. The relentless ache inside him wouldn't give up. It hurt every bit as much as when he'd woken up in the hospital to the news that Kenny and Aaron were gone.

Something kept nudging at him—an emotion he wasn't sure he could handle at the moment—and Luke kept trying to stuff it down. Why did this hurt so much? Facing a life without Stella made him feel as if he couldn't breathe. Was this another panic attack? No, this was different. It was loss and pain and the sensation of something wonderful slipping through his fingers.

He heard Nick's footsteps coming down the stairs. Luke knew that he was due for a tongue lashing from his brother. He'd been out of touch for almost fifteen hours, which wasn't cool at all, especially since Nick had been hitting up his phone, filled with concern. He'd let him know that he was safe but hadn't given him any details regarding his meeting with the Smiths. At the moment he felt as if he'd gone twelve rounds with a prize fighter...and lost. Breaking up with Stella had been brutal.

Nick looked him up and down. "Where have you been? I mean this in the nicest way, but you look awful."

Tell me something I don't know. "Thanks, bro. I can always count on you to be brutally honest." Luke didn't need Nick or a mirror to tell him what he already knew. He was a mess.

"What happened in New Hampshire? And why didn't you answer my calls?"

"I don't want to weigh you down with the details. You have enough on your plate without having to deal with my problems. I'm sorry about not calling you back. All I could really manage was a brief text."

"I want to know about your life, Luke. The good, the bad, and the ugly. You've been through a lot over the past seven months. I'm here for you if you need to talk."

He let out a ragged sigh. Bottling things up never seemed to work for him. Nick was his best friend. He needed to be real with his brother. Maybe then he wouldn't feel as if he were carrying the weight of the world on his shoulders. "Kenny's mother blames me for his death, and she thinks I'm the most horrible human being in the world. She doesn't believe I deserve anything good in my life...and I think she might be right." He tossed the words out quickly before he changed his mind about confiding in Nick.

"What?" Nick exploded. "It isn't right to blame you for what happened. That's ridiculous. It's just the grief talking. Don't worry. She'll come around."

Luke shrugged. "There isn't much hope of that happening. If you'd seen her face you'd know what I'm talking about." He felt a wave of nausea as the memory of his encounter with Dorothea came into sharp focus. "I screwed up on intel, and because of my decisions, two SEAL members died. I can't change it, even though I'd give anything to go back in time and make things right."

"It wasn't your fault. You can't take all the blame." Nick's voice was raised. The veins in his forehead were bulging. "You're not looking at it with a clear view. What about all the lives you saved that day? Do you really think they gave you the highest military honor out of pity or some sense of obligation? The United States Navy determined you were deserving of one of their greatest distinctions. Why isn't that enough for you?"

"Nick, you're talking out of loyalty to me and not being objective. You're my brother," Luke scoffed. "I appreciate the support, but it doesn't change my reality. And it certainly doesn't alter the opinion of Kenny's family."

Nick threw his hands in the air. "You served our country honorably. It's a shame that Kenny's family isn't ready to acknowledge that their son chose his path. There are always risks involved in military service, particularly in an elite unit like the SEALs."

"Navy SEALs have a mantra we live by. It says we won't ever fail." He felt a tremor in his jaw. "But I did, Nick. And Kenneth's family agrees with me. They think it was my fault. I went to Renfrew to pay my last respects and to tell them in person what happened to their son, but I never got the opportunity. There were so many things I wanted to say, but they shut me down. It's like this wound that can't completely heal because I'm still in limbo."

"You've already mourned them and honored them. Both of them received Purple Hearts posthumously based on your accounts of their bravery. Winona told you how grateful she is and always will be that her kids will grow up knowing their dad was a hero." Nick shook his head. "Why can't you be satisfied with that?"

"I don't know," he answered with a shrug. "It's just difficult for me to feel good about things in my life when others are hurting." He'd survived and they hadn't.

"You're looking for something you're never going to get, Luke," Nick pressed. "What about Stella? The two of you—"

He bowed his head. Nick wasn't going to like this. "There's nothing there, Nick. It's over."

Nick let out a shocked breath. "Over? What are you talking about? You two are great together. I saw the way you looked at her. I've never seen you so happy. So content to be in someone else's orbit. What happened?"

"It doesn't matter. She deserves way better than me," he said. "Nothing ever lasts for long in my personal life. Allison said it best. I'm not made for the long haul. I just need to suck it up and move on. I don't deserve someone like Stella." He turned away from Nick, only to have him grab him by the arm so they stood face-to-face.

"Tell me you don't love her." Nick's eyes felt like laser beams as he stared Luke down.

Luke opened his mouth to deny it, but the words just wouldn't come. He couldn't make the lie roll off his tongue. Nick pointed his finger at him. "See! You can't deny it because that's how you feel. And it's genuine and powerful. And maybe that scares you. Because love is terrifying and amazing and powerful. Running away from Stella because you don't feel worthy is the stupidest move you could ever make. And you're one of the smartest people I've ever known."

"I don't deserve a happily ever after, Nick. Not when Kenny and Aaron won't be getting a shot at one."

"I can't believe—" Nick stopped and placed his fingers on the bridge of his nose. Luke could see raw emotion was threatening to overtake him. "You're walking away from love when I'd give my right arm to be able to get a second chance with Kara. I'd crawl through fire to get her back."

Tears burned Luke's eyes and he blinked them away.

"Nick. Don't do this to me. I already feel bad enough. I can't take it if you throw Kara in my face."

Nick glared at him. Luke felt it going straight to his soul. He couldn't recall the last time they'd been at odds like this. His brother's anger was understandable, yet Luke couldn't give him what he wanted.

"Maybe you're right," Nick spit out. "You don't deserve to be with someone like Stella. Despite getting knocked down she keeps getting up. She stays in the fight." He let out a brittle laugh. "Everyone thinks Luke Keegan is so brave, but the truth is you're afraid to go after love. And that makes you more cowardly than I ever imagined."

Nick tore out of the room as if his feet were on fire. He honestly couldn't remember ever seeing his brother so angry. Luke let out a ragged breath. His brother's parting shot left him feeling as if he'd been sucker punched in the gut. *A coward?* That had been a low blow. Luke bristled. Was Nick right? Was he allowing fear to keep him from pursuing a life with Stella? If that was true, he was the world's biggest fool.

CHAPTER TWENTY-FOUR

The week after Luke dumped her had been the most miserable time of Stella's life, which was really saying something considering she'd once been ditched two days before her wedding. At this point she was fairly convinced that nothing could ever fill the void in her life left by Luke's absence. The memory of him would always loom large in her life, and in her heart. So many times she wanted to pick up her cell phone and text or call him. But what would have been the point? He'd made himself clear. She'd laid her heart on the line and he'd barely blinked. Heat suffused her cheeks at the memory of her telling him she loved him.

What had she been thinking? It had been foolish to believe a man like Luke would want something permanent with her. It had felt like love, real enduring love, but she'd been wrong. *Again.* And somehow this time was more brutal than before. Because she loved him in a way she'd never loved anyone else. Not ever.

With Rafe it had been about the humiliation and the wedding that wasn't and letting everyone down. It had never been about the loss of Rafe. Not really. It took meeting Luke to come to that realization.

This time around she was mourning the loss of a man who knew her inside and out, warts and all. She enjoyed spending time with him, whether they were going to the movies, skinny dipping at the lake, or walking Coco Chanel down by the marina. He made her laugh at the silliest things. And she felt like her truest self with him. The best part of her shined when he was in her orbit. She would never adjust to him not being in her life.

"Hey, Stella." The familiar voice called out to her, drawing her out of her thoughts. She turned her head just in time to see her mother walking up her patio steps with the help of her cane.

"Mom. I didn't know you were coming over so early. I could easily have dropped Tess home." Stella stood up and quickly walked over to greet her mother. Tess was visiting today and had taken Coco Chanel for a walk on the beach. Stella hadn't expected her mother to come so early to pick her up.

"Well, I wanted to check on you." Her mother leaned heavily on her cane as she made her way to the table and sat down. Stella knew her mother didn't enjoy being fussed over. She had an independent spirit that she wanted to maintain. Stella pulled out a chair, resisting the urge to do anything else for her mother other than offering her some refreshments.

Once Stella came back from the kitchen with two tall glasses of peach iced tea and a bowl of cherries, they dug into the treats.

"You're spoiling me," Leslie said in an excited tone as she bit into a cherry. "You know they're my favorite."

Stella managed a smile, even though it was difficult. "Cherries might just be the best thing about summertime."

They sat for a few minutes drinking their iced tea, eating cherries, and gazing at the beautiful waters of Blackberry Beach. It was a tranquil setting despite the turmoil roiling around in Stella's heart.

"I'm so sorry about you and Luke," her mother said softly.

"It's okay," Stella said with a shrug. "Life goes on." Stella spoke past the huge lump in her throat that had been sitting there for a solid week. She looked down instead, fearful that her mother might see the devastation in her eyes. It was a natural instinct for Stella to bury her emotions. At this point, she wasn't even sure she knew how to stop doing it. It was a defense mechanism born out of her desire not to be an object of pity.

Her mother reached for her chin and lifted it up so their eyes met. "No, it's not, Stella. It's never okay to lose someone you care about. Stop pretending it is."

The words slammed against her chest with a force that left her breathless. She hadn't fooled her mother one bit. And she was now picking at Stella's scab.

Stella simply nodded, her eyes burning. It was only a matter of time before she'd burst into tears, and she didn't want to break down in front of her mother. It was ridiculous to cry over a broken heart when her mother had been bravely fighting a terrible disease for years.

"Stella, I want to apologize to you."

Stella frowned. "For what? You haven't done anything."

"When Rafe called off the wedding, you went inward. I knew you were devastated, but I wanted to help you heal and I thought not talking about it was the way to support you." She wiped away a tear from Stella's cheek. "I realize now that I shouldn't have let you stuff all those feelings down. As your mother I should have forced you to scream and shout and cry out from the rooftops."

"Mom, it's all right. You didn't do anything wrong. You've had your own health issues to deal with and you were just following my lead. I was so worried about everyone feeling sorry for me that I went inward. In my own way I was protecting myself." Stella reached out and wrapped her arms around her mother. "Please don't blame yourself for a single thing."

"Just don't bottle all of your feelings up on the inside this time. Let them out. Please, Stella. It's okay to let it all out." She reached out and began patting Stella on the back. "I'm asking you to do it now. Scream. Vent. Rage. Do anything. Just don't bottle it up."

She shook her head. "I can't."

"Why not, sweetheart?" Leslie asked, her beautiful face creased in concern.

Stella's lips trembled. "Because if I do, I might just shatter into a million little pieces." Before she knew it, Stella was sobbing, shoulders heaving. She tried her best to hold it in, but something inside of her broke. She missed Luke. She ached for him. Just to see him and talk to him, to be held in his arms and chuckle with laughter at his corny jokes. That was all gone now. She'd barely gotten a chance to love this man before the rug was pulled out from under her. No matter what had gone down between them, Stella knew that Luke was a man worth loving with all of her being. And she knew it was likely that she would continue to love him even if he could not return those feelings.

"Let it all out. I'm here, Stella. I'm not going anywhere." Her mother pulled her into an embrace and Stella started wailing.

"Why did this happen to me again? I love Luke in ways that I never loved Rafe. Yet here I am again. Blindsided. Alone. Heartbroken. And still in love with this incredible man who doesn't want me. And I'm angry that he doesn't feel whole enough to go on this journey with me, because I was all in."

"Of course you were, sweetheart," her mother cooed as she rubbed her back. For the next fifteen minutes, Stella poured her heart out to her mother, who listened to every word like a trusted confidante.

Her mother swept her palm across Stella's cheek, just like she used to when Stella had been a little kid with a skinned knee. "It sounds like Luke is processing some things related to the loss of his team members. That's a big issue for you to grapple with, honey."

"I know," she answered. "But I'm in love with him. I would've stuck by him while he sorted things out." Her mother gripped her hand in a gesture of support.

"Stella! Stella!" Tess's voice rang out, filled with panic. Her little sister pushed past her gate and ran toward them, her face full of alarm and her pigtails askew. "I didn't mean it, Stella. I'm sorry."

"What didn't you mean?" Stella looked around for Coco Chanel. "Tess! Where's Coco Chanel?"

Tess's face crumpled and she let out a wail. "Coco Chanel pulled really hard and ran away from me. I tried to catch her but she was too fast."

Stella jumped up from her seat. "We need to find her. Which direction was she headed?"

Tess shifted from one foot to the other. "Umm I think she went left. No, right," Tess corrected herself.

"You think?" Stella asked with a roar. Time was of the essence in trying to find her runaway poodle before any harm befell her.

"We need a search party!" Tess shouted with too much enthusiasm for someone who'd lost Stella's most prized possession. Stella had to stop herself from raising her voice at Tess. It wasn't her fault. Coco Chanel was a very strong-willed creature. Maybe she'd caught the scent of another dog and decided to hightail it after. Tears pooled in Stella's eyes. Coco Chanel was so little. What if she wandered into the road?

"Stella, let's mobilize," her mother suggested. "I'll call Lucy and Dante and your dad for starters. You head to the beach, and I'll get in my car and ride around. Make sure you have your cell phone. Tess, you stay here in case Coco Chanel finds her way back home. And call anyone you can who can help us find her."

"Okay. Sounds like a plan," Stella said as she grabbed

her cell phone and headed down the beach, calling out for Coco Chanel every few seconds. Stella let out a sob as she looked into the distance in the hopes of spotting her four-legged sweetie. Panic gripped her as tears slid down her cheeks. What would she do if she couldn't find Coco Chanel?

What on earth had she done in this lifetime to deserve such an awful streak of bad luck?

* * *

Luke disconnected from his phone call with Cecily Evans, the head of the Maine Association for Search and Rescue. Despite the fact that he'd just endured one of the worst weeks of his life, he now had a reason to celebrate. He'd been hired as a member of the search and rescue team, with training starting next week. He couldn't wait to tell Stella. Luke groaned. He couldn't tell Stella. No doubt he was the last person she wanted to hear from.

Stella was the first person he thought of when he woke up in the morning and the last thought he had before he went to sleep. Her absence was weighing on his heart like an anchor. He was in love with her. Living without her didn't make an ounce of sense. Nick was right. He'd made a mess of his relationship with Stella because he was afraid. Afraid to mess up. Afraid to love her. Afraid that he wasn't meant for the long haul.

But he'd faced fear plenty of times as a SEAL. He'd never backed down once from a mission. And

having Stella in his world felt imperative. Everything
in his life was better with her in it. Luke needed to
win her back. Maybe if he laid his heart on the line,
she would forgive him. He racked his brain trying to
come up with a plan. Roses and a card just wouldn't
cut it. He needed to bring his A game when he
approached Stella.

A scratching sound emanated from the closed garage
door. Luke ignored it until it continued, even growing
louder. He took a step closer to the door. A critter was
definitely in there. He looked around for something to
arm himself with, settling on a mop from the pantry. He
wrenched open the door with one hand and held the mop
high in the other. He let out a cry of surprise as Coco
Chanel came barreling out of the garage.

"How did you get in there?" he asked her. In return,
Coco Chanel glared at him, as if blaming him for her
predicament. He put the mop down and scooped the
poodle up in his arms. Coco Chanel rewarded him by
giving him a very sloppy kiss on the mouth.

There was only one reasonable explanation for how
Coco Chanel had come to be in the garage. But for the
life of him he couldn't figure out why his nephew had
stashed Stella's dog there in the first place.

"Miles!" he called out. Within seconds, he heard his
nephew galloping down the stairs. When Miles entered
the kitchen, his entire face dropped when he saw Coco
Chanel in Luke's arms.

Luke scowled at Miles. "Do you mind telling me what
in the world is going on?"

"Huh?" Miles asked, playing dumb.

"I'm going to give you ten seconds to explain to me why you had Stella's dog locked up in the garage." Luke looked at his watch and began counting out loud.

Miles threw his hands up in the air. "It wasn't my fault. It was all Tess's idea."

Luke felt his eyes practically bulge out of his head. "Tess? Miles, you need to start talking. Fast."

Miles drew in a deep breath. "Tess brought Coco Chanel over here because she wanted everyone to think she was missing."

"Why?" he asked, knitting his brows together. Of all the ridiculous pranks to pull!

A sheepish expression appeared on Miles's face. "Because she wanted you to race over to the beach to try and find Coco Chanel." He wrinkled his nose. "She said it was a way to get the two of you back together."

Luke felt his mouth hanging open. "Miles, do you have any idea of how worried Stella probably is right now? She's crazy about this pooch."

Miles hung his head. "It wasn't my idea. I was just going along for the ride."

Luke pulled out his phone and dialed Stella's number. It went straight to voicemail. "Well, it looks like you're going for another ride," he said. "The three of us are heading over to Stella's house, where you and Tess are going to explain everything and apologize profusely."

Miles groaned and slapped his hand to his forehead. "Can you at least let Miss Marshall know that it wasn't my idea?" he asked in a pleading tone.

"Let's go, buddy," Luke said, reaching for his keys

with one hand while Coco Chanel burrowed herself against his chest. "Let's go reunite Coco Chanel with her mama."

* * *

By the time Stella headed back to her house, she was a nervous wreck. There hadn't been a single sighting of Coco Chanel, and to make matters worse her phone had died midsearch. She was hoping and praying that her mother or someone else had located her baby and hadn't been able to get ahold of her. Thankfully, Coco Chanel had been chipped, so any local vet would contact her if she was found. But it was the *if*s that were driving her crazy. What if she'd been hit by a car? Her baby was out there somewhere innocent and defenseless. Just the thought of it caused her eyes to well up with tears.

When Stella was within a few feet of her back patio, she stopped in her tracks. Luke was standing there with Tess and Miles. The sight of him caused a swarm of butterflies to flutter around in her stomach. A white T-shirt and a pair of khaki shorts had never looked so good. Before she could even say a word, Coco Chanel ran toward her.

"Coco Chanel!" she cried out as her dog began jumping up at her. The dog had a huge grin on her face as if she'd been on a grand adventure. Her tail was wagging like crazy. "Where have you been? Mama's been so worried about you." Stella scooped up her poodle and nuzzled her face against her fur.

After a mini reunion, Stella swung her gaze up and made eye contact with Luke. "Where did you find her?" she asked, trying to keep her voice from quivering. Seeing him only added to the emotion of Coco Chanel being missing for the last few hours.

"She was at Nick's house, courtesy of these two," Luke explained, jutting his chin toward Tess and Miles. "They hatched a plot to get us back together."

"What?" Stella asked, practically shouting.

Tess began talking a mile a minute trying to explain her thought process and how she'd come up with the twisted plan to reunite her and Luke. It was quintessential Tess, and Stella was having none of it.

She wagged her finger at her sister. "Tess! How could you? I was worried sick. And you had me traipsing up and down the beach in this wretched heat!"

Tess hung her head. Stella could see tears running down her sister's face. "I just wanted you and Luke to get back together. I thought if he heard about Coco Chanel being missing, he'd come right over to help you look for her."

"It wasn't my idea," Miles said with a shrug. "Tess bamboozled me."

Luke shook his head at his nephew. "Stop saying that! You went along with it."

"Tess, I know somewhere deep down you meant well," Stella continued, "but your method was cruel. And it was all a waste of time. You know that Taylor Swift song you like so much? We are never ever getting back together? That's pretty much Luke and me at this point. So no more ploys or tricks or plots. Do you understand me?"

She looked at Miles. "That goes for you too, Miles. Stay out of grown folks' business."

"We get it. It'll never happen again," Tess said. "We're going to go inside for a glass of lemonade and to call off the search party." She wiped a hand across her brow. "This has been exhausting."

Stella resisted the urge to strangle her little sister as she and Miles marched inside the house.

"What absolute nerve!" Stella said as soon as they were out of earshot. She was pretty certain steam must be coming out of her ears. Her sister had done a lot of outrageous things in her young life, but dognapping had to be at the top of the list. She would make sure her parents instituted a proper punishment for Tess.

"I'm kind of glad the two of them came up with this harebrained plot," Luke said, his eyes focused on her like laser beams.

"What? Why? It was ridiculous and manipulative," Stella said, sputtering. "I don't appreciate Coco Chanel being used as a pawn. And you weren't the one out there in the blazing sun crying her eyes out." She forced herself to look away from him. It was dangerous to look into his stunning brown eyes. A person could get lost in them.

He quickly swallowed up the distance between them. "Because I've been trying to figure out how to talk to you. This past week has been agonizing."

Stella bristled. "Why are you saying this? You broke up with me. Remember?"

"I'm in love with you, Stella. When you said those words to me last week, I was such an idiot. I let fear do the talking for me. I should have just told you that I was afraid of messing things up. I was wounded by the things Kenny's mother said to me. It played on all of my fears and made me doubt that I could honor you the way I want to. The way you deserve.

"And I see you. I really truly see who you are, right down to your stubborn, sassy center. You're kind and funny and you listen when I talk to you. You're the most genuine person I've ever known. For those reasons and so many more, I've fallen in love with you, Stella."

She shook her head. "You walked away from me... from us."

"I know I did. But I knew within one day that I'd made the biggest mistake of my life. And I won't ever be able to say I'm sorry enough for putting you through that. But that wasn't about you. It was about my not feeling worthy enough for a woman like you, Stella. I'm a work in progress. I'm not finished. Not by a long shot." For the first time in forever, Luke reached for her, gently taking her by the wrists and pulling her close.

"I love how you cry at sad movies and the way you treat Coco Chanel like she's a princess. Your smile knocks me off my feet and the way you laugh with such abandon makes me happy. What we have is something I never dared to dream about because I didn't think I'd ever get so lucky." He reached out and brushed her hair away from her face. "It took a speech from Nick and some wisdom from Winona to remind me that at the end of the day, love is the only choice that makes sense."

Tears pooled in her eyes. "I love you, Luke, but I just

don't know if I can be hurt again if you change your mind." Oh, how she wanted this. She loved Luke in a forever type of way and she ached to be with him, but her heart could only withstand so much. How could she trust that things wouldn't fall apart?

"It's impossible for me to promise you that we'll never go through challenges. That's a part of life. But I vow that I'll always be by your side, supporting you and loving you. I won't ever walk away from us again."

Luke reached out and linked their hands. Although being touched by Luke gave her butterflies, she tugged her hand away. He'd caused her so much pain. How could she believe he was truly committed to her? The stakes were so high. Her heart was in peril now that he owned it.

Luke winced as soon as she pulled away. "Stella, if it takes me the rest of my life, I'll show you that I'm all in. I had one bad moment where I tried to tear it all down, but in my heart I couldn't stop loving you. And I never will."

In that moment her heart rebounded. Love was always a risk. Luke had never broken promises to her; he'd told her all about his struggles from the beginning. Despite everything he'd been through, he was laying it all on the line for her. He was trying to make things right. He'd brought so much joy to her world. Because of Luke she believed in love again. Because of his tenderness and dedication her heart had come back to life.

"Say it again. Tell me you love me, Luke Keegan," she said in a raspy voice.

He held her face between his hands. "I love, love,

love you, Stella Marshall. And I want to be a better man for you. I want to make your life better simply by being a part of it." She saw the raw emotion on his face. "I want you, Stella. That's never going to change."

"Luke," she cried out as she launched herself into his arms. "I love you too. And I always will."

EPILOGUE

SIX MONTHS LATER

Luke parked his car in the pebbled driveway of the cottage by Blackberry Beach that he now shared with Stella. When he stepped out of the car and slung his duffle bag over his shoulder, he took a moment to soak it all in. It never got old looking around at the cozy house and grounds he now called home.

The past few months had been a whirlwind, from the moment he arrived home in Mistletoe till the moment he'd popped the question to the love of his life. It had all culminated in him and Stella exchanging vows in front of half the town. A honeymoon in Cape Cod had followed. Thankfully, Lucy and Dante hadn't minded at all that Stella and Luke's wedding came so soon after their own. Their joy had been effusive.

He hadn't seen Stella in three days. Luke was now a member of the search and rescue team working out of southern Maine. He'd completed his training a few weeks ago and was actively engaged in the field. This particular search had finished with a happy ending when the two hikers were found safe and sound. Although they were extremely dehydrated with scrapes and bruises, they were going to be fine. Working side by side with Nick had made the rescue even more meaningful. He hadn't spent time like this with his younger brother since they were kids. And he lived with the knowledge that he was learning the ropes from the best.

The front door flew open, and Stella was standing on the threshold with her arms stretched wide open. "Luke!" she called out, so eager to greet him that she met him halfway up the walkway. Luke dropped his bag to the ground, then lifted Stella up by the waist and placed a tender kiss on her sweet lips.

"Luke," she murmured against his mouth as the kiss ended. "I'm so glad you're home."

Home. Having a place to belong to meant the world to him. He would never regret his Navy SEAL days, but they hadn't given him everything he needed to be whole. Even though it had taken him years to realize it, Stella was exactly what he'd been searching for. Above all else, she was his soft place to land when the world around him became too intense.

After they headed inside, Stella led him toward the sitting room, where Luke sank down onto the couch. Stella cuddled up beside him and he placed his arm around her. She felt so good resting against his chest. Gratitude rose up inside of him.

"How are you feeling about tomorrow?" Stella asked, stroking his cheek with her palm. "Are you nervous?"

"I feel good, Stella. No matter what happens, I'm not going backwards. I'm way too invested in our life to allow that to happen."

In the past few months Luke had taken steps to deal with his trauma and the deaths of his SEAL team members. Once a week Luke attended a group meeting for survivors of trauma. He wasn't bottling his emotions up anymore, and his panic attacks had decreased in frequency. Although he was a work in progress, Luke knew he would make it through the storms of life with Stella by his side. Tomorrow they were driving to New Hampshire to meet up with the Smiths, as well as Winona and the twins. Dorothea had reached out to him and invited him to come for a visit. She'd turned a corner on her grief and wanted to honor her son's memory. It was clear from their conversation that she was eager to know more about Kenny's days as a SEAL. Luke was happy to oblige. He had so many wonderful stories to share with them.

Stella leaned over and placed her lips on his. Every time they kissed, Luke's brain short-circuited to the point where he couldn't think of anything but his amazing wife. He was the luckiest man on planet Earth, without exception. If Stella hadn't given him unconditional love, he might not have made such tremendous progress on his journey. Being Stella's husband made him believe all things were possible.

"This is the life, Mr. Keegan. I can't believe I ever wanted anything other than this," Stella said, linking her fingers with Luke's.

Luke raised her hand to his lips. "Thank you for standing by my side. This is all I'll ever want or need, Mrs. Keegan."

Stella's lips twitched with mirth. "Are you sure that's all you'll ever want?"

Luke frowned. "Of course. Don't you believe me?" he asked, his tone teasing. "And here I thought you knew how devoted I am to you."

She shook her head, causing her brown tresses to swirl around her shoulders. "I'm just wondering if you're open to more blessings?"

"Like what?" he asked, totally confused by the look of amusement on her beautiful face. Maybe it was the stress of the search and rescue, the emotion of the hikers being located, and the long drive home, but he felt clueless.

She took his hand and placed it low on her belly. "A baby with your gorgeous smile."

Luke froze. Was this for real? A baby? "How?" he sputtered, causing Stella to giggle. "Not how, but . . . wow. Are you serious? Please tell me this is really happening."

Stella wiped a stray tear away from her cheek. "It's happening, Luke. We're having a baby."

"It's just so incredible. So utterly fantastic." He reached over and pulled Stella against him so her head rested against his chest. "Honestly, I never dared to dream my life could be so full. I must be the luckiest man who's ever lived."

"And I'm the most fortunate woman. A year ago my life was in turmoil and then you came strutting out on the gymnasium floor to surprise Miles. That's where it all began."

"Why does everyone keep saying I was strutting?" He playfully winked at her. "There's a difference between swagger and strut."

Stella rolled her eyes. "Whatever you say, lover boy. All I know is, you brought love into my life and now we're bringing a baby into the world."

Luke sat up straight on the couch. "You and Lucy pregnant at the same time? I'm not sure if Mistletoe is ready for this." Lucy and Dante were expecting their first child in early summer. There was bound to be a celebratory mood when word got out about their bundle of joy.

Stella's face lit up with excitement. "I can't wait to tell her the news. She'll be so excited for us." She clasped her hands together. "It'll be another dream coming true. We've always wanted to raise kids who were close in age."

Luke threw his head back and laughed. "You might want to wait before you tell Tess. If you do, it'll be all over town in a heartbeat." He'd grown to adore his pint-sized sister-in-law, but he'd learned very quickly that she was a chatterbox who loved to spread breaking news.

Stella grinned. "It's early days, so I'm definitely not going to tell her anytime soon."

"How are you feeling?" he asked, hoping she would have an easy pregnancy. Either way, he knew Stella would be an incredible mother to their child. And he would be with her every step of the way.

"Happy," she said, beaming. "It's pretty amazing to have nothing else to wish for. All of my dreams have come true."

"That's exactly how I feel," Luke said, pressing a kiss

against Stella's forehead as his hand caressed her belly. Never in a million years had he imagined that coming home to Mistletoe would help him heal and show him he was worthy of love with the woman of his dreams. Love was a journey, and he was charting a course with Stella. Luke was putting in the work on himself, but he now knew that with love, anything was possible.

Don't miss the next book in the
Mistletoe, Maine series!

Coming Winter 2023

ABOUT THE AUTHOR

Belle Calhoune grew up in a small town in Massachusetts as one of five children. Although both her parents worked in the medical field, Belle never considered science as the pathway to her future. Growing up across the street from a public library was a huge influence on her life. Married to her college sweetheart, she is raising two lovely daughters in Connecticut. A dog lover, she has one mini poodle named Copper and a black Lab, Beau.

She is a *Publishers Weekly* bestselling author as well as a member of RWA's Honor Roll. In 2019 her book *An Alaskan Christmas* was made into a movie (*Love, Alaska*) by Brain Power Studio and aired on UPtv. She is the author of more than forty novels and published by Harlequin Love Inspired and Grand Central Forever Publishing.

Fall in love with these small-town romances full of tight-knit communities and heartwarming charm!

THE BEACHSIDE BED AND BREAKFAST
by Hope Ramsay

Ashley Howland Scott has no time for romance while grieving for her husband, caring for her son, and running Magnolia Harbor's only bed and breakfast. But slowly, Rev. Micah St. Pierre has become a friend...and maybe something more. Micah cannot date a member of his congregation, so there's no point in sharing his feelings with Ashley, no matter how much he yearns to. But the more time they spend together, the more Micah wonders whether Ashley is his match made in heaven.

THE SUMMER SISTERS
by Sara Richardson

The Buchanan sisters share everything—even ownership of their beloved Juniper Inn. As children, they spent every holiday there, until a feud between their mother, Lillian, and Aunt Sassy kept them away. When the grand reopening of the inn coincides with Sassy's seventieth birthday, Rose, the youngest sister, decides it's time for a family reunion. Only she'll need help from a certain handsome hardware-store owner to pull off the celebration...

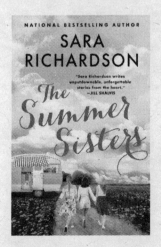

SOMETHING BLUE
by Heather McGovern

Wedding planner Beth Shipley has seen it all: bridezillas, monster-in-laws, and last-minute jitters at the altar. But this wedding is different—and the stakes are much, *much* higher. Not only is her best friend the bride, but bookings at her family's inn have been in free fall. Beth knows she can save her family's business—as long as she doesn't let best man Sawyer Silva's good looks and overprotective, overbearing, older-brother act distract her. Includes a bonus story by Annie Rains!

HOW SWEET IT IS
by Dylan Newton

Event planner Kate Sweet is famous for creating happily-ever-after moments for dream weddings. So how is it that her best friend has roped her into planning a best-selling horror writer's book launch extravaganza in a small town? The second Kate meets the drop-dead-hot Knight of Nightmares, Drake Matthews, her well-ordered life quickly transforms into an absolute nightmare. But neither are prepared for the sweet sting of attraction they feel for each other. Will the queen of romance fall for the king of horror?

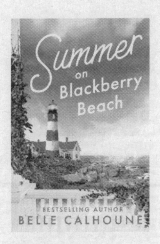

SUMMER ON BLACKBERRY BEACH
by Belle Calhoune

Navy SEAL Luke Keegan is back in his hometown for the summer, and the rumor mill can't stop whispering about him and teacher Stella Marshall. He never thought he'd propose a fake relationship, but it's the only way to stop the runaway speculation about their love lives. Pretending to date a woman as stunning as Stella is easy. Not falling for her is the hard part, especially with the real attraction buzzing between them. Could their faux summer romance lead to true love?

FALLING FOR YOU
by Barb Curtis

Just when recently evicted yoga instructor Faith Rotolo thinks her luck has run out, she inherits a historic mansion in quaint Sapphire Springs. But her new home needs fixing up and the handsome local contractor, Rob Milan, is spoiling her daydreams with the realities of the project...and his grouchy personality. While they work together, their spirited clashes wind up sparking a powerful attraction. As work nears completion, will she and Rob realize that they deserve a fresh start too?

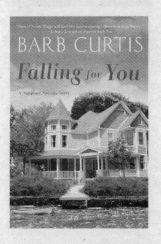

Discover bonus content and more on
read-forever.com

HER AMISH
SPRINGTIME MIRACLE
by **Winnie Griggs**

Amish baker Hannah Eicher has always wanted a *familye* of her own, so finding sweet baby Grace in her barn seems like an answer to her prayers. Until *Englischer* paramedic Mike Colder shows up in Hope's Haven, hoping to find his late sister's baby. As Hannah and Mike contemplate what's best for Grace, they spend more and more time together while enjoying the warm community and simple life. Despite their wildly different worlds, will Mike and Hannah find the true meaning of "family"?

THE AMISH FARMER'S
PROPOSAL
by **Barbara Cameron**

When Amish dairy farmer Abe Stoltzfus tumbles from his roof, he's lucky his longtime friend Lavinia Fisher is there to help. He secretly hoped to propose to her, but now, with his injuries, his dairy farm in danger, and his harvest at stake, Abe worries he'll only be a burden. Yet, as he heals with Lavinia's gentle support and unflagging optimism, the two grow even closer. But will she be able to convince him that real love doesn't need perfect timing?

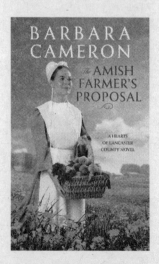